Tl

Holly Bridgwood.

Wild Pressed Books

First Edition.

This book is a work of fiction.

The publisher has no control over, and is not responsible for, any third party websites or their contents.

The Seagull's Laughter © 2019 by Holly Bidgood.

Contact the author via the publisher.

Editor: Tracey Scott-Townsend

Cover Design by JDSmith Design

ISBN: 978-1-9164896-5-3

Published by Wild Pressed Books: 2019

Wild Pressed Books, UK Business Reg. No. 09550738

http://www.wildpressedbooks.com

For my children, Kim, Noomi and Iduna.
I hope we will always tell stories together.

The Seagull's Laughter

PART ONE

1

Malik

Iceland, 1974

I listened to the sharp crack as Snorri dropped ice cubes into two crystal glasses on the table between us. I continued to watch his face for any clue as to his thoughts, but his expression remained mild and affable – concealed, even. With calm concentration he filled the two glasses with water. His eyes did not seem to explore any memories and admitted no recognition of me. His fair complexion hid his age; the two missing fingers on his left hand, stunted ends blackened by frost, were the only marks he wore that alluded to his past, to the time and place at which our lives had become intertwined.

The walls of his study, similarly, were empty of pictures or maps. No artifact peered down from the bookshelves, no carven figure, grotesquely formed, reared its bald skull; square teeth bared menacingly, blackened eyes glinting with the dark polar winters. There was nothing in the room that alluded to the time that he had spent in the Arctic. The ice in our glasses, enveloped by pouring water, glittered in the afternoon sun and threw spots of dancing, ethereal light about the walls. Once the glasses were full, Snorri placed the lid back on the jug, the jug back on the table, and reaching to the highest shelf of one of the bookcases, brought down a leather-bound book. The binding was blank.

'Rasmus,' said Snorri, and tapped a long finger against the first page, the first photograph. The image was grainy, a little unclear, but I recognised the man I knew to be my father: the heavy eyebrows, the sincere countenance, the informal but confident stance. He was standing on the deck of a ship with one foot squarely planted on a crate and one elbow resting on his knee. In the distance rose great icebergs, like castles and mountains, indistinct in the hazy stillness of the day and the passing of time. I traced the print below with my finger: *Polar Explorer, Charles Rasmus Stewart, Angmagssalik, Greenland, 1948.*

'A newspaper cutting,' Snorri explained. 'We received a lot of publicity: he knew how to make sure we did not go unnoticed.'

The book was filled with photographs chronicling the expedition: sleds and dogs appeared with ghostly clarity from between the pages, interspersed with unshaven faces discoloured from the chill of the air and inset with wild eyes. *The wilderness enduring.* My heart ached as I looked upon this bleak and distant landscape, teeming with life to the trained eye, but a frozen wasteland to those who only visited – like aliens from another world.

The images were distorted as the watery sun spilled again through the open window in rays and splashes. The room was comfortably cool. Outside, the wind blew with a gentle whisper, laced with an iciness that took the breath away, following its path over the glacier, across the barren flood plain and now to the openness of the Atlantic.

The final page of the album: a different image altogether. Against a hazy backdrop that previewed a cluster of skin

6

tents under bleak, snow-strewn mountains, there stood my father – the depiction of him with which I was now so familiar, never having encountered the man in flesh and blood – dressed in kamiks and bear-skin trousers as though he himself were one of our people. His hands, head and face were exposed. Beside him I recognised the towering figure of Snorri, curiously unmistakable in the same native attire, though the age and quality of the image almost obscured the features on his pale skin. And on my father's other side, small and unremarkable, stood a woman. Strange, that while I knew my father only from old photographs, I had never encountered an image of my mother. She looked young, some might say little more than a girl, her face full and round; and although the monochrome nature of the picture kept forever hidden the bright colours of her sewn-skin costume, her hair still fell to her hips in a striking raven-black cascade. There stirred no emotion within me, for I found myself unable to reconcile this unexpected image, immobile and un-living, with the mother I had known, the woman who had brought me into the world. But what else could I see? From the folds of her large skin hood there peered a face over her shoulder, a new, innocent face, black hair and plump cheeks, eyes screwed tightly shut.

'The child,' I began, though did not see the need to say any more as Snorri nodded his head and smiled wistfully.

'Yes. You could not have been more than a few months old.'

I looked again with some discomfort. I could not reconcile my existence with this moment of which I of course had no recollection. The two people who were responsible for my coming into the world, together in the same image – and I, too, was there: the life they had created. I was relieved that my eyes had evidently been closed when the photograph was taken. Without their strangeness I looked like a normal Greenlandic child, the evidence of my cursed nature hidden from the judgement of the world.

'And the girl standing beside you?' I added, resting my

finger on the figure, eager to deter the path of my wandering thoughts. Snorri hesitated, appeared almost bashful as he no doubt apprehended my meaning, the possibility of an accusation against him.

'But you were married,' I said; 'you have a family.'

'So did your father.' he answered, and at once the topic fell from his lips. For a moment there was silence, and the air became heavier as the wind dipped momentarily. 'I was very sorry to hear of his passing.'

I sensed the sincerity of his remark, though I knew their friendship to have come to an end many years previously. I only nodded in response. I had not known the man.

Stirring himself into motion, Snorri took a seat, silently and almost apologetically in the chair opposite mine. The early spring wind picked up once more and sent a sharp gust through the open window. The panes rattled. The ice in our glasses had all but melted.

'I would very much like to know,' he said, 'how you came to be here. In this country, in my house, so many miles from your home.' As the query came to an end, the wind made a sudden exit from the room, leaving in its wake an open, peaceful sort of quiet in which one could almost hear the swell of the tempestuous sea and the creeping advance of the ancient glacial ice.

'I was guided here,' I said quietly, unabashedly, 'by a helping spirit.'

My heart sank in my chest as I mentioned my absent friend. I considered telling Snorri, there and then, that my helping spirit had in fact gone missing, and it was the continued search for him that had brought me here, to Snorri's home. But I could not bring myself to say it – what would he think of me? I fought the bizarre urge to smile as I thought about how I would ask Snorri if he had seen *Eqingaleq*: an ancient figure padding along the Reykjavík streets, perhaps, in worn sealskin kamiks and bearskin trousers, suspiciously eyeing up the passers-by with their plastic umbrellas. But they would not be able to see him, of course. Snorri would not be able to see him.

I glanced back to Snorri and saw that he was looking at me thoughtfully. Yet there was no hint of derision in his gaze, no eyebrow raised in scepticism nor patronising sympathy – something I had come to expect from those who knew only the culture they had been brought up in. But this man had spent time in the far north, that much was true, he had lived amongst my people, taken a woman there; adopted our clothes and customs as his own. My heart warmed towards him that he should understand.

'As it is just the two of us here,' he said, 'perhaps you might like to tell me your story.'

'*My* story?'

'The story of the path that has brought you here, and the reason for your journey.'

I looked down at the photographs on the table. Disconcerted by the blurred faces of those people who had since passed away I instead studied the shapes of the mountains in the distance. I saw reflected in them the warm recollections of home, the landscape captured so teasingly in these old, grainy images. I closed my tired eyes, and the windswept Icelandic coast evaporated and was lost.

2

Where I come from, fields of ice stretch to the horizon and the mountains reach to the sky. There is only one long day and one long night by which the lives of those who live there are mapped out year after year. When the sun shines in the short summertime, it casts its perpetual light upon both the waking world and the sleeping world. When the winter darkness falls and the bitter cold sets in there is no respite brought by the morning, for the blackness is enduring.

But sometimes the sky is alive with leaping, dancing colours: pillars and prisms fall from the atmosphere and rise again, forming a path across the heavens and illuminating the endless fields of ice in ethereal light. In midwinter this is the only light – this, and the meagre but welcoming flames of the blubber lamps – for Sun and Moon, brother and sister, will not be seen together in the wide sky. Their own fate was sealed in the blackness of the long night when, the lamps all extinguished, they found each other in the dark, seeking the warmth and comfort of living bodies yet each believing the other to be somebody else. Now Moon pursues Sun across the sky, and Sun, ashamed, will not look upon him.

Beneath their eternal chase, the world moves to the same rhythm, steadily and sometimes secretly. Over and under the ice there swells a great force of life: the seal, with its deep human eyes; the bear, the lonely hunter who roams the frozen expanses in search of a kill; and the lingering fox who hopes to steal a scrap of meat. The raven and the sharp-eyed gull patrol the skies and see all below, though they are not friends. The hunter will take from this only what he needs for his family and community, and in harmony the same rhythms of nature will ebb and flow like the summer tide.

The White Man came late to our way of life, though before my time and before my mother's. He found our people living at the end of the world and on the edge of existence, an uncivilised people untouched by the Western world, eking out a primitive existence from the land.

But civilisation comes at such a high price. Now there are few of our people who remember the ways of our ancestors: few who are able to flense a seal using tools fashioned from bone, few who can recall the uses for each and every part of the animal. Now the landscape is a hindrance, an obstacle to overcome, for our imported houses are ill-adapted to the northern temperatures and our tinned food creates waste for which there can be found no place.

Now there is no one who, by transcending his earthly body in trance, can appeal to the Mother of the Sea when she takes back into her long flowing hair the creatures who have fed our existence for many thousands of years. She does this only when she has been wronged by the people; now there can be no hope to appease the hurt she has suffered through all our wrongdoings.

My own ancestry cannot be denied. Like so many others of this generation I am the result of the union between the gull and the raven: a White man and a Greenlandic woman. Since early childhood Eqingaleq has appeared – only to me – as my helping spirit, yet sometimes I still feel that my wings are white. But Eqingaleq has remained with me: he would

12

only guide one of his own, and never one who, like the gull, would fiercely fight with him over the same scrap of meat. We all know, however, that the gull will win.

Did I expect him to guide me down the path of our ancestors? Perhaps that is not his purpose. We are fast-footed and wild, divided between two paths. Yet the world in which these two paths collide is neither here nor there. We were never meant to remain in this abandoned place.

At one time a boy would grow up to become a hunter and provider; now he grows to be unemployed. My own mother could not have concerned herself much with the fate of her only son, however, for she drank herself to death before I had grown to truly understand the lure and destruction of this new vice.

Guided by Eqingaleq, he taught me how to fashion harpoons, to hunt the seal and the hare, to steer a kayak amongst the pack ice, yet there seems little use for these skills when the voices of our ancestors can no longer be heard.

I grew into a man, and the girl I thought I loved bore me a child but would not marry me – did she see in me the white wings and goggle eyes of the intruder from the West? A reminder of this new half-formed world of material comforts and spiritual desolation.

The divided soul cannot endure forever; sooner or later a choice must be made, whether conscious or not, whether intuitive or calculated, long-awaited or spontaneous. There comes a point at which, the blubber lamp having burnt out and the once-good meat having been thrown to the dogs, one path becomes non-traversable – perhaps it had always been closed off.

My own turn of fate came one spring afternoon, when the hare's pelt had just begun to turn its summer brown, when

Sun dared show herself in the sky for a few hours a day and the dog sleds could no longer be driven across the fjord for it had begun to thaw and fragment into opening water. I was sitting on my front doorstep in the last few rays of weak sunlight, resewing a seam on the soles of my sealskin kamiks with sinew thread when, hearing the crisp crunch of ageing snow I looked up from my task and beheld a man approaching. A White Man, dressed in jeans and bright orange rubber boots. This was the only impression I received, for as he drew closer and mounted the few wooden steps to the front door the fleeing sun cast her rays from directly over his shoulder so that, squinting, all I could see was a looming silhouette against a backdrop of colourful, snow-strewn houses. The dogs howled and pulled at their chains.

The figure cleared his throat and, in curiously-spoken Danish, asked me if my name was Malik, Ketty's son. Still peering up at his obscured features – boot and needle clutched in alternate hands – I answered in the affirmative, adding that he may be disappointed to know that Ketty was no longer around. He coughed, made no more mention of my mother, but said bluntly that he was a friend of my father's.

My father? Now there was a character I did not often hear mentioned – ever, in fact. Eqingaleq, from where he sat dozing against the wall of the house, pricked up his ears.

I suggested that I should pour us both a cup of coffee, for I had just made a pot in anticipation of completing the mending of my boots. I added that perhaps he should join me on the step. This would save him the hassle of removing his own boots, I pointed out. At any rate, I thought to myself, the house was quite dark and rather empty – for cruel fate had so dictated that I should be its only occupant – and certainly no warmer than the crisp, spring air.

Once he had awkwardly murmured his consent, I sprang up and slipped inside for the coffee. The veiled darkness by which the man's features were obscured was making me a little uneasy.

14

The arrival of springtime was a blessing for me, if only for the opportunity to spend at least some of my waking hours outdoors, once the cold had shed some of its bite. The interior of the house could by no stretch of the imagination be considered a homely place: in addition to its severe lack of warmth, laughter and indeed furniture, every inch was filled with unwanted, unpleasant memories of my incapacitated mother engulfed by the suffocating smell of liquor, passed out unceremoniously on the floor or sprawled, slurring bitter nonsense, across the kitchen table. I had tried my best to better these living conditions, but there was nothing I could do without a family of my own to bring the place to life. Since I was denied my baby daughter, for reasons I struggled to comprehend, there seemed little hope that the walls might be scrubbed of their unwelcome memories. The front doorstep had its memories, too, for I could not count the number of times I had found my mother face down there in the snow. But at least here the sun's rays had the power to alleviate the vestiges of much of this past unpleasantness.

When I returned with two cups of fresh coffee my visitor had, as bidden, taken a seat on the step. I could see him more clearly now: the thick grey hair uncovered, the straight mouth, the beaked nose and calculating blue eyes. It was his eyes that made me shiver with unease, though I did not know why. There was something familiar about his face, I thought, but I could not place him.

He shifted his feet, apparently ill at ease as I scrutinised his features. He accepted the coffee with a polite nod.

He was an Englishman, he announced, when I had barely managed to sit down and before I had the chance even to prompt him. He had arrived that very morning, on the year's first supply ship from Denmark, and once in the town had sought me out, for shortly before leaving his country for the journey here he had received some news which concerned me directly. I was certainly intrigued: how could the outside world, I wondered, find itself linked to *me*? I lived at the end

15

of the world; I was a ghost caught between two peoples and two conflicting ways of life – one dying, one dominating.

It was not good news, my visitor continued, pulling at the neck of his jumper and trying unsuccessfully to conceal his discomfort. He had come to tell me that my father had recently passed away, a heart attack at the young age of fifty-five. He was very sorry, he said, to have to bring me such news. I nodded, if only for the sake of a response. This was not bad news, nor was it good news; it was simply news from a distant land that concerned people other than myself and could surely have no foreseeable impact upon my own circumstances. I had not met my father. I had not met anyone who had known my father well, save for my mother – who had always refused to discuss the matter, exploding only with profanities if I dared encroach upon the subject – her brother, and perhaps the man now sat on my front doorstep, shifting uncomfortably and letting his coffee go cold.

I watched the steam rise and dissipate, along with my shallow breath in the cooling air. Had this man come to tell me only that the one existing link between myself and the world outside was now no more?

'Did you know my father?' I asked, for it seemed that he had told me all that he had to say.

'Not well,' he answered. There followed a pause, then he added: 'But I'm sure he will be greatly missed.'

I nodded again, suppressing the almost overwhelming and totally shameful urge to laugh out loud. I knew well enough to ascertain that this last remark was one of condolence, but why should he feel the need for such formalities when the deceased had been and always would be a stranger to me? I heard Eqingaleq give a loud snort, presumably for the same reasons, and I shot him a stern glare, admittedly more for my own sake – that by feigning offence I might conceal from him my sense of detachment. He was not to be fooled, and only stuck out his tongue in response.

My visitor roused himself as if to indicate that our meeting

16

had come to an end. But he did not rise, and instead said quietly: 'I am leaving in five days' time: for England. I will be attending your father's funeral... If you would like to pay your respects, I may be able to get you passage on the ship.' His cold blue eyes met mine, yet I had no ready answer for such an unexpected proposal. The silence that followed was long and uncomfortable. His gaze lingered for longer than I would have liked as he studied the strangeness of my own eyes, curiously, warily, as did so many others. Even those who were laying their own eyes upon my cursed ones for the hundredth time.

As I had given no indication that I might respond, the grey-haired man with the beaked nose promptly stood up, thanked me for the coffee – though he had not touched a drop – offered his stilted condolences once more, and took his leave. I watched him trudge away down the road, hunched over, keeping his gaze on the ground. The sun had gradually, prematurely, sunk below the mountains, and the surrounding houses rose as hazy shadows around the man's solitary figure. The lights from those houses which were occupied spilled from the windows and caused a morphing shadow to play about the man's feet: a sharp-beaked, web-footed shadow with great white wings.

I shivered. Sun had forsaken those beneath her and would not return for some time. I retreated into the house, reluctantly, as needs must. I lit the lamp and sat for a long while in thought. Outside the evening was still and quiet, and the only sound I could hear was that of Eqingaleq sharpening his bone carving knife, a habit of his during the long winter evenings. I do not know that I thought of anything in particular. My head was filled with the voices of thousands of years, the wilderness of the ice fields and the ancient strength of the mountains. I imagined the deep eyes of the seal, the unfocused eyes of my mother, the richness of the ocean and the unknown emptiness that lay beyond. And my own eyes: one dark, like the eyes of my people and my ancestors; the other pale blue, almost colourless, its pupil a mere pinprick in a pool of shallow water. This was a signpost to my mixed heritage and the curse that ran in my blood, which had branded me an outcast from the moment of my birth...

...You'd thought yourself an orphan anyway, said Eqingaleq, as he ran a bony finger down the length of the knife blade, testing its sharpness.

An orphan. I leapt to my feet, donned my parka and mended kamiks. I blew out the lamp, burst into the open air and set off at a run down the hill towards the harbour. There were few people about; the town appeared to sleep now that the children had ceased their play and were hidden indoors. Their calls, cries and laughter had been replaced by the forlorn howling of the dogs chained up outside many of the houses beside dilapidated sleds or the skeletons of those which once had been functional. A cruel wind had begun to blow, bringing with it the fresh smell of salt water.

A chill ran down the length of my spine as I stood looking up at the dark, towering bulk of the supply ship, the company's logo tattooed on its side. There shone no lights around this now deserted place. The ship waited, empty and silent, and the sea wind whistled around its shadow.

In the semi-darkness a raven alighted on an abandoned crate. It ruffled its great wings, cocked its head at me and emitted a low croak which sailed upon the wind. The Doctor's house! Of course, where else would the man be staying? I set off urgently in this direction, my legs stiff from the cold. Eqingaleq, still in his raven form, soared like a demonic shadow some way ahead to be sure I would not lose my way, though even in the dark my memory served me well.

The house was distinctive for it stood highest atop the hill. It was a grand red-painted house outside which the Danish flag could be seen always, waving and dancing in the breeze or rippling furiously in the frequent winds.

My hammering upon the door was answered by the

Doctor. I saw on his winter-pale face a look of mild, questioning surprise as he opened the door. I announced somewhat hastily that I urgently required to speak to the man with a beak instead of a nose. The surprise turned to bemusement, though eventually he appeared to ascertain my meaning and so disappeared inside. The door having been left ajar there could be heard the sound of what seemed like many murmured voices, the lively chink of glasses and the occasional ripple of laughter. The light which spilled out onto the doorstep was warm and welcoming and seemed to belong to a different world than the one in which I stood now, shivering in cold and in anticipation. Eqingaleq, once more in his human form and evidently gripped by an insatiable curiosity, crept with silent feet to the crack in the door and peered in. I hissed at him in nervous irritation. He only looked at me humorously, then winked, and the glow from inside the house illuminated his crooked, painted face and danced in his deep, black eyes. As he curled his fingers around the edge of the door, ready to slowly ease it open, it was flung suddenly aside and the light spilled blindingly onto the doorstep. Eqingaleq yelped in surprise and hid himself in my shadow.

The beak-nosed man peered down at me, once more appearing the tall dark stranger for the light by which he was backed. I hastily declared, lest I lose my nerve, that I would like to take him up on his offer, that I would accept passage to England and that I sought to attend my father's funeral. I assured him that I had a passport, one that I had obtained a year or two ago with the intention of travelling to Denmark. I had not had the courage to embark on the trip, but of course I kept this bit to myself.

Again there was silence while he observed me down the bridge of his nose, apparently in cold calculation: not so much as a smile touched his lips.

'I can pay my way,' I blurted out, fearful that my acceptance of the offer might have come too late. I could feel Eqingaleq's imploring eyes upon me, but in determination I kept my own gaze fixed upon the man in the doorway. I wished that I could better see his face so that I might remember where I had seen it before.

'We leave on Saturday morning,' he said coldly, 'at nine o'clock. Don't be late.' With that he gave a curt nod and, before I had the chance to proffer my thanks, or indeed to question, he abruptly closed the door.

The night time returned. I began to shuffle in the direction of home. My urgent task having been brought to a spectacularly non-dramatic close, my adrenaline began now to dissipate, and the cold and the dark set in once more. I found myself shivering to the bone. Now was the time for doubt.

Pay our way?! Eqingaleq hissed in my ear. *With what, exactly?*

My teeth chattered in my jaw like live things. *We can sell the dogs*, I said.

We both knew we would not be needing them, wherever the beaked man might take us.

3

Rasmus

1948

Snapshots of his childhood sanctuary under the stairs and those books which he had coveted with all the passion of his soul came to him uninvited but not altogether unwelcome, as he sought sleep on that first night crossing the North Atlantic.

He had taken the book with him into his customary hiding place under the stairs. Here he would sit for hours, relishing each turn of the page with fingers that trembled with excitement and the fear of discovery. He traced the words with his fingers, fixed his torch on the grainy images and drawings. There were heavy-bearded men dressed in skins against the cold, icebergs as big as houses, dogs pulling sleds, tents in the wilderness...

In those stolen moments, the cupboard under the stairs transformed into a vast glacier, hundreds of miles thick, and the polar winds swept across with such force they could knock a man from his feet. He would pull his scarf tighter about his neck (he took care to make sure this necessary item remained stashed with the books – props were essential). As he pored over the book on his lap he would imagine he were Adolphus Greely, famous polar explorer stranded in the icy wilderness of Ellesmere Island for years on end; or Sir John Franklin, who had vanished from the face of the earth in his attempts to discover the Northwest Passage to the continent. Some said that Franklin and his men had resorted to cannibalism in the face of starvation. This was the part of the tale he had liked the most as a boy: the hardships of those who dared venture so far north.

Sometimes, in the winter, he woke to find his home town covered by a thick blanket of snow. On those days he was Robert Peary, making a heroic first attempt to reach the geographic North Pole; sometimes the snow would still fall during his expedition, and he must brave blizzards and sub-zero temperatures. Frostbite and starvation were constant threats, but always he reached the top of the world. Planting his homemade flag, he allowed himself to picture the day when he, too, would be known for his feats of Arctic exploration. Charles Rasmus Stewart, weather-beaten face set with grey stubble and ringed by a fur hood, looking at the camera with weary eyes that had seen things of which others could only dream, or horrors one could only hope to forget. *Just like Peary.*

The ship tossed like a sailing boat on the fierce swell of the sea. The wind that blew that evening was already infused with an iciness that made the tips of his fingers tingle with excitement. As he stood up on the deck, the fog had lifted from his senses and his spirit had soared with the seagulls that trailed the laden ship. Strangely, this time it was not Peary whose image he saw before him, but that of Knud Rasmussen, an explorer who did not discover, but learned; and did not conquer, but stayed. That was what Rasmus longed for now: to learn from the people of the Arctic, those whom he most admired. He wanted to learn not only how to survive, but how to *live* in this place that lay so close to the world's end.

Once he arrived in east Greenland he would stay, for a few months at least, in the settlement that was named Angmagssalik, before undertaking the journey to Greenland's west coast. To stay first in Angmagssalik, he had foreseen, was essential: he must learn to drive the dogs in the native way, the huskies that would pull the sledge across the ice cap to the opposite coast. This was the only way to travel in the glacial wilderness. He would require skin clothing too, and to further his knowledge of navigation even in the most adverse weather conditions.

Rasmus shivered with the thrill of adventure and anticipation: his first polar expedition. He had spent a good many years planning the journey, but he had dreamed of it his entire life. The advent of the war had of course brought his ambitions to a temporary halt – a regrettable turn of events, yet it had given him the chance, at least, to build up his survival skills and brush up on his navigational expertise. The fantasising and planning of this – as then hypothetical – expedition had kept him going through even the most challenging obstacles of his wartime career.

The desire to conquer the harsh Arctic landscape, just as those explorers who had gone before him had done, was his life's ambition; yet he was driven first and foremost by an emotion so strong it almost frightened him. He wanted to become one with the Arctic wilderness. He wanted to become one of the people who called it their home.

His companions on this journey across the Greenland ice cap were to be two old friends – or one old friend and an acquaintance, at least.

Rasmus and Snorri had both studied at the Royal School of Military Survey as young men. Though British-born, Snorri's mother was from Iceland – the almost-Arctic, in Rasmus's eyes. Rasmus was intrigued by the man's matrilineal heritage; and Snorri, in turn, was soon won over by his new friend's boundless enthusiasm for the northern climes. They had become firm friends. Snorri was good-humoured, his manner calm and relaxed. The gentle tone of his voice could put anyone at ease. Rasmus could not think of a more suitable companion during months of isolation in the seemingly endless polar wilderness.

If only, he thought, he could say the same about the third member of the party: the man known as Birdie.

4

Malik

1973

For days I twisted and turned in a bed of sea-sickness, moaning and awaiting a drawn-out death. Surely this suffering was a punishment, administered to the vagrant, uncaring one who had left his home. The ship leapt upon the waves, jerking from side to side as though the very ocean tried to drag it into its depths. It lolled and rocked at the foundations, and my body protested violently. This was not the natural rhythm of the waves and water below a well-crafted kayak; the ocean shook us to the very bones, attempting to hurl us back to whence we had come – for one should not intrude who does not have the right.

I had taken a very rushed leave of my home town, unsure almost to the last minute of the path I would take, or the one which would be handed to me. I was anxious also that I might anyway be refused passage on the ship. Eventually, however, encouraged by Eqingaleq, I had knocked on all those doors which had been opened to me during my short life. I had thrown my heart wide open yet kept the explanations to a minimum. Last of all I had said goodbye to my daughter. She was still much too young to comprehend that I was leaving, yet I could go nowhere without first seeing her and embracing her, for I did not know when again I would be near her. To my shame I could not stop the hot tears that sprang to my eyes, and I held her close until her mother impatiently remarked that my leaving was my own decision and no right did I have to seek sympathy. I did not tell her that the decision did not feel like my own, but that of a force far stronger than myself. I could not deny my blood.

Every detail of my hasty departure was hurled about my head with the perpetual rocking and jerking of the ship. Pictures and memories replayed themselves over and over again with obsessive clarity, until in my sickness they became distorted. Then I saw instead the demonic white faces of bears, the open beaks and beady eyes of birds, and the twisted features of the spirits, laughing and chanting. Then there came into view the crooked countenance of Eqingaleq: his large, flat nosed pushed to one side, broken and misshapen, stealing the symmetry from his face. His dark, ancestral eyes were as old as the land and as deep as the sea: kind, wise and troubled. The painted black lines on his skin drew his face into changing patterns, up into the nest of his wiry black hair.

We had reached land again, he wished to tell me. My relief was to be short-lived, however, as I remembered we had arrived only in Denmark. From here we must endure a second sea journey to England, our destination.

That night as we left Denmark I found myself, in a trance-like state of unconsciousness, face to face with the Mother of the Sea. I was unsure as to whether or not I had desired to behold her; and embarrassed for I did not know why I had come. Knowingly she looked upon me, her long, raven-black hair reaching out like fingers of seaweed in each and every direction. Her eyes revealed a knowledge of centuries. And in a voice saturated with the rushing of waves she told me only that I should tread carefully, that the gull's wings can be folded and hidden away so that only he who dares to look closely can perceive them.

I listened, for surely she should know: she who was courted by no other than a gull who disguised himself as a man. Wearing eye goggles fashioned from bone, set with a slit before each eye, he was able to see yet his watery eyes remained hidden, concealing the truth of his species. He approached her father and asked if he might have her hand in marriage, for so much did he admire her human beauty. The request was accepted, the marriage was made. Soon after the girl, along with her parents and brother as was the custom, moved to the home of the suitor, on an island off the shoreline. But once the bride beheld her new husband's hideous, watery eyes she knew him for what he was. The family fled, clambering into a boat and beginning to row back to the mainland. Yet the gull unfolded his great white wings and pursued them over the stormy sea. The girl's father, fearing for his own safety, grabbed hold of his daughter and threw her overboard, that the gull might reclaim her and be content. She caught onto the sides of the boat and desperately clung on, but one by one the old man cut off her fingers. When they had all been severed she sank to the ocean bed, where still she lies. Her fingers became seals, walruses and narwhal. These creatures she keeps entangled within her long, greasy hair, until such time as the shaman, visiting her from his community, consoles her and washes the centuries of accumulated salt and mud from her locks. Only when this has been done will she release the animals back into the sea, to the skill of the hunter and the use of the people.

To her, surely, I must listen.

I awoke with the taste of salt on my lips. Free from sickness, and invigorated I sought out the beak-nosed Englishman. There were many questions I wished to ask, and ask I did; yet he answered only in brief sentences, of the yes or no variety if it were appropriate, and even if it were not. Yes, he had known my father well. He had worked with him. Yes, he had been to Greenland before. No, he had not met my mother. How many of these statements did I believe, I wonder? The man was distant, curt, almost unresponsive, yet there was no one else to whom I could turn; I was entirely in his power and under his protection. What choice did I have but to trust him? Reading my thoughts and my suspicions, Eqingaleq put his mouth to my ear and whispered: had I noticed that despite the man's age the corners of his mouth and eyes bore no wrinkles? It was as though never once had they been creased in laughter or joy. He did not recall ever encountering such a characterless face.

And the man's eyes: it was as if they were full of water, colourless and shallow.

England, too, appeared colourless. The sky was hung with heavy, grey clouds that leaked a perpetual, irritating drizzle which seemed as though it might persist for ever. The faces by which we were surrounded looked as though they had never seen the sunlight. I knew that here the winters did not wallow in constant darkness, yet it was easy to imagine that this weather, this bleakness, might continue throughout the entire year.

Where I had come from the summer skies, for the most part, stretched for cloudless mile upon cloudless mile, an expanse of blue, and the sunlight glinted off the glacial ice, blindingly and brilliantly. The rain, when it did fall, was sudden, fierce and refreshing. It did not linger upon the soul as it did here. Beside me, Eqingaleq shivered despite the warmth of his bearskin trousers: it was not that this new country was cold – we were accustomed to freezing arctic winters, after all – yet the dreariness of the weather seemed to penetrate to the very bones.

28

Never before had I beheld so many people in one place, each a stranger to the other. At the harbour, while we had disembarked, I had seen many men laughing and talking, yet here upon the concrete streets there passed no signs of recognition between those who hurried along, around corners and over roads, heads bent to the weather and eyes at their feet. I realised how small must be the world from which I had come.

It need not be said that I drew some strange looks from those passers-by who deigned to lift their eyes from the ground, no doubt drawn by the sight of my sealskin kamiks. I had otherwise dressed in blue jeans, a shirt and my old, Norwegian fisherman's jumper, that I might the more blend in. Yet I could not disguise the colour of my skin or my ink-black hair, any more than my scrutinisers were able to veil their curiosity.

We had arrived just as the skies were beginning to darken, and as night fell we – that is, the beak-nosed man and I – sought lodgings. We would continue to our destination in the morning, I was curtly and irritably informed in response to my questioning.

The room had only one bed, in which the Englishman slept soundly while Eqingaleq and I lay on the floor, huddled together under my anorak, both our heads resting on my backpack. I was unable to sleep, though not so much for the discomfort of my excuse for a bed: this new country was noisy, deafeningly so. In my town, up north, there was not one man who could dream of importing a motor vehicle from Europe – even if he could afford to, for there were no roads on which to drive one after all – yet here it seemed as though there were millions of them. Each time a car passed in the street below I would hear its rumble in the near-distance, growing ever louder until its engine was all but a roar intruding upon the comforts of sleep. Eventually, the sound would die away, only to be replaced by the approach of another vehicle. The air, too, was thick with the oppression of row upon row of towering buildings, a labyrinth of endless streets lined with faceless brick walls. When finally I fell into an exhausted slumber, as dawn fast approached, I dreamed of space, colour and light; yet upon waking became choked once more by my surroundings.

In the morning light I was unsurprised to find that it was still raining. I peered out of the grubby window, then rested my forehead against the cooling glass and breathed a mist before my eyes. I felt weak from the swell of the sea, and hungry and dizzy from too many sleepless nights. My breath on the window pane obscured the view of the city, and I could instead allow myself to imagine that behind the mist there rose mountains, or that the unspoiled purity of snow on ice merged everything into a wonderful and tranquil peace. Unwilling to permit me this moment, my humourless companion barked that I must get a move on, or I would cause him to be late.

'But where are we going?' I asked, turning to face him across the small room. This was a question I had voiced many times, yet the answer had not been forthcoming, for reasons presumably beyond my understanding. He had not mentioned the funeral of my father since we had sat awkwardly together, as strangers, on my front doorstep. He was no less a stranger to me now.

'It doesn't matter to you where we are going,' the man replied in a voice edged with irritation – anger, even.

'I would like to know where we are going,' I repeated. 'You've brought me this far but you haven't told me –.'

'Shut up and get your f-ing shoes on,' he growled.

I felt an anger, though weary, rise within me that I should be spoken to in such a way. Behind him, Eqingaleq strained his features and made frantic motions with his arms, indicating that I should drop the subject and do as I had been instructed. But I was not about to step down so easily. The anger by which I was spurned was, perhaps, directed towards myself, for I had accompanied this stranger to a country about which I knew very little – indeed I could barely speak the language – and for reasons that were beginning to be lost to me. The curiosity and sense of purpose I had felt upon leaving my home I could now barely recall. Once so sure of myself, now I was lost, and I could feel the cold hand of fear beginning to claw at my heart.

'I would like to have something to eat first.' It took all my energy to keep my voice from shaking.

'You'll get nothing.'

I was unsure anyway whether I would be able to stomach even a morsel of food. Ignoring Eqingaleq's arms flapping in warning, I continued nonetheless, unaware, in the dizzy heat that spread across my cheeks, that the Englishman was moving quickly towards me: 'I am not going anywhere with you until –.' Before I knew what was happening, the man had raised a thick hand and landed it with all his strength against my cheek. The blow sent me to my knees, my own hand raised instinctively against the point of impact. I cried out in pain, in shock, and my eyes welled with tears.

'We are leaving,' he said, 'Now.'

Eqingaleq helped me to my feet.

5

The first train journey of my life somehow marked a catastrophic leap into the chaos and machinery of the modern Western world which, until this moment, had been known to me only in books, photographs or hearsay. The beak-nosed man, having hauled me into the throes of a new day with the usual carelessness and insensitivity he had come to exhibit where I was concerned, had all but dragged me into the carriage of this new mechanical monster. I was sleep-deprived and nauseous, and overcome by uncertainty. The soporific rhythm of the train, however, soon sent me into an unwilling slumber which I could not fight. My senses, which had been overwhelmed by this tide of new information and experience, found opportunity to desert me for one long stretch of thoughtlessness. When eventually I slipped back into the haze of consciousness, as the train came to a standstill, I saw only brick, concrete and grey rain.

Leaning towards Eqingaleq I whispered *were we not still in the same place?* He said he did not know, for he too, had drifted from his senses with this strange sorcery of rhythm.

Some helping spirit you are, I reproached him, though light-heartedly and with a weak smile. Were it not for his

33

presence and companionship I might have found myself unbearably alone.

We helped each other off the train and together followed the thickset figure of the Englishman. Purposefully, and with long, determined strides he sought his path ahead and did not once turn his head to ascertain that I was at his heels. There was no need, I surmised, for he knew full well that I had nowhere else to go. And besides, what difference would it make to him if I were to duck unseen into the flowing crowd and disappear from his sight, never to return?

It seemed logical, to the people-pleasing, apologetic side of my mind to assume that the man were carrying out some sort of selfless favour towards me. The decision to leave my home had been my own, and were it not for the guidance of this white man who had taken me aboard the ship, I would be utterly lost in a foreign country and, so it seemed, a different time. Perhaps, then, the treatment that I received from him was entirely warranted; perhaps it was as much as I deserved and as much as he could give. Could I expect him to feed me as well as guide me? Although this idea welled foremost in my mind, I could not fight the resentment that grew and grew each time I laid eyes upon the man, and for this I was ashamed. While it was true that he had violently laid his hands upon me in anger, it seemed entirely likely that he was grappling with emotions which could find no other expression – we were, after all and as far as I could tell, on our way to a funeral. Perhaps he and this late father of mine had been close. Perhaps he was bereaved.

Eqingaleq did not agree. The man had revealed his white wings in the clear light of day, he said, the moment he had hit me. The man's hideous eyes, he said, turned him cold to the very bones. Half-heartedly I reprimanded him for his assumptions: we should not condemn the man simply because we had not yet seen him smile, or because we could see no light in his watery eyes. We must learn to see the good in those whom we needed to trust.

We bickered in hushed tones as we trailed the man in question, stumbling over our sealskin boots in our haste to keep up. Leaving the train station, which appeared identical down to the very last detail to the one from which we had boarded the train, we moved onto endless grey streets no different from those which had crowded the window of last night's lodgings and suffocated me as I slept. We walked for what seemed like hours. I worried that the unyielding surface of the streets would wear through the soles of my skin boots, those boots which had held strong for years.

At long last we turned from the streets, and passing through an ornate iron gate left behind the blank faces of the buildings. In their place rose great, leafy trees, like ancient giants, the likes of which I had never before seen with my own eyes. As we walked the distant roar of the traffic grew quieter, softer, and faded away. I realised with wonder that in its absence I could hear the rustle of the trees' magnificent canopies above my head. My feet came to a standstill, I peered upwards towards the grey sky, raindrops fell from the leaves into my eyes and onto my cheeks; everything was wonderfully still and quiet. The suddenness of this change threw my exhausted mind off balance, and for a second I forgot where I was.

This moment, however, was short-lived, for at once the Englishman hissed something that I could not catch, and Eqingaleq dragged me onwards. Ahead of us I saw gathered a group of people whose figures stood out like unmoving, dark silhouettes, each and every one dressed in black clothes which cut a stark, terrible contrast with the surroundings. To my horror the grey-haired man led us directly to the gathering, stopping only on the outskirts. I sensed one hundred pairs of eyes turn upon me, some in curiosity or surprise. Some were still frozen in sadness, others in an array of emotions I could not decipher. Nonetheless I could feel the mêlée of thought and emotion my arrival had caused move like electricity through the air. Not a word was spoken, save for the continued drone of a man, also robed in black, who continued to address the crowd.

I might have turned and fled, had not the sun decided, at that moment, to finally make an appearance. It was as though the sky opened and flooded the world with a brilliant, unexpected light that spilled colour upon the greenery and fell in broken rays beneath the broad canopies. The gathering was not overshadowed by the trees, and thus basked in warm sunlight; across the patch of bright sky that showed overhead there flew a gaggle of geese, honking their joy of freedom. Through their keen eyes I imagined the drab city sprawled beneath, like a stain upon the earth, and at its limits the beginning of lush, green fields strewn with drops of the recent rain, glistening in the sunlight. . .

I winced as the grey-haired man elbowed me sharply in the ribs.

'You might at least *try* to look bereaved,' he hissed through clenched teeth.

I realised with a sudden rush of nausea that this gathering of black-clad folk was in fact the funeral to which I had been promised passage. I had not known what to expect. The experience that I had fabricated in my imaginings, and mentally replayed countless times during the journey to this place, had been one of profundity: a picture in which I was to be found in deep contemplation to finally be so near to one to whom I owed my existence. In reality, however, I was taken so much by surprise that all understanding of the proceedings abandoned me; my mind wandered and came to dwell only on the mundane and the general.

How bizarre, I contemplated, that the deceased should be confined to a wooden box before being placed into the ground: forever removed from the very earth from which they had come. I shuddered involuntarily at the thought of my elusive father's body decomposing alone in its wooden tomb; his soul would not be at peace until the earth had reclaimed his flesh, blood and bones. Looking around the graveyard I saw that the ground was littered with slabs of rock standing on end, and though they were engraved with letters I could not read I understood that under each one, beneath the grass, must be buried such a box as the one in which my late father now lay. A box that housed the remains of a body denied final peace with the earth.

How very different had been the burial of our ancestors! In my place of home, where the earth was so hardened by perpetual frost, it had been custom instead to heap stones over the bodies of the deceased. As a child I had often been drawn to these heaped mounds of rocks outside the town where, peering through the windows between the stones I could still see the bones of he who had been laid to rest so many years before. And in the shadow of the mountains they looked out over the fjord, those mountains and the sea beyond. During the short summer the water was littered and strewn with floating ice glowing serenely in the perpetual light; in the winter it became solid as far as the eye could see, and creaked and groaned in the dark with the movements of the spirits who lived beneath. This was the rightful place for the dead.

I stole a look at the man who had brought me here. His expression was cold. I could sense a feeling of urgency and expectation beneath this calm demeanour, as though he were waiting for something to occur. My skin prickled.

Concurrently there ran a ripple through the gathering. The man robed in black had stopped speaking, and those present began to disperse. The beaked man grabbed me roughly by the arm and steered me along in the direction the crowd were taking. Again we were on the streets, but thankfully not for long, for rounding a corner we passed through a doorway and into one of the buildings. I stood bewildered. Around me, the black-clad people were removing their coats and exchanging remarks. Some smiled, even laughed, though each one avoided my eyes. Once each and every coat had been hung by the door, my sombre companions disappeared through a door to the left, and I found myself alone. It was warm and welcoming inside the house: a collection of shoes was neatly arranged by the front door, many coats hung above them, and only the uppermost ones were black; the light glowed pink and orange, the white walls were hung with pictures. Just as I became aware that I truly was alone, that even Eqingaleq did not stand beside me, the figure himself appeared from the guests' room and, eyes bright with excitement informed me that we were in the house of my late father.

He may be dead, he whispered, *but his soul looks out from moments captured in time.*

Photographs? I asked, and Eqingaleq nodded, his skin glowing strangely in the artificial light. *Yes – and of his wife. And children.*

I had begun to feel dizzy. It was warm inside the house, so warm, and the air seemed still and saturated with unfamiliar smells. I had not eaten for some time.

I turned my head at the sudden sound of voices, sharper than the low murmur that drifted from the room into which the guests had retired. These voices were raised in heat and anger. I stumbled across the hallway and past a staircase. I pushed open the door that led into what transpired to be a kitchen, and there beheld the beaked man, wings aloft, screeching at a woman who in turn shrieked back. My knowledge of the language was limited, but I understood enough, sensed enough, to know that the cause of this unsightly noise was none other than myself. As each beak was opened in turn, or both together in cacophony, I heard only an intimidating shriek of a war cry in the form of my own name: Ma-*lik*, Ma-*lik*, Ma-*lik*. The sound was unbearable, it felt as though my ears bled. Then the heat and the exhaustion took a tight hold upon me, and I dropped into an encompassing darkness that thankfully, and at long last, was silent.

6

Rasmus

Rasmus and the man known as Birdie had met during the war, both deployed on naval operations in Arctic Norway. Rasmus was sure he had once known the man's real name, but it had long since slipped his memory; the nickname he had acquired on account of his prominent, pointed nose, reminiscent of a bird's beak. It was a ridiculous name for such a stern, humourless man, and yet it seemed to have stuck, though no one could remember who had first thought it up. Rasmus had often wondered whether the man might be a direct relation of the famous 'Birdie' Bowers, who had accompanied Captain Scott on his ill-fated expedition to the South Pole. He had asked him once about this possible family connection, jokingly adding that this could be the reason for his ending up, like Bowers, freezing his nose off at sub-zero temperatures in close proximity to the pole (be it South or North). His laughter soon faltered to a stop as the man responded with a sincere look of non-amusement. He had not mentioned it again.

Whatever the vocation of Birdie's forefathers, the man certainly knew how to negotiate polar conditions. Whether he, like Rasmus, felt at home in the north, Rasmus had never been able to decipher; come hardship or adventure the man was continually straight-faced, his expression blank as a post, entirely unreadable. He rarely spoke, and when he did the tone of his voice did not vary. It was only his eyes – unnervingly clear, like pools of shallow water – that seemed alive, and his gaze was piercing, heavy, somehow challenging. There was something about the shadowed steadiness of his eyes that filled Rasmus with a deep unease. Had he ever seen the man smile? He could not recall.

Nevertheless, he had come to view the man as a partner, so often had they found themselves working together during the war years. Birdie's arctic survival skills were almost as refined as Rasmus's; he appeared to have the same determination and natural inclination to master the elements. These skills put to good use, they both rose quickly through the naval ranks and achieved a sort of respected notoriety.

Following the war, they each returned to neighbouring home towns. They saw little of each other. Yet it was Birdie who, in fact, first introduced Rasmus to Judith – the young woman who was to become Rasmus's wife. Rasmus recognised at once the look of longing for this woman in Birdie's eyes, usually so guarded and unreadable. And so he had married Judith, fearing that if he hesitated then Birdie would get there first. Besides, the war had been over for a couple of years already; it was about time, he thought, that he found himself a beautiful young woman. And he loved her, of course.

His spirits were inexplicably low on their wedding day, though he did his best to mask these feelings. Even the sour look on Birdie's face – who he had, in all honesty, invited solely as a witness to his, Rasmus's victory – did not cheer him up.

Throughout his life, he contemplated, he had hoped that

one day he might make the Arctic his home. Now that he was a married man he doubted that possibility. His blood ran cold with the thought that he was no longer free to follow his own path. Now he had responsibilities; the dream of an escape would never again be so tangible.

The chill of the arctic wind had found its way into Rasmus's bones as he stood up on the deck of the Danish supply ship bound, at last, for Greenland. There ran a pang of guilt through his body as his thoughts turned now and for the very first time to his wife, the one thing that truly anchored him to his home in England. They had married shortly before he had set sail. Judith was quiet, sensible, a good ten years younger than him; a good match, a good wife... Yet still there churned an unwelcome anxiety in Rasmus's stomach: was this to be his life from now on?

And what was it that he had said to his wife before he left on this journey? *You will always be in my thoughts.* That was it. He wondered if he had perhaps read that line in a book somewhere; it had not come from his own heart.

7

Malik

Many weeks passed before I finally found relief from the grip of exhaustion. My recovery was slow, for each time I drifted into consciousness there would appear the same white walls and floral curtains and it would dawn on me that I was being cared for in the house of my late father, and by my late father's wife. This realisation, no matter how many times it was replayed, would without fail send me once more into the pit of nervous exhaustion which I seemed doomed to inhabit until such a time as I were able to forget where I had come from – and indeed whom. My coming into this world had been a gross act of betrayal against the woman who now attended to my sick bed; I had been born to another woman, one who had entered my father's heart – and his bed – while his wife had stayed at home, unknowing.

Each time she came to attend to me, with food, with water or a kind heart, I would imagine grasping her by the hands and apologising with all the strength of my soul. I longed to let her know of this incredible hurt that bore me to the bed with leaden limbs. But of course I could not carry out such a gesture: I lacked the linguistic skills for a start. And what, regardless, could I possibly say to ease the years of pain she must have suffered, to entreat her not to hate me for the simple fact of my existence, or to soothe the injustice that she must now care for me in her own home? I could utter only a heartfelt *thank you* once my needs had been seen to, and once alone again would weep bitterly into the pillow.

I was in no doubt that she knew my identity – this I could see in her eyes.

My feverish dreams were awash with the beating of wings and the terrible scream of the gull. Feathers brushed my cheeks, obscured my vision and suffocated me as I slept. In my waking hours, however, there was no sign of those birds by which my dreams were haunted, and I knew that the grey-haired, beak-nosed man was nowhere to be found: he had left me. In place of the relief that I ought to feel in his absence I trembled with fear, for now I was alone in this place and without a guide – however unpleasant he may have been.

For the first time in years I recalled the story of the raven who decides to accompany a flock of migrating geese southwards across the sea, so strong is his love for one of these beautiful white birds. It is too far for the raven, who cannot rest upon the surface of the sea like the geese; *but fear not*, says his beloved, *you may rest upon our backs as we sleep upon the waves.* The geese, however, soon grow tired of this requirement, for the raven is much slower than they. The flock flies onwards, and the raven finds his inky black wings enveloped by the cold Atlantic, and cannot struggle free.

How foolish I had been.

I would rise only to use the bathroom occasionally, and finding I had little desire to explore my surroundings, would always return promptly to the safety of the bed and the guilt-ridden clutches of sleep. Seemingly not content to follow my hopeless example, Eqingaleq would spend his

44

hours pacing the floor examining the pictures that hung on the walls, books and trinkets lined up on shelves, and the faces that stared out unnervingly from framed photographs. He had come to the conclusion, he revealed one day, that the room in which we dwelt appeared to belong to a young woman: there were remnants of her childhood dotted here and there, he said, though from the photographs it seemed obvious that she had since grown. The drawers, however, were all but empty of clothes, and aside from the presence of the two of us, the room appeared otherwise uninhabited. Sometimes, in the dead of night when he was sure that there moved not a soul in the house, he would creep downstairs, sealskin boots inaudible on the woollen carpet: a silent detective, an invited intruder. Though when he returned he would confess that he did not know what, if anything, he was looking for, and whether or not he had found it. Some evenings he would stand and gaze out the window for hours at a time, immovable and lost in thought, his features graced in turn by sorrow, trouble, nostalgia, peace... I did not feel the need to join him, for I knew what lay beyond those floral curtains; I knew, also, what it was that Eqingaleq could see within himself – those memories that caused the corners of his eyes to crease in melancholy and remembered smiles.

I was awakened one morning by the sound of a bird outside the window. It was not the coarse laughter of the gull – whose ghost of a voice so often accompanied the long, tremulous nights – but the sweet notes of a songbird welcoming in the bright morning. The room glowed a dull gold, an indication that beyond the closed curtains the sun had broken free from the clouds that so often seemed impenetrable. I pushed back the covers and got out of bed. My legs were steadier this morning, and my mind clearer. There was no sense in hiding in this room for the rest of my days – I would have to face the world sooner or later. I wiped the sleep from my eyes, pulled on my old jeans and jumper and quietly, cautiously, opened the bedroom door.

Sunlight flooded in through a window at the top of the staircase, blinding me momentarily. I followed its golden pathway down the steps and to the closed door that I knew opened into the kitchen. I could hear the busy sounds of clashing crockery, running water and muffled voices. I took a deep breath, my heart mimicking the frenzied drumming of the shaman as he ventures into the darkest areas of the spirit, and pushed open the door.

I was met again with the blinding rays of the morning sun climbing into her new eastern sky. Once my eyes had adjusted to her brilliance, I saw that this time there were present no squawking gulls, only my kind carer and – as Eqingaleq whispered in my ear – a young man who must be her son. The former busied herself about the stove, the latter sat eating at the table. As both had their backs to the door, I stood unnoticed and uneasy for a few long moments. Eventually, I cleared my throat quietly, and the young man spun around in his chair with such fierceness that I almost turned tail and ran, like a startled hare. The glare that he fixed upon me was one of suspicion; my cheeks burned as he looked me up and down, evidently sizing me up. His mother, however, smiled and wished me a good morning, and motioned that I should take a seat.

I returned the greeting and placed myself tentatively at the end of the table. The woman returned her attentions to the stove, while the young man, obviously affronted by my intrusion, hissed something at her that I did not understand. She replied calmly, without looking at him; he responded only with a noise of disgust and a look of disdain in my direction, before pushing his chair back violently and flouncing from the room. He let the door slam with just enough force to support his apparent objections.

My cheeks were on fire. 'Sorry,' I said, barely audibly, but she only shook her head as if in assurance that I need not apologise.

I watched her, a little self-consciously, as she prepared breakfast. There was a grace to her movements that put me somewhat at ease. Her long, dark hair, plaited down her back, was littered with strands of silver-grey, like mountain streams through rocky gorges. It framed her face in wisps of pure silver, softening the sparse wrinkles in her creamy skin and lending a brightness to her countenance that spoke to me of compassion and kind-heartedness. How different it seemed to the sharp-beaked solemnity of the man who had brought me here. But I did not want to think of him.

I watched her as she brandished a wooden spoon and ladled hot porridge into a bowl; I heard the gentle hiss of the gas stove and the strange quiet that descended once it had been turned off. The kitchen smelled of coffee and sweet honey. Rays of the morning sun streamed through the window, warming my back and turning my hands golden. As my hostess placed breakfast on the table before me, I had to blink back the shameful tears that threatened. I thanked her with what I hoped she would see was all my heart, and she smiled, and sitting across from me drank her own coffee in tranquil silence, neither watching me nor ignoring me as I ate and was restored.

After I had finished, she rose to fetch the coffee pot, poured us both another cup, and sitting back down said: 'My name is Judith.'

She said it clearly, a little slowly, as though concerned that I might not understand. 'Judith,' I repeated, and offered her another heartfelt, perhaps rather meek smile. 'Thank you, Judith. *Qujanaq.*'

Her eyes were illuminated when she smiled, though there was a sadness within that light that I felt partly responsible for. I told her that my name was Malik; she nodded and again my cheeks began to glow heatedly, for my name was undoubtedly not new information. Now that we had introduced ourselves, perhaps I might feel less of a stranger in her home, though how I wished that I could say more to her! Any words of English that I had once learnt were twisted up and strangled by the nervousness that gripped me, and although the silence that hung between us was not entirely awkward, I feared that it were wasted on my part.

The coffee was strong and entirely unlike anything I had come across in my home town, which was situated even further away from the country of the coffee's origin. The tins of fruit that stocked our new supermarket shelves, the packets of frozen vegetables, the processed meats: all the food that had been imported tasted bland and almost offensive, as though with each mile it accrued in its journey from its origin a part of its very soul was left behind. To eat the meat of a seal recently hunted, however, was like tasting the very essence of life itself.

On this occasion the food I had been given was at least sufficient to fill the uncomfortable emptiness that had begun to spread within me, and the hot coffee seemed to warm the blood that ran through my veins so that my aching muscles were soothed.

When I had finished I rose to wash the bowl and mug. Judith also got to her feet, but I only shook my head at her somewhat embarrassed insistence that the work was hers to carry out. I intended to earn my keep, of this much I was sure, though quite how I would go about it – aside from clearing up after myself – was something I had yet to figure out.

At Judith's suggestion – thankfully, for surely I would have been too embarrassed to ask – I ran a bath. This was not a luxury I was often permitted, having been previously required to simply boil a kettleful of water, often melted ice, for a quick standing wash in the cold emptiness of my kitchen. When I was a child my mother would occasionally boil enough water for a sit-down affair which could be enjoyed by each of us in turn. For no one but myself – Eqingaleq, being not of this world, did not require washing –

such an extravagance seemed unnecessary. Of course, in the house in which I now found myself, the effort involved in running a hot bath was so minimal as to be almost mundane: how gleefully surprised I was to discover that hot water came straight out of the tap! My hostess, who had accompanied me upstairs in case I needed assistance getting to know my new surroundings, could hardly hide her hilarity at my reaction. As I leapt back, a little too dramatically having submerged my hand in the running water, perplexed as to why no kettle had been filled first, she attempted to stifle a giggle but soon gave up as I too broke into reels of laughter. My hand, however, burned fiercely. Judith bid me run it under cold water. I did not say – could not say – that I feared this small affliction would be the first in a series of attacks from a world that I did not know how to negotiate.

My hand was soon forgotten as the rest of my body found relief in the deep water. I sank up to my chin, half-closed my eyes and tried not to think of anything: how I longed to be free of troubles for just a moment, a wonderful, suspended moment.

Eqingaleq dangled his bare feet into the water. *Well*, he said, *what are we going to do?*

I opened my eyes and shot him a warning look. It went unnoticed. Hoping that an attempt at nonchalance might deter his questioning for now, I sank lower still in the water and let my eyelids sink also. *Go home, I suppose.*

You suppose?

Irritation began to rear its unwelcome head. *Yes*, I said, trying not to let it enter my voice, *I don't see what else we can do.*

There was silence for moment. I wriggled my body gently a few times and felt the water billow around every joint, crease and curve.

You're telling me that after all this, you are going to give up, turn around and go home?

49

I opened one eye and fixed it upon him. *Like I said, I don't see what else we can do.*

We don't have any money to get home, he said.

I know that.

So what's the plan? He gestured to where I lay in the water, my nakedness half-submerged. *Sell your birthday suit?*

That's very funny.

Eqingaleq rubbed the palm of one of his hands against his heavily wrinkled forehead, as he always did when faced with a dilemma. Such things tired him. *We've come all this way,* he said.

I sighed. *I know, and it wasn't easy. But what is there for us here?*

What is there for us back at home? Not enough to keep you there.

I made a mistake, I said.

He only shook his head slowly. *You followed the path that was laid for you.*

Please, I moaned, not wishing to be burdened by riddles and remorse, *let me have my bath in peace.*

Again there descended a moment of silence. Although he seemed to have taken notice of my tired plea, Eqingaleq's observations were not exhausted. *She seems very kind,* he said. His voice was little more than a whisper, as though he were afraid the woman might hear from wherever she was in the house, or perhaps that in my clearly volatile state I might snap at him.

Yes, I said.

He drew his brown feet from the water. *I wouldn't give up just yet.*

I emerged golden-skinned from the bathroom to find that Judith had left a neat pile of clean clothes on the bed. They were a little on the large side – the hems of the jeans had to be turned over several times before they no longer trailed on the floor – and the checked shirt had more than one hole around the cuff which would have to be sewn up later. I presumed they must be her son's cast-offs, but I was thankful for they were certainly in better condition than the old clothes that I had owned for so many worn-out years. Once dressed, however, my skin crawled uncomfortably beneath my borrowed clothes. I knew that I could not continue to live on charitable donations, whether the path of my life would continue in the direction I had thus far been steered, or turn and take me back the way I had come.

8

Rasmus

His first glimpse of white, rugged peaks; from between them protruded the smooth curve of one of the many fingers of the ice cap, spilling over the mountain pass like a dog's lolling tongue. The ship ploughed through broken sea ice below an endless blue sky. Icebergs the size of castles: ghostly presences in the glint of the sunlight. Seals plunged into the water's inky depths, peeped their granite heads above the surface, eyes almost human. Rasmus's fingers were stiff in the freezing spring air.

The supply ship pulled into the tiny harbour amidst the screeching of gulls and the creak of shifting icebergs on the still sea. News of the explorers' visit must have already reached the settlement for a great many of its inhabitants – possibly even all of them, Rasmus thought – were gathered at the harbour. The children squealed and pointed excitedly as the ship approached, though Rasmus could not help but wonder whether they were more excited by the arrival of exotic explorers or the boxes of Danish treats bound for the village store.

As he stepped off the ship, Rasmus found himself surrounded by beaming faces and curious eyes. The men shuffled forward to shake his hand and, he guessed, bid him welcome in their own guttural language that he could not understand. The women watched him with bright eyes, infants peering out from the hoods of their mothers' skin parkas. The children tugged at his woollen trousers and jumped on the toes of his rubber boots. Rasmus's heart swelled with elation. He glanced over at Birdie and Snorri, who had disembarked from the ship just after him, and the laughter broke from his lips: Birdie, welcomed in the same way, grimaced down the length of his nose as though he were under siege, recoiling from the attentions of the crowd.

Their accommodation was an old hunter's hut on the outskirts of the village. It was impossible to tell how long it had stood uninhabited: the entire structure was in a state of disrepair yet inside the smell of blubber and dried blood still hung heavily in the air. Birdie turned up his sharp nose, made a point of throwing open the door to the hut in a fruitless attempt to air out the place.

Rasmus delighted in the aroma, was sure that his own nose would grow accustomed to it soon enough. He and Snorri set about unpacking the equipment that they had brought with them for the journey across the ice cap – camera, compass, tent and sleeping bags... the sled and dogs they would purchase here in the village in due course, as well as skin clothing and anything else they might require to survive the harsh conditions they were sure to encounter.

Rasmus was toying with the idea of trying to light the old blubber lamp – a task requiring some skill, which he was not sure he possessed – when a visitor arrived. A young man with a round face and dark eyes that creased at the corners as he smiled broadly in greeting. His bearskin trousers bristled in the cold air. He held out his hand as he introduced himself in perfect Danish: 'Qallu. I am to be your guide.' Rasmus took the man's hand in both of his and shook it warmly. Snorri, smiling in his usual calming way, did the same.

'Please come to my house for coffee,' said Qallu; 'you must be tired after your journey.'

The pungent atmosphere of the hunter's hut was left behind as the three of them accompanied the young man through the village. Dogs howled and pulled at their chains, and tore, semi-wild, at scraps of raw meat. Qallu's sealskin kamiks crunched into the deep snow that blanketed the ground as it did the mountains. Rasmus smiled to himself as the sun warmed his cold-chapped cheeks.

Qallu lived with his young wife and his sister in a little wooden house not dissimilar to the hut in which Rasmus was staying and which Birdie disliked so much. Stepping inside they passed a bucket filled to the brim with bloodied seal intestines; the skin of the animal lay dejectedly beside it, coloured red, waiting to be cleaned, then sold or made into kamiks. Inside the house the pervading smell of blubber and blood was woven with the aroma of fresh coffee and cigarette smoke.

Rasmus accepted a cup of coffee and a cigarette, smiling politely at Qallu's wife, who had made the offer. Her pregnant belly swelled enormously under her clothes; the couple's first child, Qallu told them. He had caught a polar bear that winter, he went on to say, puffing out his chest with pride, for only the very best hunters possessed the skill to take on the great bear. And his wife had sewed him a new pair of trousers from the bear's hide. Qallu danced around the small room, showing the guests his wife's handiwork. His wife and sister howled with laughter.

The ice had been broken.

Rasmus heard Snorri chuckle; saw Birdie wrinkle his enormous nose. Perhaps he was simply a little confused, Rasmus thought, for he was unsure just how much Danish the man was able to understand – yet another thing that he did not easily give away. Rasmus had his Danish mother to thank for his proficiency in the language, something that

55

enabled him to communicate with the people of the Danish-governed island. Until, he hoped, he learned to speak the Greenlandic language.

Qallu often acted as a guide for visiting tourists and researchers, he told them: the reason for his immaculate Danish. He knew the land like the backs of his hands; he could read the approaching weather in the sky, smell a change in the direction of the wind, and navigate his way home through the white-out of a sudden blizzard using nothing but his keen senses. A hunter must come to know his environment, he told them, if he is to be successful.

Qallu told them anecdotes from his many hunting expeditions while the young woman Rasmus understood to be his sister handed the guests plates of *mattak*. Rasmus kept his eyes half fixed on her. He noticed the graceful movements of her body, plump beneath her clothes, and the fall of her raven-black hair down her back. Occasionally her dark, narrow eyes would flicker over to where he sat, or wander over the faces of his companions as they listened to Qallu's stories, oblivious to her interest. She could not have been much older than a teenager, he thought.

He chewed the *mattak* that she offered him, the thick skin of the whale, a delicacy. The raw flesh felt good between his teeth. He rolled the cube of meat around his mouth with his tongue. The taste was somehow primeval. He licked the tang of salt from his lips.

'Ketty is a wonderful cook,' Qallu said, throwing a wide grin at his sister. 'Perhaps the next time you come to my house she will prepare a meal for you.'

9

Malik

The city felt no less oppressive the more I wandered its labyrinth. Around each corner could be found a replica of the street from which I had just turned: an unchanging facade of brick walls, concrete roads and distant, unattainable sky. The sheer monotony of it all hounded and chased me until I thought I might go mad.

It was alarming how much of the sky overhead was claimed by buildings, and how little sunlight – on the rare occasions that the sun showed herself – filtered down to the level of the street. Even the rain seemed to have lost its fierceness by the time it hit the pavement. I was gripped by a strange longing for the elements, which more often than not steered me to the graveyard. There, where the skies were fractionally more open, I would stand before my father's grave as though in wait.

Here I was able to think more clearly. I thought about how the decision to accompany the beaked stranger to this place had not been entirely my own; the hands of fate were upon my back, the songs of the spirits in my ears and heart. Their ancient voices were now so distant that I could barely perceive them. Sometimes, thinking I sensed a murmur, I would stop still in my tracks and listen intently, but I could hear only the passionate drum of my heart and the roar of the sea over which I had travelled: far from the familiar embrace of my ancestral home I could not be certain of my fate.

The graveyard – where the ancestors of this land lay confined in a boxed eternity – offered up no more of a helping hand in my time of need. And although this place of the dead instilled within me a certain peace that could not be found in the rush of the city streets, there grew in my soul a sense of such isolation that it seemed for all the world as though I had been forgotten. I would be left to while away my remaining days in limbo – neither lost nor journeying, neither abandoned nor loved, in a place that had called to me but was not my home.

After an endless number of days spent negotiating the immediate area yet coming to feel no more orientated than when I had arrived, I began to venture further. Past the graveyard and along more grey streets I came upon an area where the buildings appeared to open up, creating a window to the sky above. I felt horribly exposed as I crept out into the open, like an arctic fox who has spotted a good scavenging opportunity and is reluctant to let it slide, whatever the risks involved. Like the fox I slunk into the square, concrete clearing, head and tail bent towards the ground, checking from side to side for signs of danger as I wound a path around those of the people around me and eventually reached the centre. Here there rose great walled mounds of earth from which shone the sun-seeking, rainbow-coloured heads of flowers; and between them, a bench. I took a seat and a deep breath, for it seemed as safe a place as could be found. From here I could watch as the people went about their business, without feeling under observation myself. Some rushed about clutching bags in both hands, some walked in leisurely couples sharing stories and smiles, children charged about uninhibited...

I laughed out loud upon suddenly catching sight of Eqingaleq, who was peering with unbridled interest through one of the shop windows. Perhaps drawn by the glorious array of smells he pressed his crooked nose up to the glass and with slender, painted hands shielded his eyes against the glare of his own reflection. How bizarre he looked – though of course he was visible to my eyes only – dressed in furs and kamiks, his golden-brown skin decorated with black-inked geometric patterns and weathered creases. Perhaps this was how I appeared to those pale-skinned people around us; though only my forearms were inked and my dress was mundane, it was possible that those who shot a glance in my direction saw an exaggerated representation of my heritage.

I caught precious snatches of conversation from my lookout post. At one point a young couple took a seat beside me on the bench, I perceived somewhat apologetically, and began to talk together quickly and animatedly. I did not feel ashamed for being a party to their discussion for it was entirely bewildering – though I was pleasantly surprised to discover that I was able to catch more than a few words – rather the feeling that welled within me was one of elation. Here was my calling, the next step along the path: if I could understand, if I could converse, the way forward would become clearer to me, and a great deal easier.

When I arrived back at the house I was, admittedly, relieved to discover that no one else was at home. I shuffled into the kitchen, warily, to make sure that I was indeed alone. Pleased by the lack of human company I approached the wireless radio that sat like some sort of watchful animal before the window. I had seen one of these before, at the doctor's house in our town, though did not know how to operate the thing. Fortunately, it took only a couple of minutes of prodding at intimidating buttons and fiddling with obscure dials before the box began to emit a loud booming which, once I had located the feature that controlled the volume, transpired to be the voice of a man. I clapped my hands together in glee. Eqingaleq eyed the thing suspiciously from an opposite corner of the room and I rolled my eyes towards the heavens to indicate that some of us must move with the times.

The hours rolled into oblivion with the day's last embers as I sat as still as a rock at the kitchen table. I listened enraptured as the wireless' words wove themselves into stories and images of my mind's own fabrication; and the four walls dissolved into space and light, and the glow of the sun began to dissipate into expectant twilight. Occasionally I would hear a word, or even a phrase that I understood, though this happened too seldom to allow for comprehension of the particular subject matter. Instead the snippets of meaning combined and grew organically into dream-like trains of thought, mystical and bizarre.

So absorbing was this experience that I nearly jumped out of my skin when Judith entered the kitchen, followed closely by her son. Automatically I rose to leave – anticipating that this would be the polite way to behave – but Judith only pressed a gentle hand to my shoulder as she passed, in reassurance that I need not be disturbed on her account. The young man dithered a moment in the doorway, having shot a reproachful glance in my direction, but his mother caught his eye. She raised an eyebrow and gave him a look that, although silent, appeared to elude perhaps to a discussion they had shared earlier, of which I had naturally been the subject. I pretended not to notice. The lad sloped over the threshold to the kitchen and proceeded to pour himself a glass of water before stiffly taking a seat, deliberately and painstakingly avoiding my gaze.

He was introduced to me as "Michael", and shyly I greeted him; still he kept his eyes down. Had I been asked to guess, I would have said that he appeared slightly younger than me. His face, lacking the grace of his mother's, yet not entirely dissimilar, had about it a look of late adolescence. His pallid skin was blotched watery red in places and his features were thin and somewhat drawn, as though having recently shed the roundness of youth they had yet to find their true complimentary shape. His hair, a murky brown, was parted in the middle and fell straight and lank to his shoulders in a way not unlike the framing of curtains around a window. His ears were not to be seen. There was a certain lack of harmony about his features which was only exacerbated by the determined pout he had adopted for the occasion, or perhaps wore all the time.

Preparations for the evening meal were conducted in a bizarre silence, accompanied only by the intrusive blare of the wireless on which I could no longer concentrate. For some time, I sat twiddling my thumbs, heart rate increasing little by little until finally I plucked up the courage to offer my assistance, managing to entreat Judith – who politely insisted that I need not trouble myself – to let me cut up the vegetables. Having located a meaningful task, I could breathe a little more freely. Eqingaleq, similarly, appeared to have found courage. Abandoning his place of safety in the corner he began to poke at the wireless with long, searching fingers, ignoring my hisses of caution. The boy remained in his seat. I could feel his eyes upon my back.

Once I had reduced all the vegetables to tiny, neat cubes and Judith was adamant that I could contribute no more for the moment, I asked, in my now customary array of bungled words, self-conscious gestures and apologetic smiles, if I might go outside into the garden until the food was ready. Of course I might, was the accurate impression I received in response, there was no need to ask permission.

I slipped through the door, framed by yellow and white check curtains, and quietly pulled it to behind me. Immediately my long bated breath escaped my lips in a sigh

61

of relief: to be free from the silence, uncomfortably saturated with too many things unsaid, and Michael's eyes upon my back, colouring my ears a deep, burning red. I could hear the lowered voices of the kitchen's two remaining occupants, silence abandoned, locked now in strained conversation amidst the endless rambling of the wireless. Occasionally the young man's voice would leap up in volume, only to be hushed back down by the reasoned words of his mother. My heart twisted in my chest and pained me, for I could not understand their words. Had I been able to understand, perhaps I would have suffered more.

The birds reeled their dainty dances in the early twilight that followed the sinking of the sun behind the house and lent a strange unearthliness to the stillness of not-yet-evening. The light fell like that of the midnight sun: she who, in my country, sinks only fractionally below the horizon at this time of the year, bathing the broken fjords in a perpetual late-summer gloaming, to go no further until she rises for morning from the east once more.

The garden, resplendent with the darkening heads of flowers and fruit bushes, stretched before me in deepening shadow, yet I saw that the sun still illuminated the roofs of the surrounding buildings. There showed a patch of bright, open sky above, coloured with a pink-orange hue that hinted at a glorious sunset. My heart ached that I should be denied this sight, hemmed in by unassailable walls which towered over my head like low clouds wherever I ventured; trapped.

Judith's voice spoke to me quietly from the doorway, inviting me back inside.

I strove to conceal my misted eyes as we ate – sunk once more in a suggestive but not wholly unpleasant silence – awaiting the time at which I could politely excuse myself without appearing ungrateful. Having washed my plate, I hastened upstairs to the room in which I was staying but could not call my own. I stripped the blankets from the bed and, with the help of the bedposts, a chair and a corner of the dresser, constructed a passable tent in which, surrounded by pillows and a rug borrowed from another part of the room, I was able to sit comfortably, safely even. I drew one of the blankets down over the "door" and brought a comforting semi-darkness to my hiding place. The only sound was my laboured breathing, growing gradually more regular as the outside world retreated.

I was roused by a gentle knock at the door to the bedroom. My mind was clouded, as though I had been sleeping, yet I realized that I was still sitting upright in my almost-meditative position. It had grown darker still; a face peered out at me from a murky corner of the makeshift tent, and my heart leapt painfully into my throat before I recognised it to be that of Eqingaleq, almost the same colour as the surrounding twilight. His black eyes gleamed wondrously with some unseen light.

I scrambled out of the tent and opened the bedroom door to find Judith silhouetted against the waiting brightness. She apologised as, embarrassed, I blinked at her in the electric light – perhaps she thought she had woken me; perhaps she had – before handing me a slim book whose title, in the blurriness of my newly-adjusted state of consciousness, I could not read. From her careful explanation I understood that the speech which had emitted from the wireless earlier that evening had concerned this particular book, a poetry book. I recalled the glorious rhythm of the words I had heard spoken, those which, though obscure, had woven threads through my imagination. I understood, and thanked her. It seemed that she smiled, but did not immediately move away. After a moment's hesitation she asked me, in a way that tugged alarmingly at my heartstrings, if I was keeping well. I swallowed, and replied yes, thank you. Then I repeated the last two words again, so that she would know I meant it.

10

Rasmus

Qallu taught Rasmus how to lash the dogs to the sled and drive them over the inland ice. As they ran, their eager squeals carried far through the clear air, their panting breath rose in clouds above them; they wound in and out between each other, entangling their skin leashes into intricate webs.

Rasmus watched with wonder as Qallu showed him how to coat the runners of the sled in water, which would then freeze into a smooth layer of ice. So simple: the sled skimmed over the terrain, ice upon ice. During the winter months, Qallu said, the hunters would drive the sled out onto the frozen sea to hunt; but at this time of year the ice was too thin. Instead the men launched kayaks into open stretches of water, eyes peeled for signs of seals, walrus and narwhal.

Of course, there would be no animals to hunt on the wilderness of the ice cap; still Rasmus longed to learn the hunter's skills, and Qallu was an eager tutor.

Rasmus felt more alive than he had ever done. Out there on the ice, beneath an endless sky smeared with pastel colours, his breath came out ragged and his cheeks became chapped from the cold. Snorri was reminded of his Icelandic childhood, he said: when the cold is so intense that time itself seems to freeze and the glory of the present moment goes on forever. When the air is so crisp you can feel it against your skin; when your bones ache and creak as though they are part of the very earth. Rasmus recognised the passion for this place that shone in his friend's eyes, mirroring the passion in his own soul.

Birdie's eyes, however, remained shallow and colourless, as unreadable as ever. Perhaps Rasmus was simply a slave to the workings of his overactive imagination, he thought, but there was just something about the man's glare that made him think of dark winters, captive creatures, folk tales that he could not remember. Snorri remarked once, when the man was out of earshot, that as the sled had sped over the ice with them astride it for the first time he had seen the perpetual frown lift for a moment from Birdie's face. He laughed as he said this. But Rasmus did not share the joke. In that moment he felt the weight of clouds above his head; he should not have asked Birdie to join the expedition.

Nevertheless, Rasmus's spirits were high. He felt increasingly more at home with each day that passed. He had even taken steps to make their decrepit old hut more hospitable: with Snorri's help he gave all the surfaces a good scrub and set a pot of coffee on the old stove, hoping to recreate the fresh, welcoming aroma of Qallu's family home.

Qallu had given them a small slab of seal blubber to burn in the oil lamp. Rasmus placed the blubber in the crescent-shaped bowl of the lamp and arranged a length of dried grass twine around the rim, as Qallu had instructed. He found the box of matches that he had brought with him, and after a few attempts succeeded in lighting the grass wick. The lamp emitted plumes of smoke into the already suffocating atmosphere of the hut. The three men choked and coughed and fiddled with the lamp, but the wick was soon extinguished as a result of their efforts.

He must remember to ask Qallu to teach him to light the thing, Rasmus thought. Or perhaps he could ask Ketty. His heart skipped a beat as this thought occurred to him.

11

Malik

As a helpful afterthought to the book she had gifted me, Judith left a voluminous English dictionary on the kitchen table. I discovered the dictionary with some trepidation the following morning. I had risen somewhat later than usual, having passed the night within the warm, dark confines of my makeshift tent, where sleep was not snatched away by the brightness of the dawn and my dreams were permitted to resolve themselves undisturbed. In this way the strange, undulating paths of my unconscious mind were soon blurred by gentle awakening, and I recalled only that I had dreamed of the sea.

I flicked through the pages of the dictionary whilst devouring my breakfast – also left out for me – but was quickly overwhelmed by the sheer number of words contained within. There are surely more words in the English language than there were things in the world to name or describe. Did one language really require so many? I closed the book with a sigh, downcast.

The rain slaked its grey fingers over the windows.

Minutes later I stood before the open front door, boots upon the threshold, anorak donned in grim anticipation, willing myself to brave the downpour. I was not particularly keen to leave the comfortable shelter of the house, there was no particular place I desired to go; it was only the weight of an unbearable guilt that pushed me in the direction of the streets. Surely I did not deserve to enjoy the luxury of a family home – a family that was not mine and upon whom I had so ungraciously intruded. I watched the rain for a while longer, marvelling at the incredible deluge released so suddenly by the heavens. Like steel it pressed its weight upon the narrow, grey world, yet bounced elastically from the pavements, snaked viscously along the gutters and rivets in the road, and pooled thickly in swamps reflecting the low metal sky. It was soothing, the heavy fall of the rain, muting all the sounds of the city to distant memories, the murky obscurity of times gone by. The weather, when it had the mind to, could still encroach upon and dominate this manmade place. I smiled, for this seemed akin to a victory.

My feet refused to carry me over the threshold. Instead they took me to the closed door of the room to which the funeral guests had retired, the room which I had not yet entered. For a few long moments I listened with bated breath lest anyone be lurking on the other side, but hearing nothing turned the handle and ventured in.

There were a few comfortable chairs, a table... nothing to really capture my attention except, that is, for the photographs that hung upon the walls and adorned the available surfaces. For weeks I had kept myself away from this room, from these pictures whose presence had been made known to me by the inquisitive investigations of Eqingaleq. I entered now and examined them, in an attempt to remind myself of the paths that had led me here, the dangers of getting too comfortable, and the reason I deserved to be out in the cold, clawing rain.

My legs steered me in the direction of the town clearing again. The place was all but deserted. For a short while I sat on the same bench by the flowers, their coloured heads heavy in the downpour. The rain was like cold glass on my back. Eqingaleq watched me, bedraggled, from the nearest shop-fronted shelter, his features contorted into a bemused, irritated frown. *Perhaps the rain might wash away the guilt!* I had exclaimed in an unreasoned desperation whose apparent fierceness and depth scared me: *the great wrongdoing I have committed to good, kind people by the simple act of my coming into this world!* Padding wetly in my immediate shadow Eqingaleq's protestations had fallen on deaf ears.

In the room of photographs I had beheld, for the first time, an image of my father. It had seemed that a complete stranger looked back at me: I saw no familiarities in his features – save for the angular facial contours displayed also by Michael, though disguised somewhat by his adolescence – indeed the heavy brows and sharp nose were a direct contrast to the gentle openness of my own countenance. It had always been said that I took after my mother – I hoped to God in appearance only. There were no pictures of her amidst the family portraits that I had guiltily perused – why should there be? Until recently I had known no other family; now the family I had newly become acquainted with did not know my mother, except perhaps in hearsay, in anger and in unfortunate issue.

I imagined a future in which I had refused to follow the path of my fate; an alternate present continued under the mountain's shifting shadows and the wide fjords of the icy coast. Home: magisterial, ancient, serene, and lonely. There, ever wondering, I would have run like the wild wind, chilled from icy climes, never resting, in search of an answer that remains elusive. Fearful of stagnation I had chosen instead to take to the sea, I reminded myself, to alight on the backs of the white geese. Fate is not a pre-ordained, concreted road; it was up to me whether or not I allowed my bearers to abandon me to the ocean's relentless waves.

I did not have to drown.

I left my perch and my self-pity and, taking shelter with Eqingaleq in one of the shops, shook the salty droplets from my waterlogged wings. Graciously, he said nothing. The water leaked out from my every pore and fibre of being, and as I came back to the surface I caught the most wonderful of aromas. How long it seemed since I had last been greeted by the smell of freshly baked bread! A tremor of warmth and anticipation ran through me, a strange, almost forgotten nostalgia.

I brushed the sodden hair from my eyes, and in doing so caught the gaze of a young woman. Dressed in a blue apron, she stood behind a counter laden with an array of loaves, buns, slices... At the sight of this wandering stranger dripping salt water onto her clean floor there passed across her face a look of pity and a comforting smile. She buttered a bread roll and passed it wordlessly to me, poor drowned feathered thing, and my heart ached with gratitude.

I was too embarrassed to devour the gift in front of her, ravenous as I was; luckily the rain deigned to lift its steel press just for a moment, and I returned to the bench to enjoy every last bite of my long-awaited dinner. Feeling fortified and thus virtuous I threw the remaining crumbs to the splay-footed pigeons that strutted around me in hope of a spare morsel. They had barely closed their beaks around their prize when I felt a rush of air above my head, the fall of the sky and the great beating of wings, and with an ear-splitting cry of triumph there landed at my feet an enormous gull. It stretched out its white wings in warning to the smaller scavengers, its head lowered and its beak poised. It hissed at its opponents and snatched aggressively at the ground and the tiny crumbs that would surely not sustain it for long.

The shock of the bird's intrusion had caused me to leap to my feet with a small cry, scramble backwards and clutch like a frightened child at Eqingaleq's arm. I prayed that the girl in the bakery had not witnessed this display. All hopes of a meal now dashed, my visitor took to the air again, shrieking, laughing, and soon was gone. Gone where, I did not know – but it struck me, as my frenetic heart began to still, that the sea could not lie far from here, for it was to the vast open ocean that my unwelcome friend must return.

12

Despite my resolve not to drown in this new place there grew a darkness within my soul that alarmed me. I began to despise myself for the very nature of my blood: a being born into two worlds yet inhabiting none; an outlaw, an outsider, given away by the colour of my skin. Was I a fool for having forsaken my home?

This world did not move to its own internal rhythm, it was not driven by the sun's changeable dwelling in the wide sky and the rolling of the tide and seasons; here each day dawned just like the morning previous, and ambled towards its end with an almost painful monotony. Occasionally I caught snatches of beauty, such as the colourful spilling of an unseen dawn or the song of a passing bird, soon swallowed by the noise of the city – suggestions that there grew life even in this most stagnant of places.

The days were unbearably long, yet so different to the long Arctic summer days during which the sun did not set. I took to staying awake well into the still, early hours of the mornings, for this was when the world, bathed in a thick, unearthly silence, was at its most peaceful, and the inevitable threat of a new day at its most distant. In my tented sanctuary I would find solace, immersed in waking dreams of open wilderness and endless skies: the perpetual quiet of the slow world broken only by the howl of the dogs, the creak of the pack ice, a woman calling to her children under the midnight sun.

I was adamant that I must not forget who I was or where I had come from. And yet, even at the time of my leaving home I had not known this.

You were not at peace, Eqingaleq reminded me, time and time again, and in agony I nodded my head. I knew that his rationality could recall that which my wounded, fearful heart had already forgotten.

I saw no more signs of the sea over the coming weeks. No sight nor sound that might lead me to the venerable, all-knowing mother who dwelled beneath the waves, wreathed in seaweed tendrils as black as her hair. I began to fear that the great, shrieking gull had been nothing more than an omen, a fearful spirit anticipating the coming of one whom I could not call a friend.

On most days I would exit the house at the earliest opportunity, dreading the sound of a knock at the door or the chime of the bell – the signal that he had come for me, his intentions unclear. Some days, finding myself alone in the house, I would turn the wireless up to nearing full volume, drowning out any unwelcome interruptions along with Eqingaleq's squealing protestations, and sit for hours at the kitchen table, drinking cup after cup of strong coffee and listening intently to the flow of language. Late at night, once darkness had fallen, I would crawl into my makeshift tent and by torchlight pore over the book lent to me by Judith – dictionary in hand – until my strained eyes could no longer be kept open. Always I feared the tap-tapping of a sharp beak upon the window: the ominous visitor, goggle-eyes peering through the crack in the curtains through which the meagre candlelight flickered on and off as though it were about to be extinguished. I feared the darkness; I longed instead for the openness of the polar nights, where once I was overlooked only by the broad sky.

The days, clouded as such by apprehension, slipped by at an alarming speed with little to distinguish each from the other. This cloud tracked my every move. It found me a shaking wreck at the street's end, terrified of rounding the corner and meeting the unknown, the watery eyes of the gull; it hung over the town clearing, and over my head, scrambling my thoughts and judgement so I could not understand the words of those around me.

This uncertainty, this fear, could not persevere endlessly; each day I trod the steps of a man condemned, single-minded and silent, clutching at swathes of time that forever slipped from my grasp for the violent shaking of my hands. Yet I was anxious for its end.

Late one afternoon I arrived back at the house to find that the great, shrieking gull had, this time, followed me home. Pursued by the relentless rain, I had scurried into the house like a half-drowned rat. I left my coat and kamiks – plastered with sodden fallen leaves in red and brown – at the door and sought out some dry clothes upstairs. I roughly dried my hair with a towel before pulling on my old fisherman's jumper against the chill that had begun to seep into my bones. Finding that I had a strange longing for coffee, something hot to warm me through, I thought I would try my chances in the kitchen.

I regretted this forwardness immediately, for there he perched, on a chair by the table. Had I heard the slap of his webbed feet on the pavement, or the swoop of his broad wings overhead? Or had he flown before me, not seeking the sea after all, as I had expected? It seemed he had planned to lie in wait, anticipating my arrival – he prepared, I unaware – knowing that I could not turn back. I could not now slam shut the door and run from the house, from the town, the city, the country...

I reminded myself that I had barely come to know the man; but what was it about those aqueous eyes that filled me with a nameless dread? They were fixed upon me now, where I stood frozen in the doorway. I knew malintent when so plainly I saw it.

As my eyes flickered around the room I saw that Judith and her son were also present at the kitchen table. But before I had the chance to greet them – politely, as only I knew how – the man's eyes narrowed and he barked in Danish: 'What the hell do *you* want?'

Eqingaleq put a heavy hand on my shoulder, and squeezed gently. We make what we can of our fated path; I would not be left to drown.

Striving to keep my voice steady I informed him that I had come in search of a cup of coffee, for I was cold, and thirsty. At the mention of the word *kaffe*, Judith rose accommodatingly from her chair and bid me take a seat as she fetched me a cup. Luckily, there was an empty chair positioned at the opposite side of the table to the glowering visitor: a barrier between us. I sat down in a dripping silence; each set of eyes in the room was averted from the other in painful deliberation, save for the sharp, beaded pair belonging to the grey-haired man: they were fixed glaringly and unabashedly upon me. It was Judith, however, whom he addressed, in his own language, his voice raised. I caught only the word *Eskimo*, spat out from between his thin lips like a curse – derogatory, accusing. Heat rose to my cheeks.

Judith did not reply, only set the steaming mug of coffee on the table before me. I thanked her, and attempted a smile, though the sickening anxiety that twisted within my ribcage was loathe to allow it.

The man's eyes flickered, his beak quivered, but he withheld his apparent mounting rage for just long enough to allow me to reach for the mug with an outstretched hand. Then he whipped it furiously and wordlessly from my grasp, and striding across the kitchen hurled its contents down the

78

sink. Droplets splashed the wall behind. He set the mug back down on the table with some force and took his seat, equality restored: those who by their blood do not deserve the kind gift of coffee must go without.

My blood beat thickly in my ears, deafening in the tense, uncomfortable silence; the skin between my thumb and forefinger smarted from contact with the hot liquid, spilled in fury. I realised that my hands were shaking, though whether in fear, in pain or in anger I could not tell. Then, to my surprise, it was Michael's turn to take hold of the offending mug, which he refilled from the coffee pot on the counter, his movements slow and deliberate, his hands steady. All eyes were upon him, then the coffee was before me again and I did not know what to do. As if in response to my thoughts, the boy pushed a plate of biscuits across the table. I sensed the coiled, hot-blooded energy that beat beneath his cool exterior, and feared I would receive similar treatment from him if I did not take one. I took one. Triumph, suppressed, flashed across the boy's eyes, and the look that passed between him and the beaked man was one of mutual hatred. Yet I did not feel that, in acknowledgement of a common enemy, I had acquired an ally.

Ignoring her son, the man spoke in a low voice to Judith, while I struggled to sip my coffee with tremulous hands, and tackled the biscuit, trying not to choke. Then –

'You're trying to learn English!' he said to me, without warning, and I could not tell whether this remark was meant as a question, an exclamation of surprise or of amusement. I did not like the use of the word "try". In response to my answer – a single word in the affirmative – he only snorted, and I saw a condescending glint in his eye. 'You have high hopes for yourself.'

I would not allow myself to be provoked. I sat with my hands wrapped around the coffee mug, its rim almost touching my lips, and drawing comfort from its warmth I stated flatly that I liked languages, and wished to learn.

Once more, the man guffawed, alarmingly loudly. 'Trying to better himself!' he exclaimed, as though the others present were able to understand his observations – though I could tell from their expressions that this were not the case. *'The Noble Savage!'*

I was unsure what was meant by this last comment, understood only that it was not an expression of kindness. He took a swig of his own coffee, as if it were beer, and slamming the mug onto the table called arrogantly to Judith, in his own language, for another cup. As she rose to oblige she caught my eye and offered me a look of empathy, of concern and of warning. It would seem the man's tone and manner required no translating. Wordlessly I tried to convey that there was no need to worry, that I knew what I was doing and with whom I was dealing, but I am not sure that she believed me. I am not sure that I believed myself.

The visitor's eyes followed his hostess as she carried out his bidding, then they were upon me again, stripping me bare, to the very bones. 'I see you've made yourself quite at home.'

'Judith is very kind,' I muttered. A wave of guilt crashed over my head, soaking me once more to the skin and beneath.

He translated this remark, mockingly, to the woman whom it concerned. She did not indulge his disrespectful tone, only brushed the silver-tinged hair from her face with a prim hand, smoothed down her skirt and sat back down, her expression blank and unreadable.

I remembered first arriving at the house on the day of the funeral, when I had found the two of them at each other's throats, screeching, acts abandoned, masks thrown aside. I wondered why the man stayed, demanding hospitality despite the coldness with which he was greeted, despite the blatant wish that he would leave, and the uncomfortable atmosphere that accompanied an unwelcome guest. With this thought, however, my blood turned cold, for could not the same thing be said of myself? Perhaps he stayed for the same reason that I could not leave. Could it be that we had this in common?

When no response to the man's remark was forthcoming, he took his coffee, without thanking she who had made it, and with a sneer provided his own rebuttal: 'She's a Christian, her god tells her she must be kind; to orphaned, homeless children, even those born outside of civilization. The uneducated, savage ones.'

Red waves of anger began to lap at my beating heart, in full knowledge that I was being provoked. He was manipulating me into expressing my defence, showing an unpleasant side of myself and rising to the bait.

'So it is her god who allows you into her home; not her.' I said quietly. If I could draw his attention to the unspoken discomfort that accompanied his presence, then perhaps he would leave when I could not.

His anger was calm, calculated. I found it terrifying. '*You* are the reason I have been invited into this house,' he said, voice lowered threateningly: 'Her god may tell her to offer you kindness, but her heart wants you gone. She hopes I will oblige.'

'But you won't accept the responsibility,' I accused.

'And why should I accept responsibility for you?' he asked disdainfully.

My teeth clenched, I answered: 'Because you brought me here.'

He laughed, the nauseating cackle of the gull, a sound so sudden and piercing that my nerves, already on edge, could not withhold this onslaught and my bones leapt in my skin. Judith looked alarmed and her son winced at the sound, already disgusted, so it seemed, by the tactless man at his kitchen table. He looked as though he would dearly like to strangle the man. He hissed to his mother, but she only shook her head, apparently deterring him. Her lips were pursed, her body was taut, coiled like a serpent ready to strike yet waiting: perhaps for the right moment, or simply exercising painful self-control in a fragile situation. With deft fingers she fiddled with a string of wooden beads on her

81

opposite wrist, rolling and twisting them in quiet distraction, rolling, rolling and twisting. When the cord broke on her self-restraint, who would bear the brunt of her agitation? The beaked interloper, or the dark stranger who could no more speak to defend himself than he could see his own place in the world?

I ought to take responsibility for myself, this much was true, and could expect this of no one else. Poor Judith, to have this helpless stranger thrust upon her in such a way, a wretched burden with whom she could not even communicate.

'You shouldn't ask this of her!' I exclaimed, anger – or fear – bubbling ever closer to the surface, 'I don't know why you thought that this would be acceptable.'

'Acceptable!' he echoed. 'You talk of this as though it's a social call? A regrettable turn of events? Just the level of intelligence I would expect from someone like you.'

Of course this had been his intention, I thought: a pre-meditated intervention, the staged scene of a play in which lives were made to collide. My anger almost dissolved, there and then, into salty self-pity and helpless exhaustion. Slowly I closed my eyes. Heavily I opened them again, and said, perhaps by way of weary defence, 'She is kind. I try to see the goodness in people.'

'And what about that wretched explorer, eh?' he spat, 'have you found the goodness in him, that deceitful bastard? Or are the dead easier to condemn?'

I looked at him, and he showed his teeth in a grimace of triumph, of covetous knowledge. 'That man was an arrogant, ignoble little liar,' he said soberly, evidently savouring the sound of the words. 'Cavorting with native women, sharing his bed with savages. A man in his position, from a decent family, with a well brought-up, *educated* wife – it was disgusting. Unforgivable. He may be dead, but the *consequences* of his actions –,' this word he spat out as though it were poison, looking pointedly at me, his eyes set

82

with a dark, unsettling glint, '– must be borne by the family who survive him. That sort of behaviour does not go unpunished.'

There passed a laden moment in which no one spoke.

'I see no goodness in you.' I said quietly.

He continued as though he had not heard me, though I saw his face redden and knew that I only antagonised him. 'It is sin enough to be born a savage; worse still to relate to a family of decent, civilised people, that disgraceful fiend notwithstanding. You'll go the way of your mother, and that's more than you deserve.'

I had risen to my feet, fists clenched, hot-headed and sick with provocation. Judith had risen also, anticipated dissention perhaps. In a lowered voice she said quite calmly, 'I think you should leave.'

The signal to move had barely reached my feet before I realised that she addressed *him*, not me. He leapt up, and fiercely pushed his chair aside. He said something that I did not understand, his voice raised unpleasantly. Then he pointed at me, spat, turned on his heel and stalked out, slamming the door behind him.

The scene swam before my eyes. I thought I might pass out. No one moved; no one spoke. Once the heat from his presence had dissipated, my feet finally sprang into action. I was halfway into my boots, having thrown open the front door – though my exact intention – or destination – was yet unknown, before Judith laid a hand strong with dissuasion upon my shoulder, and closed the door in a way that could be considered compassionate. My head reeled. It was all I could do to submit to her wishes, and instead I tore myself away to the room upstairs, a hotness welling behind my eyes.

The current of panic coursed through my veins; I was surrounded by feathers, in my eyes, ears and throat, choking me until I feared for my life. Still, through the throbbing of my blood I could hear the low voice of Eqingaleq, singing and chanting, weaving stories into the fabric of my makeshift shelter.

A-ya-ya-ya...

Then I was no longer in England, in this unknown and unending city, cowering far above solid ground in a tent thrown together from woollen blankets...

I found myself in a tent sewn from skin. The warm smell of its heavy, enveloping fabric grounded me in the world from which we all must borrow before one day returning to ourselves. I had come to fetch the knife which I had left with my sleeping-skins. By the edge of the water the ice was streaked crimson and black with fresh blood. The narwhal, like the now dormant kayaks, had been hauled ashore where it lay lifeless, this graceful grey haunter of the sea, its great white tusk reminiscent of the mast of a ship keeled over in the grip of the pack ice. A creature almost of myth, it had taken three hunters to take its life. My heart swelled with pride as I recalled the agile glide of my skin kayak over the waves thrown into a tempest by its struggle; the weight of the harpoon gun in my bare hands; the exhilarated cries of the other hunters in the success of the chase.

I had sharpened my knife the day before, in anticipation, and I had sharpened it well for it cut cleanly into the animal's blubber with fast, angular strokes. In just a couple of hours the ice was littered with slabs of meat and blubber; my hands, like those of my companions, were stained red up to the elbows, shocking in the sun's fierce glare. Blood smeared the front of my overalls.

Qallu cut small pieces of the whale's nourishing skin and we chewed contentedly, savouring the goodness of this *mattak*: I could taste it now, feel its toughness between my teeth. Never before had I tasted it so fresh.

The world around us had fallen into a tranquil stillness: serenity in the wake of a life taken, a struggle ended. The only sound was that of our voices and laughter, carried upwards and lost in the vastness of the broken pack ice and the blue, empty sky. My cheeks stung from the cold.

I had feared that the son of a white man would find no solace with those whose arctic blood ran pure. But at that moment I knew who my people were. If only it could have lasted; if only I could have stayed forever in that most wonderful, archaic of places where each life draws sustenance from another and the world moves in harmony. If only I had not had to return home to find my own mother – loveless, lovelorn stranger – sprawled, like the narwhal, on the cold floor. Intoxicated up to the eyeballs, she stared at nothing for her eyes were clouded over and her body lay lifeless.

This creature did not speak to me of graceful, ancient beauty.

Slowly I slipped back into the weight of the present. As the final, painful stop in my train of thought was banished to the dark recesses of my mind I breathed again, strangely at peace. My breath was no longer ragged, the beat of my heart no longer frenzied to the point of collapse. I felt light, but not light-headed. The house appeared to be still and quiet, reflecting the calm following the storm, or so it seemed in the blanket den of my making. For the first time since my arrival I appreciated that the noise of the roads could not be heard from the back of the house, in which my guestroom was situated; the birds, too, did not sing. Darkness must have fallen – I had not noticed.

As once before, my solitude was encroached upon by a rap at the door. I wondered if it might be Judith come to request, after all, that I pack my bag and leave. I formed an apology on my tongue before I had even opened the door, only to find Michael on the other side. A bizarre demon with his curtained face half hidden in shadow, he looked as though he, too, had formulated an opening sentence in which he had now lost faith, and instead gaped at me somewhat gormlessly. Eventually, with a shrug of his shoulders he mumbled: 'Brought you a drink.' He thrust a glass into my hand and proceeded, before I could protest or politely decline, to fill it half-full from a bottle of dark, strong-smelling liquid. Having filled his own glass, he then murmured something indecipherable, but which I took as a toast, as he slammed his glass against my own, threw his head back and downed the entire measure in one enormous draught. He smacked his lips; his eyes watered. Pouring himself another he indicated that I drink up. I did not want to appear impolite: I took as brave a swig as I could manage, spluttering a little as the liquid burned the back of my throat. Once the overpowering taste had dissipated there spread a languorous, comforting warmth to my toes and fingertips. Colour rose to my cheeks, and I downed the rest.

Michael, though he still wore the guarded non-smile with which he had greeted me, seemed pleased. He raised the bottle of spirits, as though acknowledging its apparently medicinal properties, and with a curt nod of the head was gone. My head reeled. I closed the door and fell into the tent with a sigh, and the veil of sleep engulfed me with a suddenness I could not fight. With my last flicker of consciousness there drifted into my head a hazy afterthought, one that seemed to have forgotten to rear its head when surely it must have been conjured: how strange it seemed that, of all the photographs in the explorer's house, there was not one of the Arctic.

13

Rasmus

Rasmus watched silently, barely breathing as Ketty trimmed the wick of the blubber lamp with the blade of a small bone knife. Outside the evening sun cast its light on the melting snow and glowed against the tiny, rectangular windows. In the murky darkness of the hut, Ketty replaced the wick around the edge of the lamp's bowl. Rasmus kept his eyes fixed on her as she struck a match and held the flame to the wick. Time seemed to stand still; then, with a splutter, the twined grass took the flame. Ketty blew out the match, looked up to Rasmus and smiled, triumphantly and joyfully.

Her skin glowed gold in the new light of the blubber lamp, her cheeks round and hued with pink. Her eyes were dark, inviting.

'Thank you,' Rasmus said hoarsely, when he had found his voice.

For a moment longer they held each other's gaze.

'You are welcome,' Ketty whispered.

After she had made her goodbyes, Rasmus saw Birdie follow her with his watery eyes as she made her way out of the hut. He did not like the way the man looked at her.

The bright nights of early summer were playing havoc with the rhythms of Rasmus's body. He could not sleep, and instead passed long hours picking his way along the shoreline under the strange face of the midnight sun, his head aching and his thoughts in a whirl. He knew he was growing restless. Distracted. He had perhaps allowed too much time in Angmagssalik to prepare, he thought; he was anxious to set out on their journey across the ice cap, so long anticipated. Yet at the same time there was a wilful part of him that did not want to leave. His stomach twisted at the thought. This ambivalence towards his journey worried him: he was about to embark on the adventure he had dreamed of since he was a young lad poring over pictures of famous feats of polar exploration. It was the trip of a lifetime, the culmination of his life's work and ambition. And yet... he felt as though something within him had become disconnected.

Sometimes, on his midnight walks, Rasmus would end up joining in with the youngsters' many games of football in the lingering light. He would lose himself, then – caught up in a glorious sense of belonging, in the idea that he was free.

14

Malik

The following morning, I awoke early with a fierce headache and a strange feeling of calm conscience. For the first time since my arrival, I joined Eqingaleq at the window. I pulled back the garish flowered curtains that I had determinedly kept closed to obscure the urban reality which they concealed, ripping open the same crack through which Eqingaleq's eyes had peered apprehensively.

I must face my fate, I said matter-of-factly. All hopes and expectations of returning to my homeland had left along with the beaked man. Grimly, Eqingaleq nodded, for the thought surely had been his own. The contours of his face – creased in solemnity – alarmed me a little, so unbefitting did their contortions seem on the canvas of his usually open and honest countenance.

I'm scared, I stammered in the shadow of his graveness, which mirrored that of my own heart. *Scared that I might do the wrong thing. I could accept my fate but for I knew what it was. What if I take the wrong path – one that was not laid out for me? What happens then?*

He smiled softly. *You cannot choose your fate, only guide it. No path is wrong.*

But why am I here? I wanted to know. *There is no path back for me now.* He *will not take me back; Judith will not allow me to leave when I have nowhere else to go: I am meant to be here.*

I gestured at my surroundings: the walls by which I was enclosed; the endless labyrinth of buildings, streets and strangers.

But why? What am I supposed to do? My voice threatened to break.

You will know, said Eqingaleq. The weight of years – thousands of years – settled momentarily on his brows, before his ancient face broke into a wide smile and he indicated the clear sky above the roofs of the surrounding houses. I looked with him, and saw that the morning heavens were streaked with purple and gold. *Even in this world,* he observed, *there can be found beauty; even when the source cannot be seen.*

The beak-nosed man returned to the house that evening. In the darkest corner of my blanket tent I cowered, sick with anxiety, as I heard his voice downstairs. Its high-pitched tone resounded throughout the house and echoed painfully in my head, his words unintelligible. I prayed silently that he would not seek me out in my corner of the house. I did not have the strength to hold my ground against him. I did not know what it was that he wanted from me.

Thankfully he did not venture upstairs, nor did he linger for long. I heard the beating of his great white wings as he left.

I longed to ask Judith who he was, this man who had brought me to her home and into her life.

Every evening, I helped Judith in the kitchen. While striving to make myself useful, I would ask her the names of things – the different vegetables as I cut them into chunks for the soup, the cutlery and kitchen utensils, a squirrel that appeared on the window ledge – anything that came into sight. Sometimes – often in fact – I would have to ask her to repeat the word more than once, or to remind me a few minutes later, the sounds having already slipped my mind. And I would repeat it over and over again, slowly and clearly, syllable by syllable until the sounds fitted comfortably around my tongue. Once it became apparent that my hostess did not at all mind these impromptu lessons – as I had feared she would – I dared even to ask her for full sentences, abstract notions and ideas that lay beyond the realms of our immediate culinary environment. I was filled with a great warmth to be able to utter the words *I think that. . .* even if the thought must remain incomplete. For this brought me, at least, one step closer to the ability to communicate, to relate. As soon as I was able I would ask about my father – her husband – for in this way I felt that my path would be made clear. I did not wish to believe that my journey had been or that it would continue to be meaningless.

For the time being, however, I could almost lose myself in these stolen evening moments. To an outsider they could be mistaken for family life. Occasionally Michael would slope into the kitchen, hands in pockets, the bottom of his wide trousers wet from the rain. Mumbling an incoherent greeting he would sit down heavily and twiddle his thumbs until his evening meal appeared on the table. He would offer a grunt of thanks before wolfing down the contents of his plate as though he had not set eyes on a decent meal for days. Once finished he would disappear upstairs, his departure followed by the muffled, thumping sounds of loud music. Often he would make his exit back the way he had come: through the front door and out into the darkening evenings. I often wondered where he disappeared to. From the cocoon of my blanket tent I would hear him returning in the early hours of the morning, sometimes drunk – so I assumed, given the unevenness of his footfall, the clumsy bumps and crashes and muttered curses. It filled me with dismay to hear these noises, for I felt as though I were a child once more, listening with bated breath and beating heart to the sounds of my mother coming home at night, drunk once more.

Michael had not spoken to me again since the evening of the beaked man's visit. There seemed to be a degree of awkwardness in his mannerisms towards me, a steadfast reluctance to make eye contact.

One evening, however, he approached me uncertainly as I was seasoning the soup. He had spoken to Judith first, in a low voice, stealing snatched glances in my direction through the drapes of his unwashed hair. My stomach had turned a somersault in unfounded fear that he might mean some ill towards me. His mother motioned him to the stove at which I was positioned over the pots. Shuffling towards me in his wide blue jeans and oversized shirt he shoved his hands into his pockets, tossed his head slightly so that his hair was momentarily parted from before his face and muttered to the floor, 'Got you a job.'

I stopped stirring the soup. It was difficult to tell if I had in fact heard him correctly, and whether it had been me he had addressed. 'A job?' I echoed.

He shrugged, threw back his hair again. 'Yeah, you know. Like, working. For money.'

I nodded, and though bewildered, managed to thank him. Michael, too, gave a vague nod of the head. He briefly made eye contact and upturned the corners of his mouth into something that could have been interpreted as a smile, or perhaps he had frowned, before sloping away and taking up his customary, expectant seat at the table.

No more was said on the subject until the following morning, when the boy appeared quite unexpectedly – and rather unwelcome given the hour of the morning, for again I had not slept until the early hours – at my bedroom door.

'Job,' was all he said by way of explanation, as I squinted

at him through sand-filled eyes. I struggled hastily, my heart quickening with nerves, into my second-hand clothes, and there was no time for coffee before we were out the door.

Michael took to the pavement in lolloping strides, his hands still buried deep in the pockets of his jeans, hair swinging from side to side with the rhythm of his steps. I hurried a short distance behind him, led blindly once more through rain-soaked streets, invigorated somewhat by the cold droplets upon my face still swollen with sleep. Despite the comfort of my fisherman's jumper beneath my anorak, I shivered with the bleak chill of consciousness, and silently we trudged past unassuming facades of grey walls set with gaping, faceless windows down which the rain streamed in gleaming rivets.

Michael came to an abrupt standstill outside one of the buildings, as though he had only at the last minute become aware of its presence. I, in my absentmindedness, almost ran into the back of him. How easy it seemed, on these streets in which each building ran into the other in featureless monotony, to overlook one's destination.

The window and door frames of the shop outside which Michael had stopped were painted a colour that at one time may have been a vivid blue but had since been worn away by the weather into insignificance. A grubby, hand-painted sign above the door proclaimed *Tony's Records*. The windows were steamed up. With a nod, his hair plastered wetly to his head, Michael indicated our journey's end, and apprehensively I followed him inside.

A little bell sounded sweetly above the door as we entered. Released for a moment from anxiety as the sudden warmth of the interior wrapped itself around me, my first and only thought was that it felt wonderful to be out of the chill of the rain; although it had seemed as though it fell only lightly, my anorak was sodden. I pulled back the hood and shivered once more as a stream of dislodged raindrops made its way down the back of my neck. The low-level lighting of the small

93

room gave the impression that the day, comfortingly, had already reached an end, for the clouded light of the morning barely filtered through the fog that had settled upon the window pane. It lent a homely feeling to the otherwise bizarre, cluttered layout of the shop: floor stands and boxes in which could be seen row upon row of record sleeves, the walls adorned similarly with loaded shelves. Where these were absent there had been affixed instead a multitude of posters. Some depicted black and white photographs of sullen young men with long hair; some were garishly colourful jungles of swirling shapes and words, or surreal artwork; one showed simply a picture of a dairy cow.

I stood captivated and curious, my fingers resting distracted below the hollow of my throat, on the unopened top button of my anorak. I was startled into the moment by the croak of a man's voice in greeting. Dressed in a bright blue t-shirt with the word *Woodstock* printed across the front, he stood behind the counter in the opposite corner of the room. His round face creased into a wide smile as he surveyed the shop floor, which was empty of visitors save for Michael and myself.

'All right, man.' Michael returned the greeting and trailed up to the counter. From the depths of his pocket he removed a hand and slapped it against the man's own, outstretched, in a strange sort of a handshake. I hung back uncertainly as they exchanged pleasantries – news, thoughts, opinions – it was difficult to follow the flow of conversation, though most of the talking was carried out by the man who I assumed must be the proprietor. Michael listened intently. He continually nodded his greasy head, almost bouncing on the soles of his shoes in apparent enthusiasm as he did so, and repeated 'Yeah, man, yeah,' at regular intervals. When he laughed it sounded as a peculiar rasping chuckle, not wholly natural; his partner's laugh was more of a roar, alarmingly aggressive – increasingly so given the way in which he slapped his large, hairy hand on the counter top – evidently

94

in amusement. The other hand clutched a burning cigarette from which he took a long drag every now and again, expelling clouds of opaque smoke into the heat of the room. My eyes watered; I attempted to stifle a cough, and at this disturbance Michael turned around as though surprised to find me standing a little way behind him. He gestured towards me somewhat awkwardly, eyes averted from my face as usual, and muttered my name to the middle-aged man. 'Come for the job, yeah?' he added, by way of introduction.

The man gave a broad, friendly smile and held out his hand. 'Tony,' he said as, after some hesitation, I reached out and shook it in the customary manner, 'of Tony's Records.' I noticed that there hung a grey ponytail down the back of his neck, though the top of his head, while wreathed in smoke, was bald. It shone dully in the electric light.

'Pleased to meet you, Tony of Tony's Records,' I greeted, as best as I knew how. I thought I heard Michael give a loud snort. Perhaps he, too, was affected by the smoke.

'You like music, Malik?' the man asked. I chose to ignore the askew pronunciation of my name, foreign to his ears, and simply nodded in response – an honest answer, even if I was not able to elaborate.

He grinned more broadly. 'Then you've got the job!' he exclaimed, and slapping his great paw against the counter once more, threw back his round head and roared with laughter. Michael contributed his rasping laugh in accompaniment.

Eqingaleq, who had been perusing the records nearby, almost leapt out of his skin at this sudden cacophony. He looked at me questioningly, and I, bewildered also, shrugged in response. I was beginning to sweat under the stifling layer of my yellow anorak, perhaps in the heat of the room, or possibly it was the unbearable nervousness of the entire exchange. Still I dared not remove my coat lest this be considered presumptuous, for I did not know the planned length of our visit. I could take no cues from Michael for the boy had, bizarrely and for reasons I could not presume, left the house without a coat of any kind. I wondered whether he was so unaccustomed to the weather that he did not know how to manage its onslaught. Or perhaps it was generally so mild at these latitudes that he simply foresaw no need for cover. His canvas shoes were sodden, the wide hems of his jeans were wet almost up to the knees in rising damp, and the water dripped from his lank hair in streams. He appeared entirely unconcerned by the condition of his attire, and was evidently of the opinion that he would dry out soon enough in the sultry atmosphere of the record shop – indeed, he seemed to steam in the dry heat and the smoke that hung about the ceiling.

I was saved from prolonged discomfort by the attentions of Tony who, as if reading either my mind or my clouded expression, stubbed out his cigarette along with the remaining notes of his laughter.

'Get your coat off, then, Mal, and we'll show you around the place.'

Beside the shop counter there was a hook on the wall (framed by postcard-sized pictures of a similar nature to the posters that adorned the walls) on which I was instructed to hang my dripping anorak. Beside this a doorway hung with a red curtain led the way into a cupboard-sized kitchen whose sole occupants, aside from the sink, were a stove-top kettle, a box of tea bags and a carton of milk. The highlight of this brief tour, however, appeared to be the battered-looking record player that sat atop the counter, complete with a pair of worn speakers. Michael approached the thing with a manner akin to reverence, lifting the lid with a careful, respectful hand. Displaying an uncontrollable grin, he opened his arms wide to indicate the entirety of the shop, and for the first time spoke to me directly, as though in the throes of his passion he had forgotten to hide defensively behind the curtain of hair: 'We can listen to anything, man, *anything!*'

He skipped over to one of the racks of records, his sodden shoes slapping the linoleum floor – geometric patterns in yellow and brown – and disappeared momentarily behind a mop of hanging hair as, head bowed, he flicked deftly through the record sleeves with eager fingers. The chosen one having been retrieved, he placed it reverentially on the player.

'Listen to this, man,' he half-whispered, his eyes gleaming in a way I would not have thought possible given his previous, perpetual sullenness. It was as though he were extending an invitation to share in a guarded secret, some form of beauty revealed only to those few who took the time to look, to listen. With all the gravity of a revered ancient ritual he lowered the needle, adjusted the volume, and as the table began to turn the crackle of empty noise gave way at once to the sound of electric guitars.

How little I had heard such music, yet how palpable was its effect in this context. It was as though the record shop and its idiosyncrasies suddenly made sense, became real, as though the music had awoken a purpose in this confusing world – just as the trance-inducing drum songs of the shaman would bring forth the spirits. A meaning narrated by the music, by those who played, composed, and those who listened and dreamed. In the guitar's rhythms and wailings I saw the psychedelic patterns that leaped out from the posters on the walls, the sleeves of the records; colours and sounds intertwined and were made tangible. I saw another dimension to this mundane world; my senses were ignited, and my imagination took flight, its raven wings glinting in the awakening light.

I looked over to Michael, drawn by the movement of his head bobbing to the rhythm of the music, trance-like, and saw that he was watching me. For a split second it seemed that he was two-headed: Eqingaleq peered curiously over his shoulder, wide black eyes fixed upon the record player with a mixture of disdain and wonder, crooked nose wrinkled in the

97

smoke. It was disconcerting, these two faces in juxtaposition: one of the ancient spirits, one of this new world. I tried to hide the shudder that ran down the length of my spine. Imperceptibly I shook my head at Eqingaleq, for I did not like the truth of what I saw, and strove to ignore the look of warning that weighed heavily in his eyes.

Don't let yourself be seduced, he said to me later, in the neutrality of the blanket tent as outside the city lay sunken in darkness.

Irritated – fearful, perhaps – I reprimanded him in short temper for his reluctance to embrace these things that before had been of little concern. *The world advances*, I said, *we must adapt or we cannot hope to get by.*

Music is a powerful thing, he cautioned, *how easy it can be for one who is not on his guard to get caught up in its magic, swept away, to fall into a trance.*

And you who said we must learn to see the beauty in things! I scoffed. *Even where it may not be obvious. Especially here, so well-hidden. Beauty is more than what the eye can see. It* has *to be, in a place like this.*

I felt that I could cry with the elation, the confusion of this new discovery, this music. *There has to be something more.*

Just make sure that you look in the right place, were Eqingaleq's final words upon the subject. Off-handedly, I dismissed him – though how I wish, now, that I had listened.

15

Rasmus

Snorri and Birdie had both chosen to accompany Qallu to the annual summer camp in a nearby fjord. Rasmus was reluctant to join them; there were still plenty of preparations to be made in the town before their journey across the ice cap, he told them, though when he thought about it he could not see what more needed to be done. Still, there were bound to be some last minute details that required his attention.

The season had changed noticeably. The pack ice that had choked the fjord had broken up bit by bit, until all that remained were the looming castles of icebergs that cracked and shifted like awakening giants. The snow that had blanketed the town had all but melted, leaving trails of grey slush on the earthen roads and exposing multitudes of discarded tin cans and broken glass bottles.

Qallu's little boat sat low in the still water of the harbour, loaded up with clothes, cooking equipment and the components of a heavy canvas tent in which he, Snorri and Birdie would be sleeping at the communal camp. The harbour buzzed with activity: other families loaded up their boats to make the same journey, a nod to their ancestors' nomadic way of life when the whole village would relocate, following the change in the seasons and the chance of better hunting grounds. The children shrieked with uncontrollable excitement; the women passed around strips of dried seal meat. The atmosphere hummed with anticipation.

Qallu kissed his wife and sister goodbye. He ran his hands over the enormous swell of Avaaraq's belly and spoke softly to her in his own tongue as she sobbed into his shoulder. He had promised her he would return from the camp before her time was upon her: he did not want to miss the birth of his first child. Rasmus felt a pull in his stomach and a rush of warmth through his veins as he watched the tender scene between the young couple. For the first time in days he thought of his wife back in England. He tried to recall the details of their own parting before he had left for the arctic. He was sure it had been much different from this couple's affectionate display.

Ketty slid a comforting arm around her sister-in-law's shoulder as Qallu released her from his embrace.

'Make sure you look after the explorer,' he heard Qallu say to them, in Danish for the benefit of Rasmus. He glanced over to Rasmus, grinning mischievously. 'There are still many things that he does not know.'

Rasmus watched the boat's passage away from the town and down the fjord with a pang of regret. To think of the things he could have learnt if he had accompanied Qallu and the other hunters and their families to the camp! As his gaze wandered his eyes met those of Ketty. Her eyes sparkled, creasing at the corners as she smiled softly. And he knew, then, why he had chosen to stay.

Rasmus enjoyed his many evenings spent with Avaaraq and Ketty in the cosy atmosphere of their family home. It was a home filled with simple pleasures: the all-enveloping smell of the blubber lamp and the heartiness of Ketty's seal-meat stews. Once they had eaten, Ketty would tell him stories, folk tales that took place in the harsh arctic landscape. About strange demons that crept through winter darkness and snatched away lone hunters; bears that could take human form. Ketty's voice was low. Rasmus's skin prickled.

He would watch as the two women prepared new skins, in the same way that their ancestors had done for thousands of years before them, and sewed them into garments for Rasmus and his companions. They chewed the leather with their teeth, for hours at a time, to make it supple, and threaded bone knives though the hide with remarkable strength and dexterity.

Avaaraq would never accept his offers of help. This was women's work, she said; it was a man's job to hunt for their sustenance. Ketty turned her dark eyes up towards him, a piece of hide clamped in her teeth, and giggled. Her cheeks were rosy from the heat of the blubber lamp which warmed the room to an almost stifling temperature, despite the evening chill outside. Beads of sweat glistened on her collarbone, her bare shoulders. . .

Rasmus swallowed, pulled at his collar. He was sweating. He had been too embarrassed to remove his shirt as the temperature rose inside the hut. He thought about venturing outside for a breath of fresh air, but could not tear himself away. He could not keep his eyes off her.

16

Malik

The relief I experienced at having, finally, a purpose to each day, was almost tangible. There was to be found comfort in simplistic routine, a set path on which to focus my mind, whose corners careered with the cacophony of thought, and whose voices were never quiet. I reverted back to my lifelong summertime habit of rising with the sun, though it is true that there arose with me a great number of anxieties that clouded my newly conscious mind and hounded me until the day's end, like ravenous wolves in search of a kill.

Each morning I attempted to drown out the sound of the creatures' howling with the preaching of the wireless. I nursed a cup of tea at the kitchen table, bathed in early morning light, until the appearance of Judith would signal that it was time for breakfast. Always we would eat in silence, but communal silence at least, I with burning cheeks as sentence after sentence formed painstakingly in my head yet failed to make it past my lips. Sometimes I could not eat for fear that I would choke on the words that piled up in my throat. Judith would stir her porridge absentmindedly, attention fixed on the wireless, thank me when I brought her a cup of tea, shake her head at something she heard on the news, glance apprehensively at the rain that beat upon the window.

Sometimes we would be joined late in the proceedings by Michael, tired and grumpy if he was required to work that day. As if sleepwalking, he would pour himself half a cup of tea from the dregs of the pot, take only one sip, then make himself a piece of toast which he would invariably still be eating as we left the house. I watched it go soggy in the rain and wondered what it was that so occupied his thoughts that even the simplest of tasks seemed to take him an eternity to complete.

The choosing of the first record of the day was deliberated upon for even longer, yet it was in this particular undertaking and no other that he appeared entirely absorbed. He would listen just as intently, never showing any sign that he enjoyed the rhythms, the melodies, the noises, other than the slight bobbing of his head in time to the music. I strove to remember those records which most captured my imagination, so that I might retrieve one at a later date and, too apprehensive to set it on the machine myself – whether cautious of the technology itself or perhaps Michael's reaction – prop it up next to the record player in anticipation that it might be chosen again.

I could lose myself in the music, a welcome antidote to the slowness of the days and the uncertainty of where they would lead. The perpetual clouds of smoke that hung about the shop made my eyes water, my head reel; the bottomless cups of tea made me jittery; I tried not to think too much. I coveted the relative feeling of safety that the record shop offered, a cave set into the street and breached only by the outside world with the occasional tinkle of the bell above the door and a solitary, long-haired customer perusing its treasures.

Nonetheless I looked forward to the day's end, to returning to the house, to the kitchen where I could help Judith prepare the evening meal. Though, when at last this time came I invariably felt so awkward, and plagued once more by the nausea of my guilt, that I wondered what I had in fact been anticipating.

How unbearable was the silence in which we ate.

After three long, confusing weeks of this new focus of my waking hours, when we were again sat around the table over the remnants of a habitually hushed meal, Michael offered an unexpected invitation: would I like to listen to some records? He jerked his head upwards to indicate the proposed venue of his bedroom, to which he would generally disappear alone after each meal, if he did not instead vanish out the front door. I looked expectantly to Judith, for I had already risen with my empty plate, but she only smiled – as so many times before, her thoughts veiled behind this gesture – and took the plate from my hands.

I followed Michael upstairs in the semi-darkness of the evening that had descended inside the house and stood blindly at the threshold to his room while he clattered about unseeingly and eventually succeeded in locating the lamp. As the low electric light seeped like treacle into each corner of the room, the scene that met my eyes was one of chaos. An unmade bed dripped with blankets, clothes spilled out of a wardrobe and draped themselves over every inch of the carpet; unwashed bowls and mugs lined the edges of the room, crept under the furniture. A musty smell hung about the air, as though the window, obscured now and perhaps permanently by garishly patterned curtains, had remained closed for longer than the occupant cared to remember. Eqingaleq, peering over my shoulder from the darkened hallway, balked at the sight by which he was greeted. Quietly, I muttered that the boy might feel similarly, had he instead entered the room in which I was staying as a guest, and there beheld the makeshift tent I had constructed, the hiding place in which I had chosen to reside.

Michael seemed unperturbed by the disorder of his environment. With his foot he cleared a space amidst the clothing and crockery that littered the floor, and motioned that I ought to take a seat, next to the record player. How strange, I thought, that despite the overwhelming disorder of the boy's bedroom, his collection of records alone was neatly, painstakingly arranged on the bookcase.

Nervously I sat down on an orange pile rug uncovered by Michael's shuffling, and rested my back against the wall; the clutter bore down on me from all remaining sides. Michael continued to clatter about the room and, having come up with a glass bottle, poured us both a drink.

'You liked Pink Floyd, yeah?' He handed me a full glass of spirits. Nodding in response to this sudden question I failed to refuse the offering, then thought perhaps that a little of the stuff might not be all that bad. Eqingaleq raised an eyebrow. But before he had a chance to open his mouth to speak, the record player sprang into life. The music was a gradual crescendo of brass, drums, noise... Michael sat down on the rug and offered me a cigarette. I had at that moment chosen to brave a sip of the brimming glass of spirits, and spluttering, dizzy, failed once more to decline the welcome gesture.

The guitar began to wail, hauntingly.

Emboldened by the glorious warmth that trickled down my throat and spread its fiery fingers through my veins, I raised the cigarette to my lips as Michael lit it; though my eyes watered I could tell that he smiled, laughed as I tried to stifle a cough.

There were other voices, too – a choir – sombre, sorrowful, passionate...

I took another swig from my glass to soothe the burning sensation in my throat; another cautious drag on the cigarette. When the guitar spoke again I watched the reams of smoke rise and curl around its melody.

The more I drank, the more of Michael's rambling I found I was able to understand, for he grew particularly loquacious as the liquid in his glass rapidly dwindled. I listened as he

106

spoke of the music, the story and the people behind it. Each record he introduced to me as one might introduce a friend to another, that I might understand the reason for its coming into existence, the meaning within its notes. Each time the bottom of my glass was within sight he refilled it, talking still of his passion so that I did not have the chance to decline. Recklessly, I asked him to repeat the words that I did not understand, and elaborate on the ideas that most caught my imagination. It was as though the room around me evaporated into the heat of the spirits. I felt only the electricity of the music; it wove stories and pictures within my head which disappeared into an excitable haze of imagination as soon as they were conceived. I grew light-headed, though my eyelids were heavy. When I tried to speak the words could not fit properly past my lips and spilled out in an indecipherable jumble of sounds. In my own language I apologised to Michael that I was not more proficient in his. He laughed, poured me another glass.

The music again fell to silence. A blackness began to creep into the peripheries of my vision, and at once I noticed that Eqingaleq was not in the room. I did not know how much time had passed. I struggled to my feet, onto legs that could barely hold my weight. I made my goodbyes, my apologies – Michael, sprawled contentedly on a beanbag, raised a drunken finger in farewell – and stumbled from the room and into my own.

Within the shelter of my tent I caught a glimpse of Eqingaleq's lantern eyes before the creeping shadows claimed the rest of my vision. I floundered in an unstoppable tide of material darkness, smothered and claustrophobic. I tossed and turned upon storm-ridden waves, adrift in the vastness of the ocean. Were the gleaming eyes I saw those of Eqingaleq, or did they belong to *her*: The Mother of the Sea, in all her power and all her sadness? I could not reach her.

When I awoke in the morning I barely made it to the bathroom before the seasickness took its toll.

Seasickness? Eqingaleq laughed, cruelly. I swore at him,

and regretted it immediately as without another word he left
the room, and I was alone, on my knees on the cold tiled floor.

17

Rasmus

Ketty made love like a wild animal.

Her skin was the colour of chestnuts; her hair smelt of summer moss and wildflowers. Her voice was the low moan of the wind over the arctic tundra. Her hands, when she ran them hungrily over his chest, felt rough and worn from a lifetime of use; the rest of her body was as warm and soft as the earth.

Afterwards, he lay for a while beside her. Suspended in the moment, his relentless thoughts absent for now, he heard only the rushing tide of Ketty's breathing. As his faculties began to return he smelled the rich smoke of the blubber lamp that smouldered on the table, and thought that he would light himself a cigarette.

He carefully pushed himself into a sitting position and swung his legs off the side of the raised sleeping platform, enjoying the texture of the animal hide blankets on his bare skin. The hut was warm from the burning lamp and the heat of their bodies. He could just reach the box of English cigarettes he had left on the table without needing to stand up. He fiddled with the silver lid of the slim case, meaning to lift it open and retrieve the one remaining cigarette that he was sure was still inside. The lid was stuck; with a little force and a jerk of his hand he was able to open it, and a metallic object dropped out of the box and clattered against the hard surface of the sleeping platform.

It was his wedding ring. The gold shone in the light of the lamp, a searching eye turned upon his crime: judging, condemning. He grasped it with shaking fingers, plunged in back inside the tin, and closed the lid.

He had only removed it from his finger because he had been bothered by the weight of it, he told himself silently; he was not used to wearing such ornaments after all. He would wear it again once the expedition had come to an end, once he returned home: it wouldn't get in the way then, and there would be plenty of time to grow accustomed to it...

His heart sank at the thought.

Ketty's fingers played up his spine. He shuddered at her touch. He slipped the cigarette case into the pocket of his coat that hung on the back of the chair and re-joined Ketty in the bed, banishing all thoughts of the tin and its contents from his mind.

18

Malik

I dreamed, each and every night, of the vast sea and its guardian; dreams of frustration and of unendurable longing. Each night her eyes grew dimmer. Within them welled another ocean from which I turned my eyes in fear, for I did not understand. Each night the horizons grew more distant.

And yet I did not set out in search of its shores. When Michael and I drank and smoked together in the music-infused confines of his bedroom, I often felt the swell of determination rise within my soul, the rush of elation: I would set out at first light, I told myself, and not rest until there lay stretched before me the great, calming plane of the ocean. I imagined its grey fingers reaching for my feet, welcoming – soon I would be home. Yet as the evening progressed and the drink flowed I was gradually overcome by lethargy. A sickening fear began to sink its wolverine teeth into the back of my clouded conscience. By the time the fingers of dawn pulled me from my hounded sleep I was overpowered by nausea and fatigue. I would not seek the ocean; I could not. I was terrified of becoming lost, for I had no bearings in this place where every street was the same. Were my senses able to guide me correctly, I was more afraid of the watery eyes and sharp beak of the one who might await me there.

Instead I resigned myself to fate – a pathetic act of hopelessness: I would be led to the ocean if that was the direction of my intended path. Did Eqingaleq call me a coward? I was unsure whether the word had passed his lips.

There was a strange security to be found in the relinquishing of responsibilities and the resignation to remain in one place. I would tread the same paths each day: the tent to the kitchen; the kitchen to the record shop; the record shop to the kitchen again, and so back to the tent to see out the day, if not to the record player in Michael's bedroom. The wolves, too, knew my route, and trailed me untiringly, tongues lolling, saliva dripping in anticipation of the moment at which I would drop to the ground as carrion meat. They howled continuously, so that even when I dared not look I knew they were there. I turned up the record player to drown out their yowls and squeals.

One evening, however, they nearly caught up with me.

I was ambushed, perhaps, for I had taken a different route, deviated from the set paths of daily routine. When Michael laid down his knife and fork that evening he did not slope wordlessly upstairs, nor did he beckon me to listen to a new record that I really ought to hear; to my surprise, and apprehension, he informed me that we were to go out. He did not say where. My stomach twisted horribly, my heart began to palpitate. Leave the house? Again? Why prolong the day when we were so tantalisingly close to its end?

Michael did not appear to expect an answer; indeed, no question had been asked. He poured us both a drink, and I knocked it back as though it were water and I a man dying of thirst, seeking comfort in its giddy arms and the blanket stupor that would throw the wolves off course. By the time we left the house I could barely walk in a straight line. The streetlights seemed so bright it could almost have been daylight, though still I stumbled as though I could not see. Eqingaleq followed in my shaky shadow, striving to point out landmarks and street names so that we might find our way back, in case Michael were not there to guide us, in case we must run from the wolves or from the White-winged One, in case. . .

The bar smelled of alcohol and of sweat. In the low light it seemed as though the room were filled with shadows; spirits and demons screeching and chattering within these enclosing prison walls. Michael and I were surrounded by people, by greetings and laughter; my name was mentioned, others exchanged but none remembered. I think I smiled but did not feel it within my soul. I wished I had not had so much to drink, so that I might think more clearly, that I might be on my guard. Yet already there was another glass in my hand that I had not requested, not refused. And I drank to quench a thirst that would not be slaked.

Who was this young woman standing before me, where Michael had been a moment earlier? *Where are you from*, she wanted to know. I told her, but could not tell whether her interest was genuine, or nothing but a social convention. She had never met anyone from Greenland, she said. She seemed soft around the edges, long dark hair that framed her face, fell over her forehead and almost into her eyes, which were ringed with charcoal. Her lips were full and red. I found myself wondering what it would be like to press my own against them.

It is not the sort of place that is easy to leave, I told her.

But you – she said – *why did you leave?*

I had to, I said.

You had to?

I had to.

She touched me on the shoulder; the clatter of the melee of bracelets on her wrist was drowned out by the music. *You'll like it here*, she said. I did not believe her.

The wolves howled more loudly over the volume of the music and my own voice was hoarse with the strain of making myself heard. The record was one I recognised – a small comfort, something on which to concentrate. Some people danced, others tapped their feet; Michael's head never stopped bobbing when the music played. He nearly spilled the drink that he passed to me, so enraptured was he in his own interpretation of rhythm. Eqingaleq murmured a caution in my ear as I set down my empty glass – how well Michael could anticipate! I raised the replenished one to my lips.

It's the only way I can get through, I replied – did I mean the chaos of the evening or the insistent fog by which I was surrounded? Perhaps I meant the path that I was required to take in order discover the very reason for my following its course. Whatever its meaning the truth felt good upon my alcohol-stained lips. I said it again. *It's the only way I can get through.*

Through the haze of consciousness I felt a longing for the quiet and solitude of my blanket tent, yet I feared the stillness that lurked there and the thoughts that would make themselves known in the absence of this cacophony and distraction. By the time we did leave for home I had lost all track of time, and all coherency; my head was a nightmarish jumble of howling, panting and heavy footfall. I stumbled after Michael. The wolves came after me from each and every direction: I was surrounded, hemmed in from all sides by hot, rancid breath and lolling tongues, red as blood. To run would be futile. Instead I stopped at the side of the empty street and was sick – waves of shame and of hopelessness, the swell of the tide. Afterwards I found that the creatures had pulled back somewhat, though not so far that I could forget their chase.

Eqingaleq gripped my elbows and dragged me homewards. *She wants me to drown,* I moaned, *the Mother of the Sea.*

He shook his head. *You are throwing yourself in where you*

114

cannot swim, he said. *The more water your wings take in, the harder it will be to fly free. Even she cannot help you then, if you sink straight into her arms.*

'Good night out, man,' Michael said to me the following morning over a breakfast that I could not stomach. His eyes were bloodshot. Unsure if this had been intended as a question or an unfounded statement, I merely nodded and regretted my response immediately for the sickness welled again. I closed my eyes. Trying to stay still, I willed the ship to stop rocking and the tide to calm its advance. The sea had been so rough during the night that I had barely slept, and had swallowed only salt water from the storm's spray. My eyes and throat stung; my body ached all over as though I had been beaten.

The seasickness persisted all week, and I could drink nothing but water and strong tea. When Michael brought out the bottle again one evening, the sounds of a mellow guitar drifting from the record player, I could not touch the stuff despite even the pressures of social convention and the inevitability that I would not be able to finally broach the subject of my father – our father – were I not under its emboldening influence. He did not seem offended, as I had feared, only laughed amicably and assured me that I would yet learn to hold my drink.

Was this the point of it all? I wondered aloud to Eqingaleq once we had retreated into the soothing quiet of my tent: *to learn to drink oneself to excess without becoming too ill, perhaps?*

Your mother never managed that, he said plainly, and so unexpectedly that I was taken aback.

But that... that was different, surely? I stammered defensively. *She was... you know what she was like. This is different. I'm just trying to get by until I know what I have to do next, until I know what it's all been for.*

115

You remember your mother's brother? He continued as though he had not heard. *He came home one winter night so drunk he couldn't fit his key into the lock. And they found him the next morning, frozen to death on his front doorstep.*

And your point is? I tried to mask my horror at such an unwelcome memory.

Eqingaleq shrugged his bare, lithe shoulders. *Just be careful.*

I had to bite my tongue to stop the words from flowing out uninhibited; he would not be argued with, and I, in the weaker position, could not hope to win. Yet what simplistic advice! I was on the run from wolves, in search of the sea: I could not simply "take care", I could not hide and wait for the storm to pass. If I stopped, I would surely drown.

19

Rasmus

'We've delayed too long,' said Birdie, glaring at Rasmus down the bridge of his long nose. 'Summer's almost out – any later in the year and the weather will be against us.'

Although the man did not say it aloud, Rasmus knew that he held him to account. It had not been his conscious decision to stay for so long in Angmagssalik; he felt a stab of panic at the realisation that he simply did not know where the time had gone, and for a second he recognised the taste of a recurring nightmare in which the minutes, the days slipped through his fingers and he could not run fast enough to keep up.

The blubber smoke inside the hut was suffocating him.

He looked over to Snorri for validation, though of course he knew that Birdie was right. The Icelander was sitting on one of the low beds, his elbows resting on his knees and his fingers knitted before his nose. He nodded impassively. 'If we leave it any longer it will be too close to winter. We'd have to get settled here and wait for the spring.'

Birdie snorted at the suggestion. 'We leave now or we go home,' he stated.

Rasmus swallowed the lump of anger that rose up in his throat: that Birdie should think he had the authority to dictate to them what they should or should not do.

'You're taking charge now, are you?' he asked plainly.

'Don't get passive aggressive with me, Rasmus,' Birdie snapped, 'We all have a say in this. I suppose you'd have us set up sticks here in this godforsaken place for as long as it suited you.'

'But Qallu has his family,' Rasmus pointed out, searching for a line of argument that would not render him as the responsible one for any changes of plan. He twisted his hands together. 'The baby's not a week old, I'm sure he wouldn't want to leave –.' He was interrupted by the unsettling screech of wood scraped against wood as Birdie rose to his feet, pushing his chair back from the table.

'Qallu will leave when he's told to leave. Isn't that what we're paying him for?' He stalked across the room to his narrow bed, picked up a book. Propping up his pillow he sat down with his back against it and his legs stretched out languorously over the blankets. He stuck his nose inside the open book and apparently began to read.

For a moment no one spoke.

'We're well prepared.' Birdie's steely voice could be heard from behind the covers of his book. 'We can leave tomorrow.'

Rasmus could not bring himself to speak. He could not find the words to express his thoughts; even had he been able to he would not have dared to utter them in present company for fear that he might be ridiculed or patronised. His eyes wandered over to where Birdie sat: it appeared Birdie had put an end to the discussion, his face hidden deliberately behind the book.

With a sigh Rasmus leaned forwards in his seat, clasped his hands together. He had believed that in Qallu he had made a friend, a companion and teacher who would accompany them to the ends of the earth... He had not considered that the promise of a wage might play a part in their relationship, as Birdie had suggested. And what about Ketty? His chest pained him, as though it were clamped in a vice. He had been naïve, he reprimanded himself – to think that here he might have made his home, here amongst strangers.

He heard Snorri speak quietly, it seemed to him alone. 'We can't stay here forever.'

It was as though his friend had read his mind. Heavily he nodded his head. His body felt drained, anchored to the chair on which he sat. He could not imagine hauling the weight of it all the way across the ice cap.

20

Malik

The following week, seasickness already forgotten, I accompanied Michael to the bar again. I had found myself consumed by thoughts of the long-haired girl whose acquaintance I had made so briefly the week before, possibly for the reason that this was the only part of the evening that I could recall with any clarity. My bemused mind sought focus, demanded reason – and found it in the pleasing bow of red lips and gentle femininity so alien to my inherent gracelessness, and so desirable.

Although I had made a conscious effort not to unwittingly drink so much before the evening had barely begun, and indeed as it progressed, I soon discovered that even a little of the stuff – for I could not get by without at least a little to calm my nerves and dampen my inhibitions – sent me reeling. My cheeks burned with the heat of the bodies that crowded the room; the girl's cheeks, too, were flushed with colour. The music rang out so loudly that we could not hope to converse. The mutual attempt to be heard brought our hot cheeks closer together and our hands upon each other's shoulders, and our lips to each other's ears until finally, somehow, our lips met. She pressed her young body to mine; I held her close, seeking the comfort and warmth of another human being, and the simplistic pleasure of the sharing of flesh. Her hands cupped my jaw and slid up into my hair, pale, slender fingers running through the blackness of a raven's wing.

In the stifling heat of the bar, crowded and noisy, I struggled to catch my breath in the seconds that our seeking, desperate lips parted. My head began to swim. I took hold of her hand and in a moment we were outside. The cooling smell of rain hung in the air. She led me away from the bar, wordlessly, down the deserted street and into the semi-darkness of the little park that lay around the corner. We had barely escaped the glare of the street lamps before her feverish lips sought mine once more; her fingers fiddled with the buttons of my borrowed jeans, then she hitched up her short skirt. I lifted her up against the wall behind her and she wrapped her legs around my waist, drew me into her.

For once my mind was free of wandering thoughts, bent instead upon the hedonism of pleasure and the promise of release. It was only when finally, and with a breathless shudder I gave into her, as the heat dissipated and stillness fell, that I became aware of the dampened sound of wolverine paws, heavy upon wet earth. Oblivious, she adjusted her suede skirt, brushed back her hair, her ragged breath now calmed. My heart continued to hammer with the wildness of the shamanic beat. Could I tell her that the wolves were coming? I longed to bury myself in her neck, in her hair, to hold off their advance just for a little longer. I ached to tell her of the fear in my heart and the guilt by which I was hounded, longed to say aloud that I was scared I had lost my way. And yet, despite that which we had just shared, she was a stranger to me. I realised, with a wave of transient, sickening sobriety, that I did not even know her name. Had I given her my own? She had not asked.

When she kissed me again, as we parted at the bar's open doors, I felt the emptiness within it, within myself.

But was that not what you wanted? Eqingaleq asked of the night's encounter, his tone neither accusatory nor deprecating. The question was genuine; I could not answer.

The night air did little to cool the shame with which my cheeks burned, though it brought upon me a sudden and agonising sobriety. Such a drunken tryst had brought my daughter into the world, I remembered, on the evening of the day we had piled stones, soil and hollow prayers over the emaciated body of the woman who had once been my mother. The wolves had been present then, too. It terrified me, the consequences that my actions, however impulsive, could cause; the power of life, and – who could know? – even of death.

———

The next morning, in desperation, I ransacked the guest bedroom for some sort of a sign as to my supposed purpose, where all seemed chaos. I did not know what it was that I searched for; I felt like a madman, rifling through drawers and peering under furniture as though in the grip of delirium – sleep-deprived and seasick once more.

I surfaced, eventually – gleefully – with a box of watercolour paints and a pad of thick, white paper. Clutching this treasure with both arms I crept fox-like out onto the landing and down the stairs, to be sure that I would meet no other form of life. I brewed a pot of strong tea to quell the nausea, and in the welcoming silence of an empty house took up my usual place at the kitchen table.

The rain beat its slate paws against the window as though trying to break its way through. It seemed as though twilight had already fallen. As soon as my borrowed paintbrush touched the paper this immediate world disappeared, and I was taken instead to the frozen fjords of home: the rain was

123

the beat of the shaman's drum, the electric lamp over the table the midnight sun of long summer days. Silhouetted figures waved from doors that glowed with the light of blubber lamps, from red, blue, yellow wooden houses backed by fields of endless ice and distant purple-hued mountains. Sometimes the open water lay as still and as clear as glass – reflecting the blue of the sky without end, or the mountains' rugged heights – its surface decorated briefly by the sleek ripple of the returning hunter's kayak. Raven-haired women dressed in skins sharpened crescent-shaped knives against stone, their little ones encapsulated, round-cheeked, in their mother's anorak hoods. A little girl – did her soft, watercolour features seem familiar? – chewed freshly-caught seal meat.

So enraptured was I in my work – and how long it had been since I had last taken up a paintbrush! – I did not hear the gentle opening and closing of the door as Judith returned home. I looked up, the red walls of a house leaking from the tip of the brush, as her shadow fell lightly, and unintended, over the page. I was taken aback by the deepness of her gaze as it rested on the few postcard-sized paintings I had completed, spilling a sadness I had not seen before and a hurt that I could not describe. For a moment she seemed unaware that I watched her, then as she tore her eyes away and met mine she smiled meekly.

'I'm sorry,' she said, 'I didn't mean to disturb you.'

'Don't apologise,' I stammered.

'They're beautiful.' With a slight nod she indicated the paintings; the look in her eyes still lingered. I thanked her. 'Are they... are they people you know?'

'I don't know.' I hesitated, then drew towards me the picture in whose frame could be found the black-haired women sharpening their knives. I rested my finger above the foremost one, over whose shoulder peered chubby infant cheeks. 'I thought, when I had painted her, that this one could almost be my mother. I like to think so, at least: in happier times.' As this confession escaped my lips it occurred to me the tactlessness of mentioning, in present company, the woman who had born me.

Judith avoided my gaze. She moved to put on the kettle.

'She must be very worried about you.'

I looked at her in surprise, having unfoundedly assumed she knew a little of my family history, being a somewhat indirect part of it herself, though all things considered it seemed rather unlikely that my father would have discussed with his wife the life and movements of his extra-marital lover.

'She's, err. . . she's dead,' I said, and for a moment feared she might think me callous for the lack of emotion in this simple statement. She only offered her condolences, as would any human being, and I swallowed down the unexpected lump that rose to my throat, and blinked back the hotness that pricked my eyes.

The silence that followed, although filled with the busy sounds of Judith's tea making, was uncomfortable. I tried to dab more paint onto the red-walled house that took shape beneath my paintbrush, but found that it only made my eyes prickle once more. I set it down with a sigh that Judith apparently did not hear.

She sat down opposite me and slid a fresh cup of tea across the table. I had exchanged precious few words with her over the previous weeks. It is true even that I had avoided her to some extent, certain that she would immediately smell the guilt upon my alcohol-tinged breath. I shuddered to think that she might come to hear about my shameful act of lust with the unnamed girl in the short skirt – though quite why I could not explain.

'What was she like?' she asked, as I took the mug of tea.

I faltered, the mug halfway to my lips. The heat had begun to rise to my ears, before I realised that we were still talking of my mother. I could not think how to answer.

'She was. . . she was. . . lost, I think.' Even in my own language I could not have said more.

Another laden silence rolled between the walls. 'Was she very beautiful?'

'Not when she was drunk,' I said honestly, 'and she was drunk most of the time.'

Judith looked past me, out of the window, seemingly deep in thought. The rain beat louder against the glass. Eventually she turned her clouded gaze down to my paintings on the table.

'He should not have brought you here,' she said, as though speaking to herself. She did not look up from the pictures as she spoke, her voice low, and I saw the endless reaches of the painted glacial wilderness reflected in her eyes.

Why had *he brought me here?* I longed to ask. But I could not find my tongue.

Eqingaleq, who had been tracing the trail of the raindrops down the window pane with his long, gnarled fingers, looked over, curiously, as the silence rolled thickly into every corner of the room. His hands now stilled, his eyes picked out a path between me and Judith. And back again.

With one hand Judith brushed her greying hair away from her forehead.

'I don't know why he... And at a time like this,' she murmured.

My stomach churned with discomfort. I could not ask her why the man meant her ill, why I had been used as an accessory to an unexplained punishment. *At a time like this*, when she had just buried her husband.

'I can leave,' I suggested bluntly.

Swiftly she raised her head, and her eyes shot up to meet mine. 'And where would you go?' she said, knowing that this question had no answer. I was startled by the sharpness that lined her words as she continued: 'No, Malik, I will not give him that satisfaction. You'll stay here for now.'

I nodded, speechless. Again Eqingaleq looked between us, from one to the other, following as if to see who would first venture to break the painful silence that swelled like a coastal

126

fog across the table. Both he and I glanced towards Judith as she spoke, changing the subject entirely, presumably in the hope that this brief exchange might be forgotten.

'Your English is coming along very well,' she said, and although she smiled only half-heartedly and her eyes did not quite meet mine, I knew the praise was genuine. Long days spent behind the counter in the record shop, eavesdropping on mundane conversations, had proved invaluable practice, as well as being audience to Michael's many drunken orations on rock music.

Blushing, I opened my mouth to thank her. But before the words could pass my lips she had risen from her chair, and turning away muttered, 'I won't keep you any longer from your painting.' And with that she left the room, closing the door gently behind her.

21

The record player had lapsed into silence. Michael was too drunk to notice. He was sprawled almost horizontally over the beanbag on which he liked to sit, his body as limp as a ragdoll's, drool running freely from his slack-jawed mouth and his face part-obscured by his hair. The glass from which he had been drinking, now emptied, had slid from his hand and lay on its side on the orange pile rug. For a moment I feared he had slipped into unconsciousness, but as this thought crossed my mind I saw him turn his head, pucker his lips through the curtain of hair and take a drag on the cigarette that he still clutched in his other hand. It had gone out. With the cigarette hanging loosely from his lips he raised himself with difficulty into a sitting position and began fishing around on the carpet for the box of matches, eventually locating it under one of his knees. Having re-lit his cigarette he sank back down on the beanbag, spread-eagled, holding it between his lips as he puffed.

'Michael,' I ventured.

He grunted. I took this as an invitation to continue.

'Will you work at the record shop forever?'

'Nah, man,' he said around the cigarette, seemingly without moving his lips.

'What will you do?'

He shrugged his shoulders – as far as I could tell. 'Summat else.'

'Like what?'

Again, a non-complicit shrug of the shoulders; this time he remained silent. I watched the smoke from the end of his cigarette climb gracefully towards the ceiling before dispersing into the low-lit atmosphere of the room.

'Will you be an explorer like. . . your father?' *Your* father, not *ours*. . .

He gave a loud snort. The suddenness of the sound made me jump, but he did not appear to notice and continued to puff away mutely on his cigarette.

I tried to imagine Michael visiting the Arctic. I pictured him standing disinterestedly in the throes of a winter blizzard, his shirt sleeves rolled up to his elbows, his flared jeans dragging in the deepening snow, a sodden cigarette drooping from between his lips. Had I been sober this picture might have caused me to laugh out loud; as it was, in my exhausted and alcohol-tinged stupor I only scowled with confusion. The picture faded and was replaced by the black-and-white image of a bearded man – a white man – dressed in furs. His eyes gazed out from his weatherbeaten face with a look of clarity and contentedness. Although I had seen this man only in a few old photographs, I knew who he was.

'What was he like?' I heard my voice ask. 'Was he a good father?'

His cigarette burnt to a stub, Michael pushed himself up into a sitting position again. His eyes looked vacuous, unfocussed. At first I was not sure if he had heard me, but then he rubbed a hand against his forehead and his shoulders made the usual non-committal gesture. 'Dunno,' he mumbled, 'he was just. . . Dad, yeah?'

He hauled himself onto his feet with apparent difficulty and stumbled over to the record player. Moments later the heavy sound of guitars filled the room. Michael retraced his steps and, having lit another cigarette, dropped back down onto the beanbag. He lay prostrate, seemingly lifeless once more apart from the continuous column of smoke that rose from the end of his cigarette.

Tony scratched the crown of his bald head with thick, stubby fingers as he surveyed the shop. A young man dressed in a plaid shirt was the only customer to be seen this slow morning, leisurely rifling through the records in a corner of the room. I drummed my fingers against the counter. I was bored, and uncomfortable in the heavy silence that lingered over the shop floor, disturbed only by the discreet sound of the record sleeves rubbing against each other as the young man browsed through them. The record player on the counter top had lapsed into silence some time ago; Tony, for some reason, had made no move to turn the record over to the B side or replace it with another, and though I longed for the music's distraction I dared not do this myself, felt that it was not my place.

Michael, as far as I knew, was still in bed. Urged by Judith I had knocked on his bedroom door before I left the house, since he had not appeared downstairs for breakfast as usual. Hearing a muffled groan, I had pushed open the door to find him cocooned in his duvet. Only his hair was visible, protruding wildly from the lumps of blanket on the bed. Hesitantly I told him that it was time to go to work. He did not move, only swore hoarsely and mumbled something about not feeling well. I suspected that the amount of alcohol he had consumed the night before likely had something to do with the state he was in, but I did not push the matter further, and left him there in bed.

It was intensely uncomfortable being alone with Tony in the record shop. I watched him as he slipped yet another cigarette between his thin lips, lit it with a match and began

131

to puff away. His mouth opened and closed like the slack jaws of a fish. The tingle of the bell above the door cut through the atmosphere momentarily, as the only customer made an exit.

Tony removed the cigarette from his mouth and studied it. It had burned almost to a stub already. The ends of his fingers were patched with yellow-brown nicotine stains.

'You ever see a polar bear, Mal?' He glanced up at me and grinned widely. I noticed that the corners of his mouth did not seem to turn upwards when he smiled, but continued horizontally in their opposite directions.

I nodded. Truth be told I had seen a live polar bear only once, a large adult male driven too close to the village in its search for food. It had been shot immediately. Only the most skilled hunters went out in search of bears. Generally, they travelled alone, often over great distances, and could be gone for weeks at a time. When finally the hunter returned the children would run shrieking alongside his sled as it skimmed over the ice of the fjord, the dogs whining, yapping and howling. The bear – if the hunt had been successful – would already have been butchered, but the whole town would gather to see the animal's great, white hide stretched out on the ground, its eyes gleaming dully from its heavy head. The hunter's wife would sew him a new pair of trousers from this skin – the hunter's pride.

Tony took another drag on his cigarette. 'Anyone you know ever get eaten by a polar bear?'

I frowned at him: this was an odd question. I had heard of hunters being mauled when the hunt went wrong, or knocked down dead to the ground by the lethal swipe of a bear's gigantic paw – after all these animals were wild, dangerous. But specifically *eaten?*

'Err... no,' I answered.

The corners of Tony's mouth dropped in disappointment. 'Enough penguins to eat, I suppose.' He shrugged, stubbed out his cigarette.

Penguins? I studied his expressions for signs of humour,

but found none. I glanced over to Eqingaleq. He raised his eyebrows, his lips twitching slightly at the corners. Would it be inappropriate to put Tony right? I was apprehensive that he might think me rude, relieve me of my job at the shop, perhaps. Although I was not particularly enamoured with my work at the shop, I did not know what I would do without the distraction that it awarded me. I began to mentally formulate a carefully-worded explanation that I hoped he would not find offensive, but my thoughts were interrupted by the sweet sound of the bell above the door signalling that a customer had entered. It must have been a friend of Tony's, for he greeted the customer wholeheartedly and moved across the room towards the door to speak with him.

I abandoned the sentence that was forming in my head, aware of the profound feeling of emptiness that spread through my body as I did so.

When I returned to the house, I sat down at the kitchen table with my watercolour paints and painted the simple image of a swimming polar bear onto the paper. Sleek, graceful, otherworldly; snout reaching up to the surface of the water, limbs akimbo, its body curved with the suggestion of power and gentleness.

For some time, I sat looking at the bear I had painted, ruminating on what I could have said to Tony, what I could have told him about: the absence of penguins in the Arctic, of course, but there was so much more to be said. The great white bear was not merely a vicious creature to be avoided for fear that it might long for a taste of human flesh; it was a part of the land, the sea and the wilderness, just as the people of the Arctic were and had been for thousands of years. Survival, for both Man and Bear, depended on the understanding of this northerly world, and Man depended on Bear. He must treat Bear with the greatest respect and humility; neither Man nor Bear were cold-hearted killers.

I doubted that I could have articulated any of this to Tony, had he even shown any interest.

Later, in the safe space of my blanket tent I fell to sleep with my thoughts still fixed on the painting. I dreamed of running bears, swimming bears, hunting bears. I dreamed of bears in human form – of which the old stories told – who were able to slip in and out of their white-furred skins at will. Finally, I dreamed of one story in particular, of the bear-woman who, seeing the hunters approach, bit her cubs to death so they would not fall into the hands of men; and I woke up in a cold sweat.

22

I could hear Judith and the beak-nosed man arguing downstairs.

It was late evening, the window panes dark and drenched with rain. I had heard him arrive, that ominous tap-tapping at the door; recognised his shrill voice in the hallway, Judith's low and patient. It was not long before the confrontation escalated and the man's shrieks permeated the walls by which we were separated and sent my pulse racing. I could not make out what was said but my fearful imagination filled in the details.

My heart skipped a beat as I heard the sound of heavy footsteps on the stairs. But it must only have been Michael, for the feet stomped in the direction of his bedroom and I heard the door slam with an obstinate thud, followed by the blare of the record player turned up to full volume. The pounding noise of the music unsettled me just as much as the voices it drowned out.

In search of a distraction I picked up the book I had been reading, but I could still hear the man's cries in my head, like echoes – the haunt of unwanted memories – and I could not concentrate. As I glanced up from the page, my eyes came to rest on the half-bottle of spirits that I had left Michael's room with the previous evening. I had not planned to take it: yes, I had been drunk, and somehow the bottle had found its way into my hands as I stumbled back to my own room seeking a pillow on which to lay my reeling head. Michael had not noticed, sprawled semi-conscious on his bean bag, the record player still churning out its music.

I put the bottle to my lips and grimaced as I took a swig. The first taste was always the most bitter; sooner or later I would fail to notice its flavour, or the way in which it ran like fire down my throat.

The soles of Michael's canvas shoes pounded the pavement like the slap of a seal's flippers against the frozen surface of the sea. Determined strides, his expression sullen, hands thrust moodily into the depths of his jeans pockets. I hurried after him, seeking answers and a distraction from the nausea that had awoken with me that morning as I drifted into painful consciousness beside an empty bottle of spirits.

Who was the man with the beak instead of a nose? I pressed, addressing the back of Michael's greasy head as it swung, pendulum-like along the streets grey with morning drizzle. *What did he want from Judith? Why did he keep coming back?* The boy only grunted in response. His flat feet continued to smack the pavement, and it felt as though my ears bled with the sound. But the alcohol that still surged through my bloodstream spread a determination, a recklessness even, and insistently I repeated my questions.

As we reached the record shop, Michael withdrew his hands from his pockets and threw open the faded blue door. The bell above it tinkled sweetly as the door slammed into the rack behind it and bounced back on its creaking hinges. Michael turned to face me, gesturing emphatically as he walked backwards across the linoleum floor.

'He's just some deadbeat, man. Travelled with my dad. You know, like, to Greenland or wherever.'

136

My dad, he said, not *ours*.

As he reached the counter he stomped behind it and flicked up the lid of the record player. From the small pile of records that had been left next to it he selected one, seemingly without even thinking, and having drawn it roughly from its sleeve almost slammed it into place on the turntable. It was the first time I had seen him treat one of his records with anything less than reverential respect.

'Has a thing for my mum, man,' he said to the machine as he wrenched at its buttons and dials, 'it's *obvious*, man. It's sick.' The record player emitted a screech as he adjusted the needle. 'As if she'd be interested,' he muttered, as though to himself. 'And dad barely even buried.'

The crackle of white noise filled the shop. Michael flipped down the plastic lid of the record player with a hollow crash, and turning on his heel he stomped off to the kitchen amidst the sudden burst of electric guitars.

———————

The relentless tread of the pavement had worn a hole in the sole of my sealskin kamiks. Rainwater seeped into the inside of the boot and I shivered from its contact with the bare skin of my foot. When I arrived back at the house I sat for a long while at the kitchen table with the boot in my hand, looking at it. I thought of the wrinkled skin of my late grandmother's hands, like brown paper; remembered the way in which her increasingly arthritic fingers had held steady as she threaded the bone needle, pulled lengths of sinew through the tough hide, sewed on the minute pieces of brightly-coloured leather in decoration. They had held strong for years, through countless seasons, over ice, snow, rock and arctic tundra. *They were not made for the concrete of the city streets*, said Eqingaleq as he took a seat beside me.

I nodded, could not speak. I felt paralysed, powerless. I could not mend the worn sole for I had no sealskin nor sinew thread. I did not have a kayak or harpoon with which to hunt the animal for its skin, nor the tools with which to flense it. I did not even know in which direction I would find the sea and its creatures, or how far I would have to walk, barefoot, until I reached its shores.

I glanced up at the sound of the door opening. Judith entered, her hair wet from the rain, a string shopping bag in each hand. She stopped as she saw me, and looked at the boot that I cradled in my hands like a dead thing.

'My kamiks,' I said brokenly. I wanted to tell her – to tell someone – what had happened, what this meant: that the soles of my hand-sewn shoes, like the very soul within my body, had been worn down to almost nothing by the mercilessness of the city. But I could say no more. Overcome, I put my head in my hands and sobbed like a child.

I would rather have trodden the pavements barefoot than in Michael's old boots. Several sizes too big for me, I had to pull on an additional pair of thick woollen socks before I could walk in them with any degree of comfort. They were like weights around my ankles; too heavy, I felt, to allow me to outrun the wolves that hounded my thoughts and the clouds that enveloped my senses. As I trudged along the morning's usual path to the record shop I experienced the strange sensation that my feet were not my own, that they were not under my control. I feared where they might take me.

As soon as I arrived back at the house that evening, I took the boots off and threw them under the bed. For the rest of the week I feigned illness, unable to bear the thought of slipping my feet into them once more and anchoring myself to the city's insufferable streets. Instead I remained in the bedroom, curled up defensively inside my blanket tent, feet clad in woollen socks against the pervading chill of the house. I listened for the slam of the front door as Michael left for work; the gentle click as Judith followed a few minutes later, pulling the door to behind her. The house now empty, I took my borrowed box of watercolour paints, paintbrush and paper, and padded downstairs to the kitchen.

The arctic landscape spilled uninhibited from the end of my paintbrush. As I painted I ran along the rocks that lined the fjord, my feet cushioned by summer moss; paddled a kayak across the still water. I urged semi-wild huskies, howling above the hiss of the sledge runners, over winter's frozen sea. I melted pans of ice over a blubber-fuelled flame, boiled the water for tea with *mattak* and stale biscuits.

Yet all the while I was aware of an indistinct longing within my soul, a sense of incompleteness. And a fear that I could not name.

I was startled back into the present by the falling shadow of wings upon the paper. The beak-nosed man was standing behind me. I leapt to my feet, the paintbrush still in my hand, and my chair tipped backwards and clattered onto the linoleum floor. I backed away from him around the corner of the table, inwardly cursing Judith, in my fear, for not locking the front door as she left.

He looked a little surprised at having caused me to jump out of my skin, though this was immediately replaced by a glint of triumph. His eyes moved down to the painting I had been working on.

'Been thinking about that explorer, have you?' he said, his expression deadpan.

I looked down at the page and saw that I had painted into the landscape the image of a container ship. It sailed noiselessly into the serenity of the fjord, dwarfed by icebergs that glowed pink in the evening sun. A flock of seagulls wheeled and dove around the vessel, brushstrokes in the clear sky. In the distance rugged black mountains coloured by ice; a cluster of red-walled houses upon the rocks of the coast, waiting. It was as though I was seeing the painting for the first time. For some reason it unsettled me.

I saw the man's eyes flicker across to the almost-empty glass and bottle of spirits that stood beside the picture. He let

139

out a cruel laugh, his thin lips twisted.

'Your mother's son!' he said.

I did not know how much of the stuff I had drunk, had barely been aware that I was drinking it. My head swam, my heart slammed again and again against my ribcage in indefinable panic. I could not speak. I glanced around the room but could see no sign of Eqingaleq. Where could he have got to; now, when I did not know what to do?

Looking down the length of his beak, the man examined my completed paintings, spread out upon the table top. He ran his fingers over the contours of the mountains, the curve of the fjord, over the ship picking its way around the icebergs.

'I could never understand his obsession,' he murmured, as though to himself: 'such a barren place. . .'

He lapsed into silence; still he did not look up.

'What do you want from me?' I managed to say. My voice sounded pleading. I did not like it.

He shrugged his shoulders. Dislodged droplets of rain water ran down the front of his coat and dripped from the end of his sleeve, narrowly missing my watercolour paintings. His fingers continued to trace their path over the scenes that I had crafted, the memories I had put down upon the paper, and my intoxicated blood began to boil.

'I wanted you to see the family you pulled apart,' he said, without looking up.

'But what did I ever do to you; to Judith?'

His fingers came to rest on the parka-clad shape of a woman, black-haired, a child on her back. He paused for a moment, then in one swift movement he lifted the painting with both hands and roughly tore the paper in two. My fists clenched instinctively.

'He never wanted to come back from that godforsaken place, your father.' He spat the last word as though it were poison. 'But he returned to his family all the same: I suppose he felt he had a sense of duty. Of course it would have been better for everyone if he had stayed there with *her* and the

140

bastard child they had together.' He turned his colourless eyes upon me: *the bastard child.* 'But no, he came crawling back to Judith. The coward.'

I was both shocked and intrigued by the hostility in his voice. He continued, 'He didn't love his wife as she deserved, not after that.'

'But you did,' I said. His eyes shot to meet mine, his gaze hard. Although my remark had been intended as a question I got the feeling that I had inadvertently made an accusation.

'If she had any sense she would have left him,' he hissed, jabbing a bony finger towards me as though I were to blame. 'That ungrateful bastard didn't deserve her. I told her as much when she married him, but did she listen? And look what he did to her.' The finger pointed at me, directly now and unabashedly.

'*I* didn't do anything,' I protested weakly. I was shaking; my anger seemed unsure of itself, tinged with an uncertain fear. My pulse was erratic. I no longer felt the soporific effect of the alcohol I had drunk, yet my perceptions seemed to be misplaced and my judgement skewed. The man appeared larger than the room itself, and his sudden, violent movements set my nerves on edge.

'*You,*' he spat. 'You and your mother did everything. And that explorer did the rest: made Judith's life with him a misery.'

Was it my imagination or was he moving closer to me around the edge of the table?

'You didn't have to bring me here,' I said, 'you didn't have to make Judith suffer more for *his* actions.' I longed to defend Judith, to make the man acknowledge the wrong he had committed to her by unloading me into her care. She had been so kind to me, I did not want to let him hurt her more than he had done already.

'*He* did not suffer enough for his actions,' the man responded. His watery eyes darkened. '*He* went and died before he could really see the hurt he caused her. He only

141

ever thought of himself. It was his selfishness that killed him, and he deserved it, deserved all the pain it caused him.'

I did not understand. What did he mean, the selfishness killed him?

'He had a heart attack –,' I said uncertainly.

'*Heart attack!*' snorted the man with such suddenness that I leapt in my skin. He appeared to have moved even nearer; his face was uncomfortably close to mine, his beak loomed before me, threateningly, ready to strike.

'It was you,' I said. My voice shook. 'You killed him. You killed him because you love Judith. But now she won't have you, and for that you want to make her suffer.'

He laughed darkly, his face contorted by the light of the lamp overhead. As I backed away from him in panic my hand brushed over a knife that lay on the table beside me. Before I knew what I was doing it was in my hand, and my hand was raised before me.

Something changed in his eyes: a semblance of doubt, or perhaps fear.

'And you're going to kill *me*, now, are you?' he laughed. I felt his hesitancy. 'You never even met the man and yet you want retribution?' He opened his arms wide; his full wingspan. 'Go on, then.'

My breathing was ragged; I was lightheaded, my vision swam. Of course I could not kill him. But my heart pounded with anger, and a terror that I could not contain. The world felt heavy around me – my whole body ached horribly. I raised my other hand, upturned, and rested the sharp edge of the knife on my wrist. The metal was cold against my skin.

'This is what you want,' I said, my voice low. 'Isn't it? You want to ruin me, too.'

His eyes bore into mine, confidently now that the weapon was no longer pointed at him.

'A drunk, just like your mother,' he said. 'And like your father you'll take the easy way out.'

I looked at him. I had never felt so scared and I did not know there existed such darkness within me. My hands shook violently.

'I didn't kill him,' he said at length. 'I didn't have to. Coward saw to that himself.' His lips curled. 'But I'd have gladly tied that rope around his neck with my own hands.'

A wave of nausea flooded through me as I struggled to comprehend what the man was saying.

'He. . . he took his own life?'

'His final cowardly act,' he said, his face expressionless. 'And the last blow to his family. If he'd only done away with himself sooner it would have been better for everyone.'

'Don't you have any compassion?' I said.

He scoffed. 'He brought it upon himself. He was a selfish man.'

My head was swimming. With difficulty I tried to focus on the man's face. 'And now that he's dead and you can't make him suffer anymore, you're hurting Judith instead?'

With his lips pressed tightly together, his mouth fixed itself into a severe line. 'I'm trying to make her realise just what he did to her,' he hissed.

'You're punishing her for marrying him and not you,' I said. I noticed that my voice was raised. 'But she still won't have you, of course she won't have you.'

'But she'll keep *you* in her house,' he shouted. '*You* – the cause of all this.'

'*I* wasn't here when he died! I'd never even met him, barely know anything about him – why did you pull me into this?' I did not have to look down to see that the knife in my hands was once more pointed at the beak-nosed man. My hands were so unsteady I feared what they might do. He did not answer.

My body rocked as I was hit by a sudden thought.

'You must have already been on the ship when he. . . when you heard,' I said, my voice lower now. 'You didn't come all the way to Angmagssalik to tell me that my father had died;

143

you were already on the way there. You took me back with you just on a whim.'

He raised his eyebrows, as though this had surely been obvious. 'And you came with me on a whim,' he said. Then he smiled wryly. 'Could it have been the hand of *fate* crossing our paths together?' He laughed; I did not like the way that he laughed, as though he were mocking me. It frightened me, this use of the word *fate*: I got the impression, ludicrous though it must surely be, that the path of my life was in *his* hands, that all this time I had been labouring under the illusion of free will and wrongly believing in the guidance of the ancestral spirits. Had I lived my entire life in the shadow of his wings, unaware? Sickness arose in my throat.

I turned my head at the sound of the door opening. Judith stopped in her tracks, her eyes wide, fixed on the scene before her: the knife in my hands.

'The boy's drunk,' the man said to her, in English. His cruel laughter seemed to echo around the room and reverberate inside my head; it sounded like the laughter of the gull.

Wildly I glanced around the room, searching for Eqingaleq. He was nowhere to be seen. The walls seemed to be closing around me, the floor tilted dangerously. The man's watery eyes were all that I could see. I could not breathe. I dropped the knife to the floor, and turning away from those grotesque eyes I stumbled from the room, passing Judith without a word.

In the sanctity of my tent I lay prostrate, while my imagination lurched sickeningly. The harder I tried not to think about my father's death the more clearly I pictured him, the man I had never seen: his limp body, his glazed eyes and the rope around his neck.

Where was Eqingaleq?

144

My thoughts swerved to Judith. Perhaps she had been the one who discovered his lifeless body, saw what he had done. Perhaps she, too, felt that I were to blame for what had happened. Perhaps I *was* to blame.

Where was Eqingaleq?

I remembered two of my childhood friends. When we were children we had run free together in the Arctic's changing seasons, we had learnt how to drive the dog sleds and run a line through a hole in the ice to catch fish. But little by little the temptations and confusions of the modern world cast the light of uncertainty on our futures. One of my friends put a shotgun to his temple; the other, like my father, tightened a noose around his neck. He was my uncle's son. He had hung in his home for days before I found his body. I should have gone round sooner.

Where was Eqingaleq?

These lives ended, caught between two worlds and two ways of life. No other way out. I feared that I might share the same fate.

———

When I lurched into consciousness in the cold light of early morning, I saw that Eqingaleq was sitting cross-legged beside me in the tent. Unmoving, his face half hidden in the night's lingering shadows, he kept his usual silent vigil.

Where were you? I asked. My voice was little more than a groan. *He came last night. The man with the beak for a nose. He came for me, and you weren't there.*

I was there, he answered calmly. *But you had little use for me given the state you were in.*

Little use? He came for me: I needed *you.*

He smiled grimly. *What could I have done to help you? How could I have got through to you? You were drunk.*

I wasn't drunk.

He raised his eyebrows. Pathetically I fell silent.

145

I could hear the sound of rain against the window pane: a morning chorus.

He says my father took his own life.

Yes, I heard.

The rain fell heavier, pounded on the glass. *Do you think it was because of... me?* I whispered.

Because of you? You never even met the man.

I mean because of... me and Mother.

I knew too well the pain of a father separated from his child – I felt it then in my chest. *He had two families, but perhaps he felt that he did not belong to either of them.*

Eqingaleq's eyelids drooped languidly, as though he were bored, but I knew that he was only deep in thought. *Who can tell?* He said quietly.

I sat up and hugged my knees to my chest. *My mother was never kind about him.*

The rain was the only sound as Eqingaleq waited, knowingly, for me to complete the thought. *I don't want to end up like either of them*, I said at last, my voice low.

The corners of Eqingaleq's ancient eyes creased as he gave me a gentle, reassuring smile. *Then don't.*

23

I had lost track of time.

The long, dark nights and the bare trees by the street sides heralded the approach of winter; the strings of blinking lights and cardboard reindeer that Tony had draped around the shop suggested that Christmas would soon be upon us.

It was cold: a damp, dreary sort of cold that seeped into my very bones and robbed me of spirit. I could not seem to warm up. I wrapped myself in blankets and extra pairs of socks, but the dampness sat steadfastly in my chest and lungs, spread a lethargy to my limbs.

I had made up my mind: I was leaving. I had no idea where I would go or what I would do, I knew only that I should not have stayed so long in this house.

Each day, however, I would tell myself that I was not ready, that I just needed one more day to prepare and to plan what I would say to Judith, for I could not simply walk away after all her kindness towards me.

Each evening I crawled back into my blanket tent with heavy limbs; how could my legs carry me any further? I couldn't possibly leave.

We ate a stone-silent Christmas meal around the kitchen table, Judith, Michael and I. Judith had refused my help in preparing the food; instead I had lit a candle as a contribution to the absent festive atmosphere. I knew that I was not welcome here. I had heard Tony debating the topic of Christmas with a customer: that it was a time for celebration, for family. And family I certainly was not.

A bottle of wine stood on the table. Michael poured himself a glass, full to the brim, but did not offer the bottle around. No toasts were made, no glasses tapped lightly together. Judith served slices of succulent-looking red meat but kept her eyes upon the meal. Michael emptied half a bottle of tomato sauce over his plate and began to eat.

I was still trying to think of something I could say, in the spirit of things, when I noticed that Judith was crying. Her head turned down, silent tears fell over her vegetables, which she had not touched. I reached across the corner of the small table and laid my hand comfortingly on her shoulder. It rested there only for a moment before she pushed back her chair and half-ran from the room.

Michael and I watched the door close behind her. For a few minutes we did not speak.

'She thought she'd at least come home for Christmas,' Michael said.

I caught his eye.

'Who?'

'Marianne.'

He tucked back into his tomato-smothered portion, without another word.

A few days later, I came downstairs as darkness was falling to find the kitchen full of people. It was New Year's Eve. I had heard the muffled voices from upstairs; the continued open and close of the front door, footsteps in the hallway. It was not long before the brazen sound of electric guitars and rhythmic bass overpowered the sound of these comings and goings and I crept downstairs to investigate.

148

I pushed open the kitchen door and saw that Michael had brought the record player into the kitchen; it revolved at full volume on the table beside a pile of records and empty beer cans. A dense cloud of tobacco smoke hung above the heads of, I presumed, Michael's friends. They milled about the room, beer cans and glasses in hand; long-haired boys in jeans and patterned shirts, girls in short skirts and tall shoes. Some danced, some laughed, while others made raucous conversation over the noise of the music. I peered through the throng, wondering if Michael were among them. He saw me first, came swaggering across the room and slapped me amicably on the back as though I were his best friend in the world. He handed me the can that he clutched in his other hand, and roared, 'Party's started, Mal! Get some of this down you.'

I did not need persuading. I desired nothing more than a stiff drink to calm my nerves, dampen my inhibitions and help me to blend into the swelling crowd. I drank it quickly; I knew there would be more to come.

People continued to arrive, and soon the party had spilled out into the hallway and the living room as well as into the garden. I remembered that Judith had gone away somewhere this weekend, I doubted that she had known of Michael's intention to turn the house into a disco in her absence.

I was nervous and overwhelmed. The more I drank, the more my nerves dissipated. The more I drank the easier it became. I recognised a few of Michael's friends from our outings to the bar; they too clapped me on the back and gave me drinks when mine had run dry. Their conversation eluded me. I could not hope to understand when I could barely even hear their voices over the music.

Soon the room began to spin. My feet were dangerously unsteady. I stumbled from the room, meaning to go upstairs to use the bathroom, and almost careered into a young couple who were leaning against the bannister with their arms wrapped around each other and their lips locked passionately together. They did not seem to notice my intrusion. I righted myself, and felt a painful tug in my stomach as I noticed that the young woman was the one I had found myself entangled with, alone in the park, on that drunken evening. I had not seen her since. A wave of nausea swept through me. Why did I care so much? In this place of strangers I thought perhaps I had formed some sort of a connection with her when we...

I turned away, pulling myself onto the staircase and tripping up the steps into the darkness that awaited at their summit. The party did not appear to have progressed upstairs. It felt quiet, calmer, even though I could still hear the music and voices that raged in the rest of the house. I staggered to the bathroom through the dark landing, and screwed my eyes shut momentarily as I turned on the bright bathroom light. I closed the door with an uncontrolled thud. After I had relieved myself, I leant upon the sink and ran my hands alternately under the cold tap. My eyes had grown used to the light. When I looked up, I was taken aback to see my reflection staring back at me – hair tousled, eyes bloodshot. I had forgotten that a mirror hung above the sink. Even more surprising was the appearance of the face of Eqingaleq behind me in the mirror, disturbingly disembodied for the rest of him could not be seen. His expression was blank but the contours of his face were grossly exaggerated by the electric light that was cast from above our heads.

I'm not drunk, I said to his mirror image, then my voice broke out into empty laughter and I threw my hands up into the air in a gesture of acceptance. *All right, I'm drunk!*

His expression did not change.

My arms fell back down again like lead weights. In seriousness I studied his reflection. The depth of his dark eyes made me uneasy.

Why does everyone drink so much? I wondered.

He shrugged his shoulders, impassive still. *To forget.*

I ran the tap once more over my hands. The cold water felt

good on my skin; the rest of my body was numb. *But in the morning it all comes back. You can't forget everything for good.*

Eqingaleq's voice bubbled above the sound of the running water. *That's why you drink so much, isn't it? To forget. I imagine that's the reason your mother drank so much, too.*

My eyes snapped up to meet his in the mirror. *There's no need to mention my mother every time I have a drink*, I said sharply. *I know what I'm doing.*

He raised his eyebrows, said nothing.

My hands shook with anger as I turned off the tap. The soothing sound of running water stopped abruptly, and once more I could hear the mingled cacophony of music and loud voices from downstairs.

I don't need your judgement, I said, without raising my head to look at him. Though I spoke quietly, my voice simmered.

Suit yourself, he said.

I had clenched my fists, ready for a fight. But when I turned around he was nowhere to be seen.

I turned off the light before opening the door and stumbled out onto the landing, where I almost ran into a figure standing outside the bathroom door. I stopped dead. At first I thought it might be Eqingaleq, waiting to reprimand me, but as my eyes adjusted to the reclaimed darkness I saw that the figure was a woman. The window at the top of the stairs cast a grey light over the wreaths of her long hair and the curve of her neck. I could not make out her features, as they were only a suggestion in the dim light.

From her surprised intake of breath as I burst through the door, I knew that she was real, not just a shadow cast by my vibrant, drugged imagination.

'Are you drinking to forget, too?' I asked irritably, as though she, a stranger, had been privy to my conversation with Eqingaleq in the bathroom. My voice sounded strangely loud and brazen in the heavy, deserted atmosphere that hung around this part of the house.

151

I thought that perhaps I saw a small smile prick the corners of her mouth, but it may just have been the play of shadows in the grey darkness.

'What are you drinking to forget?' she asked me. It was as though her lips did not move. Her voice was low, soft.

'Everything,' I said.

I could not see her eyes, only black holes where they ought to be.

She held up a bottle, it glinted dully in the meagre light from the window.

'Me too,' she whispered.

I don't know how it happened.

A blur of movement and shadows in the semi-darkness; the feel of the hard mattress beneath me, her skirt hitched up around her waist. I was still wearing my fisherman's jumper. My lips tasted of alcohol and sweat.

The background noise of the music, continuous; the raggedness of her breath. The bed groaned beneath us.

I drifted into consciousness with the first rays of the morning sun. My head pounded as though I had slammed it against a brick wall, my eyes felt gritty and the bright light pained me. Throughout the night I had tossed within lucid dreams: of tides turning, fjords freezing over, the moon chasing the sun round and round in the vast arctic sky. I had run with wolves through the wilderness, flown high above the tundra on coal-black raven's wings; I had fought bears in human form and carefully combed clean the long, black hair of the Mother of the Sea, strand by strand, over and over again.

When I awoke, I was alone. My night-time companion, found in the darkness, was nowhere to be seen now that the sun had risen. I scrambled out of bed and peered into the depths of my blanket tent which was still raised at the foot of the bed. Empty. Perhaps I had imagined her after all, an otherworldly creature – a drunken fantasy.

But where was Eqingaleq?

Bit by bit I struggled into my jeans, nauseous from the movement of my limbs, then slowly sloped downstairs and into the kitchen. I began heaping spoonsful of coffee into the pot, but stopped as the smell of it only made me feel worse. I noticed that it was mingled with another aroma as well: smoke. I turned around and saw that the back door stood open. I tripped into the garden, blinking in the daylight.

The first thing that my eyes landed upon was a metal dustbin which had been placed in the middle of the garden. It was on fire, or rather a fire had been kindled within it. Flames licked the edges, smoke spilled out into the early morning air. Michael was standing beside the fire, clad only in jeans and a t-shirt, despite the winter chill. He looked as though he had not slept. His hair, though still lank, was in disarray, and his face was drawn and his eyes shadowed by dark rings. He appeared to be having difficulty holding himself upright, swaying on uncertain legs. I could tell that he was still drunk.

He looked up at the sound of my approach. His eyes narrowed; the ferocity of his glare took me aback and stopped me in my tracks. I saw that he held a piece of paper in his hands. He followed the line of my gaze, then raised the paper up into the air, above the open dustbin.

It was one of my watercolour paintings.

'Don't!' I cried instinctively.

He released the paper. It drifted down in graceful arcs and disappeared into the flames. I was struck by the image of the glacial ice melting from the page in streams, then rivers.

I gaped at him.

'What's the matter with you?' I shouted, rising quickly to anger.

'What's the matter with *you*, man?' he screeched, a rising note in his voice. He swore at me, spat in my direction. 'What's the matter with you, laying your dirty hands on my *sister*?'

Something plummeted within my stomach, as though the ground had flipped on its side and I had been tipped from the face of the earth. All at once I remembered the photographs I had seen in the front room of the house. Photographs of the whole family: Michael, the son, and a daughter too. Was it not her childhood bedroom that I had been sleeping in? She had not been present at the funeral; I had only seen the photographs... Last night, through the darkness and the drink I had not recognised her, and she, it would seem, had not known *me*.

I wondered how she had realised – too late – who this stranger was that she had met in the darkness. Given away by my black hair, perhaps? And the colour of my skin. Seeing this, she must have fled at the first sign of the morning light. Just as Sun moves across the wide sky pursued by her brother, Moon, in the aftermath of their mistaken union when each had believed the other to be someone else...

What had I done?

The flames licked higher as Michael tossed another, and another of my paintings onto the fire. The sea ice melted, the mountains crumpled, the houses went up in smoke; I could smell the burning of the ravens' feathers.

With a howl I threw myself at Michael, wrestled him to the ground. He shrieked, struggled, swore. We fought with tooth and claw until someone pulled me off him. I tore myself from the grip that held me and stumbled out of reach, my breath staggered. I looked up and saw that it was the man with the beak for a nose, dressed in his coat and boots, having presumably just arrived. He did not come after me or try to restrain me again, only stood with his arms hanging limply by his sides, seemingly at a loss.

Michael was kneeling on the grass, swearing still and trying to stem the stream of blood that spilled from his bruised nose. Judith crouched over him attentively, the hem of her raincoat trailing on the wet grass. She turned to look at me, her gaze imploring, hurt. Not waiting for her to speak, I turned tail and ran.

I ran into the house and up the stairs to the bedroom. There was no one there. *Where was Eqingaleq?* I gathered my few belongings and stuffed them into my backpack, then stumbled back down the stairs. I pulled on my anorak, slipped my feet into Michael's old boots, and throwing open the front door, I ran from the house. The boots were weights around my ankles, sinking my feet to the ground as though I were trying to run through drifts of heavy snow. I did not look back. I could not breathe.

It had started to rain. I pictured the water falling on the ashes of my paintings, the fire extinguished. Above me, unseen, the moon chased the sun around and around in the clouded sky.

24

Rasmus

His heart was full of *her* as they plunged into the frozen wilderness of the ice cap, leaving behind the dark coastal mountains.

The hiss of the sled runners over ice that stretched for mile upon gloriously empty mile in every direction, the dry barking of the huskies as they raced ahead of Qallu's leather whip. Air so cold that it caught in his throat, tore at the skin of his cheeks. This was freedom.

He remembered the stories he had heard, of pilots of light aircraft skimming the ice cap, who swore they had seen skin-clad figures of men below, waving spears. Though surely there could be nothing to hunt in such a place. It was a secret world, a place of magic and deliciously twisted fairytales. They sped through it with speed and ease. Rasmus soon lost track of the days in a satisfying haze of elation and exhaustion.

And yet, there was a part of his mind that cowered into darkness under the watchful eyes of his beak-nosed companion. In the ethereal light of the slowly-darkening nights, the man he knew as Birdie appeared to morph, little by little, into a creature that he did not recognise. The eyes that filled with shallow water, the dark hair streaked with grey and white, the "beak" that grew sharper still. He seemed a creature of myth who, like a vulture, shadowed Rasmus's every step with great wings that blocked out the sun, waiting for him to drop down dead to the ground. Every morning Rasmus awoke with his head filled with vivid images of torn flesh and poked-out eye sockets, the vestiges of his troubling dreams.

He would wake often during the night, and beyond the rustling of his canvas tent in the wind it would seem he could hear the quick footsteps of those mysterious dwellers on the ice cap, the hiss of a spear through the air, whispered voices plotting. Hunters so silent that even the dogs did not wake at their approach, out there in the unsettling twilight that he daren't look out into for fear of what he might discover. He quaked inside his sleeping bag with all the uneasiness of a trespasser. For that, he realised now, was exactly what he was.

When they rested or stopped to eat, Qallu would tell stories about spirits who lived underneath the ice – that was why it would creak – or troll-like creatures of the mountains who hunted the unsuspecting hunter. Strange tales, too, of lonely people who, having no one else to talk to, would converse with insects which soon grew into human size. Rasmus could not get these stories out of his head; the horror and desolation of it all flooded his mind until he could no longer think straight.

He felt the burden in his body, too. There were ridges of ice they encountered on the journey that were sky-reaching mountains over which they must haul the sleds, laden to a dead weight with supplies. And frequent crevasses plunged unseeing into the depths of the ice cap, like open graves, waiting. Birdie was roped into line behind him. He imagined mistiming the jump across, slipping on the crevasse's brink and teetering into the emptiness below. Or the weight of Birdie on the rope beneath him, dangling, dragging him down to that mysterious place where the ice would close over their heads and it would just be the two of them together, frozen in breath, frozen in time, forever. Or he could cut the rope, watch the man fall to his death. . .

Through the haze of his thoughts and dreams, Greenland's West Coast drew nearer. The reproachful eyes of Birdie burnt his back; Snorri's furtive, concerned glances Rasmus read only as judgement. And Qallu, the only one who laughed or smiled, the only one who found joy in the journey – of course, he had to, Rasmus thought bitterly, they were paying him after all.

At long last they reached Christianshaab. Larger than Angmagssalik; to Rasmus's wilderness-accustomed eyes it seemed almost a city. An unsettling sight, after nearly two months on the ice cap, alone save for the company of those mysterious spirits who had haunted his journey.

Gangs of excited children accompanied them into the town, running alongside the sled if they could keep up, howling like the dogs. Rasmus shrank into himself under his layers of skin clothing. He was an outsider and a fraud. He had done nothing worthy of note. He wanted to be left alone; he wanted to get out of this new place.

After two weeks of rest, Rasmus felt no more revitalised than if he had crossed the entire ice cap again in that time. He could not master the weariness in his bones.

'We can charter a plane from here to Godtshaab.' Snorri's voice dripped with forced optimism. 'Fly straight home from there. Sell the dogs, give the money to Qallu in expenses.'

Birdie snorted. 'He'd only drink it away.'

But Rasmus would not hear of taking a shortcut. He listened with mild interest as his own voice – ignoring Birdie's offhand remark – began to say something about the importance of completing the journey they had set out on and returning the same way over the inland ice; of making sure Qallu – *their friend*, he emphasised – got home safely, and the dogs, too. He was surprised to note how calm and collected his voice sounded. Inside, however, he quaked with the fear of their journey's end, the fearful uncertainty of what would await him once he had left behind the unsettling emptiness of the ice.

25

Malik

I walked without knowing where I was headed. The streets all looked the same, though I barely paid my surroundings any attention. My head turned towards the ground – ashamed in the face of her, Sun – I put one foot in front of the other, mechanically, repeatedly, in the hope that they might take me away from this place. Yet with each step I caught a glimpse of the toe of Michael's old boots, and the chance of escape seemed all the more unlikely, for clad in such a way my feet were not my own.

I needed to find Eqingaleq. He would not have stayed in the city; of that I was certain. He was a part of my being; he had always been my guide. And since my heart ached with a terrible longing for the open sea, I knew that his must, too. If I could find the sea, I would find Eqingaleq. And, perhaps, if I could find the sea I would know how to get home.

North. That was the direction in which I needed to travel. Any more, I did not know.

The hours passed. On and on I walked. After some time, I noticed that the houses were becoming more sparsely spaced, separated by clumps of trees or bleak, muddy fields. I was following a worn road marked with puddles and holes, old and well-used so it seemed, yet at this moment there were no signs of any vehicles. I stopped to listen: nothing, save for the distant, hypnotic rustling of the treetops in the wind. My heart, which had been racing, out of control, since my confrontation with Michael, at long last began to grow calmer. I watched my breath condense in clouds in the cold air. My nausea had dissipated; I could smell the wind. The sky was growing dark, though it was not late in the day, and the clouds were heavy with the promise of rain.

In Eqingaleq's absence was a sense of fear and loneliness such as I had never before experienced. Without his guidance I did not know what to do, and without him to lead me I did not know where to go. Hopelessly I continued along the road.

After another mile or so I came to a canal, and leaving the road behind I followed the path beside the water, which looked empty and still. The dark clouds gathered upon its reflective surface, turning the water to ink. I imagined taking off my shoes and my coat, and disappearing forever into those unknown depths. I had never learned to swim.

The reflection of white wings glided in amongst the clouds on the water, and painfully my heart skipped a beat. But looking up I saw that it was a swan, solitary and peaceful, its feathers glinting with the sunlight that no longer shone. I saw, too, that I was surrounded by boats. Yellow, red, blue; the water lapped against their painted sides, and the narrow boats rose and fell with the gentle swell, tugging on the ropes that moored them to the banks of the canal.

I caught sight of a figure – a man – sitting on the grassy bank beside the boat that was nearest to me along the tow path. My heart rate quickened, though I fought the urge to turn around: there was no sense in going back the way I had come, after all. As I approached he looked up, and seeing me he raised the mug that he held in his hand and offered me a smile in greeting. I tried my best to return the smile as I passed by, but only my mouth went through the motions. I knew that it could not be seen in my eyes. I quickly looked away.

'You look as though you could do with some coffee, my friend,' I heard the young man say behind me.

Surprised, I turned my eyes once more in his direction and saw that he was looking straight at me. Michael's old boots brought my feet to a stop; my lips began to open, but no words sprang up to meet them. Instead, for the sake of a response I found myself nodding my head, truthfully. Without another word the young man rose to his feet and with long strides he hopped up onto the back of the boat.

Too uncertain to follow him and too exhausted to continue on my way I stood dumbly, watching as the stranger lifted a ceramic pot and poured dark liquid into a mug beside it, before topping up his own mug that he had been clutching in his hand. He jumped back onto the bank, spilling drops of coffee into the canal, and with an encouraging smile he handed me one of the ceramic mugs. Wisps of steam curled into the air; I wrapped my hands around the cup, my fingers tingled with the heat. The aroma of coffee was making me dizzy.

'*Qujanaq.*' I thanked him quietly in my own language. My voice sounded hoarse.

He raised his own cup into the air. 'Cheers,' he said. He took a swig, grimaced, and then promptly sat back down on the grassy bank, long legs crossed before him. With his free hand he tucked his shoulder-length hair behind his ear and looked up at me as though he was waiting for something.

'Well, have a seat,' he said, and gestured to the ground when still I did not move.

I sat down. Relief flooded through my limbs. I thought about removing Michael's old boots from my aching feet and throwing them into the canal, but my arms were too heavy to be of any use. I willed them to at least raise the cup of coffee to my lips, and I took a sip, eager to soothe my throat, spread the warmth. . .

The taste was vile. As I swallowed it I could not help but pull a face, and the young man let out a short laugh.

'Terrible, isn't it?'

For a second time I nodded wordlessly. The man continued to speak, seemingly unperturbed by my silence. 'Still, a hot drink is a hot drink.' He raised his mug into the air once more, his voice elevated, as though making a toast at a busy dinner party. 'And a hot drink on a cold day is a hot drink on a cold day.'

I sipped some more coffee, did not ask what he meant.

'So, where are you off to today?' he asked casually, lowering his mug from the toast he had made.

'I'm. . . looking for someone,' I answered, hesitantly.

My companion turned his neck to view the painted boats that bobbed on the gentle swell further up the canal.

'Someone who lives here?'

I shook my head. 'No, I'm searching for my friend. He. . . I lost him.'

The young man's mouth took on a lopsided tilt in sympathy.

'That's too bad, man. Hey, what's he look like, your friend? Maybe I've seen him.'

I smiled to myself as my mind conjured the image of Eqingaleq creeping stealthily down the tow path beside the water in his bearskin trousers, as the boats' owners looked on in amazement. Of course, I knew that no one but me had the ability to see him, for he was not of this world, but I did not want to admit this in the presence of a stranger and in a foreign land. I doubted that the people here would understand.

'If you had seen him,' I said simply, 'you would know.' I studied the ripples of water that broke against the manmade bank, listening to their subtle, soothing sound.

'Well, I'll keep my eyes peeled for any unusual visitors,' the man said. 'Besides yourself.'

I glanced at him, wondering what was meant by this last remark. A small smile pricked the corners of his mouth in his open, friendly face; still it crossed my mind that I should get up and leave for I knew now that to good people I could bring only pain. In the distance I heard the howling of the wolves, as again they drew closer, always on my trail.

I stumbled up onto my feet and turned to leave. 'Thank you for the coffee.'

The young man had risen also, and I had taken barely a few steps before he stopped me, speaking quietly.

'Listen, man. You got anywhere to sleep tonight?'

A sense of nausea swept up into my throat. Was I that transparent that he knew, without knowing me, that I was lost, alone?

'It's getting dark already,' he added, when I did not answer.

I tried to look at him but could not bring myself to meet his eyes, did not know what to say. The baying of the wolves grew louder; hungry yet untiring they would pursue me until I could run no more. And if I dared to rest out in the open, in the night's oppressive darkness. . . a shudder ran down my spine at the thought.

The stranger patted the shoulder of my anorak, encouraging me to take a step in the direction of the boat.

'Come on, there's plenty of room in the boat for one more weary traveller.' He laughed a little, seemingly making the effort to sound light-hearted. 'Who knows, there could be wolves out tonight!'

I stopped, my eyes shot up to meet his. He looked uneasy at the intensity of my stare, the panic that must have visibly swept through me. His gaze shifted. 'But it's all right, we'll untie the mooring rope: they won't be able to swim to us across the canal.'

I forced myself to smile – to show that I had understood that it had been a joke, a meaningless remark – and stepped after him onto the back of the boat. It rocked gently under my feet.

'Neil,' the man said suddenly, stopping and turning to face me so abruptly – or perhaps I was simply too dazed to anticipate his movements – that I nearly careered into his arm, outstretched in greeting. I did the same, and shyly we shook hands.

'Malik.'

'Welcome aboard, Malik!' He smiled, and releasing my hand he turned to move through a low doorway beside where we were standing, and disappeared inside the boat.

I peered over the side of the boat to the water below: it looked almost black, decorated with rippling silver circles from the first few drops of a new rain. A strange sensation of peace accompanied the fatigue that spread through my body, lulled by the rhythm of the water and the gentle, longed-for silence that had come to replace the roar of the city.

At the sound of quiet footsteps from inside the boat I looked up, expecting that it would be Neil returning to see why I had not followed him. The face that appeared in the doorway, however, was one that I did not recognise. It was largely obscured by a wild black-and-grey beard and thatched with hair of a similar nature. Two piercing eyes picked me out where I stood on the deck, helpless and uncertain. The head vanished as suddenly as it had appeared and I heard a man's voice call out gruffly: 'It's all right, Neil, I can see him too.' And then Neil's head appeared around the painted door frame, the glint of the failing light on his glasses, shrouding his eyes.

'For a moment there I thought I must have imagined you,' he said unabashedly. 'Come on in.'

The rain had picked up momentum; I could hear it pattering on the roof of the boat – a skittish drum beat – as I stepped under the door frame and inside. The comforting aroma of wood smoke washed over me, a fireside warmth; I wanted to close my eyes, savour the smell of Home – whoever the home might belong to. But a persistent sense of apprehension kept me alert. Looking around I saw that the boat was no bigger than it had seemed from the outside, though it was unmistakably lived-in. My elbow knocked against an old gas stove stacked with ceramic pots and pans and overhung with a variety of kitchen utensils; on my other side squatted a small cupboard, a tin basin half filled with soapy water perched on the top. Beneath my feet I saw a rug adorned with branching flowers, and quickly I slipped off Michael's muddy boots for fear of ruining it, though as I did so I was struck by the uncomfortable thought that I might be acting presumptuously.

'Just make yourself at home!' the man known as Neil said cheerfully. He was standing in a sea of cushions and woollen rugs, his back turned to a wood-burning stove and an untidy pile of chopped logs. 'Allow me to introduce you to Dennis –' he gestured to the man with the grey beard, who nodded accommodatingly '– Man with the Boat and Maker of the World's Worst Coffee. And Dennis – meet... *Malik*, was it? Mysterious Visitor and Keeper of the Silence.'

I did not know what to say.

The man known as Dennis had been looking me up and down. I could see that beneath his branching beard his mouth was sharply drawn, apparently humourless. But when he spoke his tone was friendly. 'Don't mind Neil, he means no harm.' His gaze lingered, curiously, and I knew that he was inspecting the strange, mismatched orbs of my irises, the windows to my otherworldliness that I could not hide. 'You, err, speak English?' he asked, acknowledging my obvious discomfort but misunderstanding its cause. I nodded. At long last his gaze shifted, coming to rest instead upon the cooker beside me.

'Well, get yourself sat down anyway, I was just about to make some soup.'

Awkwardly we switched places – the "kitchen" being too small to allow for the both of us to inhabit it – and heavily I sat down on a cushion, hugged my knees to my chest and peered through the glass door of the wood stove to where the flames

167

danced and flared. Dennis clanged pots and pans around. I could sense Neil's eyes upon me long before he spoke:

'What happened to your eyes, my friend?'

The noise from the kitchen ceased. A strange emptiness hung in the air: Dennis listening keenly for the answer.

'I was born like this,' I said. *Like this.* A circus freak, an outcast.

'Wow.' Neil nodded his head, making no attempt to hide his intrigue. 'They're so... *intense.*'

The atmosphere was broken by the sudden cry of an infant, half-muffled as though drifting through from another room or the depths of my imagination. I started. For one long moment I believed, with every fibre of my being, that it was my daughter, and had my limbs not been flooded and heavy with fatigue I may well have leapt to my feet and run to her.

Neil must have acknowledged my reaction to the sound, though he made no move himself. 'It's all right,' he said, waving a hand to apparently excuse his inaction, 'Martha's in there with her.'

The baby, when she was carried through from the other end of the boat by her mother a few moments later, stared at me unwaveringly with eyes as round as saucers. I feared she might burst into tears at the unnerving sight of my eyes – for such an effect they often had upon children – yet she simply watched, and continued to watch me even once her mother placed her down on one of the rugs that lined the floor, as though I were the most interesting thing she had ever seen.

Neil was again making introductions, but I barely heard. The baby's innocent little eyes sent a chill of memory through the depths of my soul. Memories I had tried – unconsciously, it seemed – to banish to the corners of my mind and escape the hurt they caused. I had not been there when my daughter was born; she was already a few weeks old when I saw her for the first time, having finally and at great pains persuaded her mother's family to allow me to meet the new child. And though, after that, I tried to be with my daughter

168

whenever the chance was awarded me, my presence in the family's household was met always with a coldness that marred the joy that a baby brings. It was not that I had done anything wrong, other than be born with a curse that was visible to all. And they shunned me, for they knew that a person cursed in such a way – that I – could bring only misfortune, above all to a child that I had fathered.

I had often tried to imagine how my mother must have felt when she saw her first – her only – child open his eyes for the first time. What must she have thought she had brought into the world?

It was a relief only that the curse had not been passed onto my daughter; both of her irises were, thankfully, the same colour. The right colour.

I sat immobilised as thoughts of her came flooding back, and for the first time since arriving in this strange country I regretted with my whole heart leaving the place where she was born and where she lived. How could I ever find my way back? How stupid I had been.

———

I dreamt of her that night, vividly and painfully, though by the time I awoke, disorientated from the heaviness of my sleep, all the details of my imaginings had long since vanished from my mind. I was curled up amidst the cushions on the floor, covered by a woollen blanket, the wan morning light lingering above me. I could not remember lying down to sleep the night before. I sat up hurriedly, flashed my eyes around the small space: perhaps Eqingaleq had returned to me during the night, to save me, to guide me. . . But the room was empty.

The fire smouldered, radiating a meagre heat that did little to mar the chill that had settled in my body during my night-time stillness. I buried my hands in my hair, massaging my aching head into wakefulness. I could feel the gentle swell of the water beneath the boat. It was peaceful,

169

quiet. Gradually I became aware of a snuffling sound, like that of a small animal drawing near. Looking up, I saw the baby crawling into the room – from the end of the boat that I assumed must contain the bedroom – hands slapping the floor rhythmically as she moved, making blowing noises through her closed lips. Just before she reached me she sat back on her haunches and grinned happily, then flapped her arms like a bird and squealed a string of nonsense syllables.

Her mother entered just behind her, hurriedly, her fingers entwined within her fair hair, which she was teasing into a long plait over her shoulder and across her chest. 'Sorry,' she gabbled. 'Sorry – did she wake you?' She slipped an elastic band onto the end of her braided hair and, her hands now free, scooped the baby up onto her hip.

I watched the baby's movements, did not answer. She had immediately busied herself with picking at the pills of wool on her mother's jumper with small, fat hands, a look of intense concentration on her pink face. Her mother shivered, exaggerating the ripple of her body for the sake of the infant, who squealed delightedly as she was shaken from side to side.

'It's cold this morning.' I could not tell whether she was speaking to me or her daughter. I nodded anyway, just in case.

The young woman slipped past me into the kitchen area. 'You must be hungry; you fell asleep last night before you could eat your soup.'

A flush of heat rushed into my cheeks. Luckily she was too preoccupied with setting the baby down upon the floor once more, a wooden spoon in her plump hands, to acknowledge my embarrassment. 'I'll make some porridge,' she added. The hem of her checked skirt brushed the floor as she crouched down to rummage inside one of the cupboards. The baby, watching her, put the spoon to her mouth and began to suck on it loudly.

I sat unmoving, did not know what to do. I felt the

170

continued absence of Eqingaleq as I imagined I would feel a hole in my heart. A creeping paralysis threatened my limbs, like a wild animal stalking the weakest of its prey. Still on my knees I shuffled over to the wood stove, opened the door and began to rake the ashes. From the wicker basket beside the stove I placed some split pieces of wood on the embers and blew gently upon the smouldering coals to coax the fire back into life. It did not take long before the smallest of flames began to lick the edge of the kindling. I added some lumps of coal, breathing in the earthen aroma as it caught the heat.

From the corner of my eye I noticed a tiny hand reaching for the basket of coals, and gently I moved the baby's fingers away before she could blacken them with soot. I spoke to her soothingly in my own language, for a moment not realising that she would not understand. She seemed to enjoy the sounds I was making, watching the movement of my lips in fascination with round, bright eyes. I said the same thing again, and then she looked up at me, serious for a moment, before a wide smile spread across her cheeks and she waved the spoon above her head as though applauding my efforts. I could not help but laugh. She looked over to her mother – busy at the cooker – to share her enjoyment. The young woman laughed too, caught my eyes, and for one long second I felt as though the world had stopped in its tracks and the weight of it had been lifted from my shoulders. Her eyes were blue, the deep blue of the ocean, creased at the edges above cheekbones dotted with freckles and lips that seemed to wear the perpetual shape of a smile. Was it the spreading warmth of the fire that had brought a new pink to her cheeks?

I heard the slamming of a door opening with too much force – breaking the spell. Neil blundered into the room, clutching a jumper in one hand, his eyes turned towards the floor as though in search of something.

'Martha, have you seen my socks?' In the same breath he caught sight of me, as I knelt still on the floor surrounded by cushions. 'Oh, morning, Malik. Sleep well?' He smiled encouragingly, perhaps to show that he did not mind my having fallen to sleep in the midst of the hospitality he had shown me the previous evening.

I nodded mutely.

'Cat still got your tongue, eh? Good, good. Martha! My socks?' He strode over to the young woman, who was rolling her eyes at him, spoon in hand by the cooker.

'I don't know, Neil, why don't you just keep them on your feet?'

I noticed the toe of a woollen sock peeping out from beneath a flower-patterned cushion, which I moved to the side and discovered the other one. I stood up, and clutching the socks in one hand I lifted the baby up into my arms, away from the stove.

'Thanks, man,' said Neil, grinning as I handed him his socks. The baby reached out her arms towards her mother, standing beside Neil, who took her from me almost apologetically. I mumbled something about the fire, eyes averted, then turned and ducked through the doorway and out into the fresh air.

The rain fell lightly, skittered across the water in thin curtains driven by the mounting wind. I took off my jumper and rolled my shirt sleeves up to my elbows, seeking the coolness of air on my bare skin, a call back to life from the drowsiness of the night and the numbness of my wearied soul. I gulped down the clear air, trying to swallow the lump in my throat: the longing for Eqingaleq and his guidance. I was truly lost now, captured within an infinite moment, unable to move forwards, cut off from everything that I had known before.

I stepped onto the bank of the canal. Felt the reassurance of solid earth beneath my bare feet. I sank to the ground where Neil and I had sat the evening before. I kept myself still, listening. I imagined I could feel the vibrations of the rain upon the earth, the relentless, rhythmical pounding of the shaman's drum as he journeyed to the Spirit world. But it was so distant now, I could not discern the beat. I had journeyed too far.

Neil picked his way off the boat, in each hand a bowl and spoon. He sat beside me and we ate our porridge in silence, the steam rising from the rims of the bowls like smoke signals.

'Those lines on your arm –' Neil gestured with his spoon in between mouthfuls of porridge '– what do they mean?'

I looked down at my right forearm, the exposed skin decorated by black lines sewn into the skin, geometric shapes, dots and patterns – the same distinctive tattoos that my ancestors had worn.

'My mother's brother drew them,' I said, unsure how to explain. 'He had the same patterns drawn on his arm.'

Neil nodded, his gaze still resting on my arm. His vision must have been obscured by the reams of rainwater that ran down the lenses of his glasses. 'It's. . . traditional?'

My turn to nod my head, mute again.

'Did it hurt?'

Sometimes my skin still prickled with the memory of the pain.

'Yes, very much.'

Qallu's hands, steady with the needle, concentrated upon his work. Sober, for once. The palms of my hands slippery with sweat, wishing I had acquisitioned some of my mother's bottled spirits after all, to dull the pain with their strength. But the pain was part of the process: to prove you had the strength and stamina to withstand it. And I was fiercely determined. *Let no one say you are not one of the People now*, I remembered my uncle's low voice, bubbling with reassuring warmth. *Your arms bear the patterns of your ancestors. This is who you are.*

PART TWO

1

Martha

England, January 1974

I remember Neil as a child – a gangly pre-teen with round glasses and a suggestion of handsomeness to his features that he had yet to grow into. His hair was shorter then, though it already brushed the tips of his ears. He allowed it to grow; soon to his earlobes, then his chin, and eventually past his slim shoulders. 'Like Neil Young,' he would say with a grin.

I loved him then, before I found out that he was gay. And if I'm honest for some time afterwards. I had thought that such feelings only existed between a man and a woman, until I caught him with the boy who worked at the butcher's.

'You won't tell anyone, will you, Martha?' he pleaded with me later, a fear in his eyes that I did not understand then. I kept his secret, yet in time the news got out nevertheless – as such gossip inevitably does. He hung his head lower after that; came to me often with bruised eyes and a bloody nose. *War wounds*, he would say with a wan smile as I wrapped sticky tape around his broken glasses.

I love him, still, though more as I imagine I would love a brother, were I not a stifled only child. Such children are ill-equipped for life in the big wide world, and I am no exception. I found myself pregnant at nineteen by a man who dominated me in a way that I believed was normal. It occurred to me, too late, that I could have told everyone that Neil was the father of my child. It may well have made life easier for both of us.

But I was determined to accept the consequences of my actions. I thought that I could make it work if I did everything my daughter's father wanted of me – if I gave him all that he wanted, he would have no reason not to love me. I believed him when he said that I had ruined his life by getting pregnant, that I had done it deliberately so that he would not be able to leave me, that it was all my fault. Perhaps I was the one who had turned his hand to violence, too – perhaps I had asked too much of him. He had once been romantic, gentle even, when we made love. And he is gentle with his baby daughter – most of the time.

'He is a good father,' my mother says, her words heavy with reproach, as though I am to blame for not appreciating what I have, for being so ungrateful. But no one can see what goes on behind closed doors; my mother has not seen the bruises that I hide in shame beneath my clothes.

'I fell down the stairs,' I tell her one day, when she inquires as to the origin of my recent black eye. It is an unconvincing lie, yet she swallows it without question. 'You should be more careful,' she warns.

What would she say, I often wonder, if she knew the truth? Continue to reprimand me for my carelessness, perhaps. *A man would not attack the mother of his child unless he had reason to.* Or, *you can see how gentle he is with the child, for she is innocent.* Perhaps: *what do you expect, when you gave him a child he did not want? You are lucky he is willing to marry you, so you will no longer have to live in shame.* I hear her voice in my head, though I no longer know if the words are hers, or my own. No matter who first spoke them, these

178

words are true to me: I am the one that he hates – he does not hurt the baby.

I would not hurt the baby, he tells me afterwards, once he has sobered up, his voice broken as he watches me hold a tea-towel-wrapped pack of frozen peas to my bruised eye. And for a moment he looks so pathetic that my heart weakens. I pat his hand, smile, tell him that it will all be okay. He promises he will not do it again.

Every time, the same promise.

Neil is angry with me, too.

'You should leave him,' he says, steel-voiced. He does not believe, for an instant, that I injured myself by falling down the stairs. 'How can you let your daughter stay in the same house as a man like that?'

'Because he is her father,' I say. I feel as though I am defending myself, making excuses for my fiancé's behaviour. I feel sick.

Every day Neil and I go for a long walk together, taking it in turns to push Boo in the pram that my mother bought – her one contribution in the role of a grandmother. Sometimes both Neil and I are battered and bruised. Other times our pain has no physical manifestation, yet it unites us. Often we ignore our bruises, talk only of mundane things – a distraction. Sometimes we compare our war wounds.

'Could we not just run away together?' Neil says one day, offhandedly, and I laugh, thinking he is making one of his usual piteous jokes.

'I have an aunt who lives in Shetland,' I say, pushing the pram as we walk.

He raises his eyebrows – the hint of a smile, the glint of an idea. 'Yes, no one would think to look there. . . '

It is only later that evening, when my daughter and I are home alone again, that the idea starts to take shape in my imagination. Why *couldn't* we run away? There is nothing to keep us here. The empty house looms around me in the darkness. I tremble secretly with excitement, the possibility of freedom. Could it really be so easy?

Once this seed has been planted in our thoughts, Neil and I talk more and more about how we might make our escape. It feels hypothetical, a shared fantasy – something to keep us going in the dark hours so that we do not give up hope.

I arrive back at home one evening to find that *he* is waiting for me.

I wheel the pram through the front door and into the hallway. Boo lies asleep inside it, swathed in blankets. I take off my coat and my hair is damp from the rain, uncomfortable against the back of my neck.

Then I see him: a malignant figure slumped over at the bottom of the stairs in the semi-darkness. I can tell immediately that he is drunk, I can smell the alcohol on his breath from the end of the narrow hallway. A flash of panic tears through me. For a few moments I stand unmoving. I hear the pounding of my heart inside my head, and the gentle sighs of the baby sleeping from where she lies in the pram. I wish that I had left the pram outside. I am thankful, at least, that I waved goodbye to Neil at the end of the street. He will never come into the house – I don't blame him.

'It's late,' slurs the shadow at the bottom of the stairs.

I swallow hard, try to keep my voice from shaking as I answer. 'We walked all the way to the park. It's such a lovely evening.'

I would not have expected a drunken man to move at such speed: in a flash he has his hands around my neck, pushing me up against the wall behind me. I can barely catch my breath. I try to pull his hands away, but there is no use in fighting, he is too strong for me.

He has his face right up against mine.

'I don't want you hanging around with that faggot, do you hear me?'

I *do* hear him. His voice is deafening. There is a splutter as Boo begins to cry, rudely awakened from the innocence of her slumber.

He releases his hands. My knees buckle, I gulp air back into my lungs. It takes a few moments before I am able to come to myself again, and when I do I see that he is beside the pram, one arm leaning heavily on the edge, apparently supporting his drunken weight – the other reaching down to touch the baby's head.

'Get away from her!' I shout in panic, though my voice sounds weak.

He turns around. I see his eyes flash with the light of the streetlamps that cast their cold yellow light through the window.

'She's my daughter – *my* daughter! I'll kill the filthy bastard if he touches her again.' Boo is screaming now, a cry of pure fear. He kicks the pram, stumbles away into the kitchen. Through the sound of Boo's crying I hear the clank of a glass bottle against the kitchen table.

I snatch my daughter from the pram and carry her upstairs as fast as my weak knees will take me, holding her tightly to my chest, stroking her head and whispering gentle reassurances in her ear. I sit on the bedroom floor to nurse her, my back against the closed door, and shudder and gasp as our tears mingle on the skin of my breast.

I have Auntie Jeanie's letter in my satchel, the reply to my letter that I sat waiting for – for four long days – watching the letterbox. *Yes, come here*, she has written, *come here and be safe.*

We leave under cover of darkness, loading up Neil's campervan with our belongings. It has not taken long to prepare – a few clothes stuffed into a suitcase, some tinned food for the journey. Neil has filled the van up with petrol.

We each have some savings – enough to get us across the Atlantic, to Shetland.

Neil drives all evening. Few words pass between us, and Boo sleeps in my arms. Neil has arranged for us to spend the night with an old friend of his, somewhere near Manchester.

'A close friend and ally,' he assures me, for I am uneasy about leaving a path for others to follow, 'We need allies. You can trust Dennis. He used to play in my uncle's band – you know, back in the sixties. He's practically a hermit now.'

I am not sure that I do trust Dennis. He eyes me up with an air of suspicion when we disembark from the van and meet in the midnight darkness at the end of a cul-de-sac. He roughly shakes my hand, which I untangle from the blankets I have wrapped around Boo, and leads us along a path beside an inky canal, torch in hand, to the narrow boat where he lives.

But Dennis is kind, though he gives little away. He offers us a bed for the night and in the morning plenty of porridge and endless cups of tea, even a little coffee. He and Neil are deep in discussions through most of the following day, about what I have no idea and am little concerned. I play with Boo beside the heat of the wood burning stove, try to keep her entertained and my thoughts occupied, but my mind is blurred by anxiety. My body, too, itches with restlessness. Why are we lingering here when we are on the run? It occurs to me that perhaps I am fearful that Neil will change his mind, decide we should return. 'We'll carry on in the morning,' he assures me as the afternoon is drawing to a close and still we have not moved on.

I nod mutely, swallow my discomfort. I tie Boo up into the sling and wander outside to stretch my legs along the tow path. She burrows into my chest, drifts off to sleep. There are swans on the water of the canal: mute, graceful. A strong breeze rushes through the trees' bare branches, crisp and clear – it is as though it has travelled here from a distant land, an ethereal force – the wind of change. I breathe in its newness; it calms me a little. When I get back to the boat I lay down on the mattress in the cupboard-sized spare room, Boo beside me, and fall asleep to the muffled sounds of Dennis and Neil in deep conversation.

I awake with a start as Boo cries out, seemingly out of the blue. I comfort her, blink the drowsiness from my eyes and carry her through to the boat's living space.

At first I do not notice the stranger sitting beside the wood burning stove. I am preoccupied with my daughter, wiping something sticky from her cheek as I set her down on the floor.

'Martha,' I hear Neil say. 'I'd like you to meet Malik: the Mysterious Stranger.'

It is only then that I look up.

'Oh,' I breathe, taken by surprise. I had not expected another visitor to the boat. I nod in greeting, but it seems he does not see me as he has his eyes fixed upon my daughter where she sits on the floor, staring back at him.

He has such strange eyes: wide-spaced, mismatched. His left eye is dark, almost black, deep as the night out here where there are no street lamps; the other is an orb of watercolour blue, deceptively large – for the pupil is little more than a pinprick – an island of rock in a vast, colourless ocean. Its washed-out blueness is completely at odds with the darkness of the rest of his features. His hair is as black as night, thick and long about his rounded face. His skin appears golden brown in the light of the fire. *One of them foreigners*, my mother would have said in hushed tones, not exactly disapproving and yet not open to acceptance either.

I shake my mother's influence from my thoughts.

Dennis is clattering about the stove, tipping chopped vegetables into a large pan, roughly slicing a loaf of bread with an apparently blunt knife and stealing wary glances at this new visitor. He must be a stranger to us all, I think, rather than a visiting friend of Dennis's.

The visitor continues to watch Boo as she potters about on the cushions and on my lap. He looks young, yet his eyes are

183

ringed by dark circles as though he has not slept in days. He responds to Neil's questions and attempts at small talk with only a nod of his head – *have you walked far? You must be hungry?*

Dennis' soup is forever in the making. There is little conversation as we wait – even Neil gives up, lulled to a tired thoughtfulness by the warmth of the fire. Boo climbs into my lap, whimpers, and I feed her at my breast, before she should make a fuss.

I feel my cheeks burn as I sense the young man's eyes upon me, but stealing a glance at him I see that he is only looking at Boo as she sucks contentedly. I am sure I detect the faint traces of a smile in his eyes: the warmth of a memory perhaps, or just the reflection of the tenderness of an infant at its mother's breast. As the fire gathers heat, he falls asleep on the cushions, even before my daughter has closed her eyes for the night.

I dream that he is pursuing us. Sometimes he is a malignant presence in the shadows, haunting my every step – at other times a bloodthirsty giant under whose stomping feet the whole earth shakes. But mostly he is simply a man, just as I remember him – no more than that, yet no less frightening. I run as fast as I can through the vast, mountainous landscape where I had been certain he would not find us, clutching Boo to my chest, disorientated by her emotive, fearful cries. If he catches us I know that this time he will kill us.

It is almost dark. I can't see where I am putting my feet. I stumble over something unseen and my knees come into contact with the hard earth. Still in my arms, Boo's cries grow more fearful. As I struggle back onto my feet, I send a glance behind me. I expect to feel his hands grabbing hold of my shoulders, seeking to inflict more bruises. He is not there; instead I catch sight of something else in the near distance, something that freezes me to the spot with fear.

It is a bear, an enormous animal silhouetted by the last rays of the setting sun. It rears up onto its hind legs. Powerful, dangerous. Boo sees it too. She falls silent, too frightened to cry. As we watch, paralysed, the bear drops its great paws back to the earth and the ground beneath us shakes so violently I almost fall back down to my knees.

It is this movement of the earth that wakes me. I open my eyes blearily, my body still rigid with the terror of my dreams: it is Boo bouncing on the mattress on her knees, eager in the first light of morning.

I push the memory of fitful dreams to the back of my mind. I dress quickly so as not to disturb Neil where he lies asleep next to me, and also because it is cold away from the protection of the blankets and without Boo's slumbering heat beside me. The boat rocks gently beneath my feet. I can hear the winter song of a robin outside the window.

It is only when I notice that Boo has crawled out of the bedroom that I remember the stranger that Neil brought to us yesterday, the tired traveller who did not speak and who fell asleep beside the fire. He has the look of another world about him, I recall, as though he has wandered alone from some remote land, as though he is lost in a place that he does not understand.

Rushing to follow my wayward daughter into the living area of the boat – my fingers working my hair into long plaits – I see that our guest is awake, messy-haired and bleary-eyed as though he has arisen from a deep coma and does not know where he is. I apologise hastily, anxious that Boo has woken him, but his eyes are fixed only on her.

His eyes. I had almost forgotten their strangeness, since he fell asleep so soon last night. They make me think of fairytales or half-remembered dreams. On someone more overbearing the effect could well be unsettling, fearful even – yet there is a look of gentle sadness behind his gaze that wards off any fear of their peculiarity.

Dennis is wary of him nonetheless. He muttered as the stranger lay sleeping, that we may well wake in the morning to find we have been robbed. As if he has anything worth stealing. I laughed as he said this, and Dennis glared at me. *And you with the baby*, he added, *you don't know what he might do.* But I only shook my head: I know a violent man now, when I see one. And he looked so young and innocent as he slept – the stranger – lulled by the warmth of the fire perhaps, and the contended stillness of Boo at my breast as she fed her way to sleep (this makes Neil sleepy, so he says). The stranger's skin is the colour of caramel. The fire's heat spilled a rosy hue onto his cheeks as he rested, though his eyes were ringed by shadows.

I see that the darkness still encircles his eyes in the morning light. Unsure of what to say, I find myself mentioning breakfast. He keeps his eyes on Boo as I set about making porridge, my attention divided, as always, between my daughter and my task. I see him move her hands away so gently when she reaches out to touch the basket of coals as he is lighting the fire. As he does so he speaks to her soothingly in a language I have not heard before. It is low and guttural, the music of a bubbling stream. I stop and look over from my place at the cooker, drawn by the look of enrapture on my daughter's face as she listens, before she throws her arms up in the air and squeals with delight.

The stranger laughs and the troubled look vanishes from his gaze; heavy creases are etched into the corners of his eyes as he smiles. First at Boo, then at me. My heart writhes inexplicably in my chest.

I am brought back down to earth as Neil lurches into the room, exclaiming something about his missing socks. I sigh inwardly, turning my attention back to the cooking porridge, back to the mundane. I hear Neil greet the stranger with a few meaningless pleasantries before he is at my side, mentioning his socks again. Irritation bubbles up in my chest; he is always leaving his socks lying around.

'I don't know, Neil. Why don't you just keep them on your feet?' The words come out a little snappier than I had

186

intended, but Neil does not seem to notice the unexplained edge to my voice. A wide smile creeps out over his face as the stranger approaches, the missing socks held in his outstretched hand. Neil takes them from him.

'Thanks, man.'

Something leaps within my stomach as the stranger turns to me, Boo on his hip.

'Fire's lit,' he mutters as he passes her into my arms. I can smell the wood smoke caught in the woollen knit of his jumper, he is so close to me in the tiny kitchen. But only for a moment. Boo's eyes follow him as he slips out the door and onto the deck. Neil's gaze, too, lingers on the doorway, now empty. With one hand he slides his glasses off the end of his nose and absentmindedly rubs at the lenses with the socks that he is still holding. Neither of us speaks a word and even Boo is still and quiet in my arms.

'Do you think he'll come back?' Neil asks.

'Well, he won't get far without his shoes.' I gesture across the room to the neat pile of the stranger's belongings: yellow anorak, canvas backpack; battered leather boots.

Boo squirms in my arms, bending her body and angling herself towards the floor, all her surprising strength pushing against me so that I have no choice but to set her down. Her limbs are whirring in a crawling motion before they even touch the floor. In the blink of an eye she has one of the stranger's boots clutched in her little fat hands. She glances at me across the room – a look of triumph, testing the water. My hands on my hips I admonish her teasingly, theatrically, and she rewards me with a big, toothless grin.

'Did he tell you where he was going?' I ask Neil, as I scoop Boo back up from the floor. 'Where he's travelling to, I mean?'

Neil shrugs. His glasses have returned to their usual place on the bridge of his nose. It unsettles me the way in which the lenses reflect the light: sometimes they are like mirrors. 'Said he was looking for his friend.'

'His friend?'

'That was all he said. I didn't want to cross-examine him, Martha, he looked so exhausted.'

I nod my head slowly. 'Still does.'

'Did he say much to you? Before I came in?'

'Not a word.'

Neil knits his brows together and chews on his lower lip, in the way that he does when he is deep in thought. I shift Boo over to him, freeing my hands to turn off the gas ring on the stove, and begin to ladle the porridge into bowls. Boo gurgles, happily sucking on a wooden spoon and paying as little attention to Neil at this moment as he is to her, each occupied with their own thoughts.

'Where do you think he's *from*?' Neil says, appearing to voice what he is thinking.

I resist the urge to say *another world*, or *the same planet as the Clangers*, though I can tell by the exaggerated tone of intrigue in Neil's voice that he is likely thinking something similar. 'You could ask him?'

Neil flashes me one of his ironic, knowing smiles.

'Oh, but that would take away all the *mystery*.' Then heaviness descends once more onto his eyebrows – Neil's jokes are a way to mask a deeper meaning, his own way of comprehending those things that touch his soul. He glances at the empty doorway, then turns to look at Boo, running one of his slender hands over her soft, downy head.

'Where could he be going to, do you think, Martha?'

I am struck by the note of concern in his voice for a stranger he has barely spoken to. I remember the rush of emotion that had flooded through me when the stranger's eyes met mine as he cared for Boo beside the fire – a feeling of being subject to something larger than myself – and I blush with faint embarrassment, wondering at the same time whether Neil has perhaps experienced something similar. But I know I cannot put it into words – I know what my mother would say if she were to hear such things said.

I set down the heavy pan, its contents now portioned into bowls.

'I don't think he's going anywhere,' I say quietly. An open-ended question to Neil and myself. 'It seems as though he's...' I struggle to find the right words. 'As though he's thinking of something else. Something only he can understand. I don't know.' I shake my head, sighing. 'You can offer him some porridge anyway, there's plenty. Is Dennis up yet?'

Neil's fine hair falls across his face as he bends down to set Boo on the floor. 'Not heard anything.' He spoons honey into two of the bowls of porridge, takes them one in each hand.

'What did you say his name was, Neil?'

'Malik,' says Neil, 'or something like that.' Then he, too, has vanished from the doorway.

Boo and I share a bowl of porridge, then I stoke up the smouldering fire and set about gathering together our scattered belongings from all corners of Dennis's house boat. It is gloriously quiet. I can hear only the music of the birds outside and Boo's low gurgles as she explores various objects that she finds lying around. Looking up I see that she has discovered the stranger's anorak. She has clamped her toothless jaws around the collar as though testing its durability. I prise it free and rub at the resultant patch of dribble with the sleeve of my jumper – I hope Malik will not notice. My stomach knots with the notion that I have invaded his privacy – I remember the way Boo's father would react when he felt such a crime had been committed against him, and I shiver, despite the warmth of the fire.

A tremor from the other end of the boat signals that Dennis is up and about at long last. I fold Malik's coat as neatly as I can and set it back in its place, immediately sweeping Boo up onto my hip as her small, curious hands reach out for it once more. I place my bag, now packed, beside the door on my way out onto the deck. I do not feel as though I have the strength to face Dennis just now. He is friendly enough, yet there is something in his gaze that makes me uncomfortable, something disapproving.

The surface of the canal ripples with a light fall of rain. A gentle morning mist lingers above the surrounding fields, the vestiges of the night's shroud. Everything is still. How peaceful it must be to travel by the waterways: hot tea on the deck, a fire below, stepping off to open the gates of the locks, watching the water flow. Such a life seems worlds away from our old campervan. A battered tin can that splutters up and down busy roads, the roar of diesel engines in one ear, the flare of angry horns in the other.

Already I am savouring the remembered taste of remoteness that I know will lie at the end of our journey – the ululating quiet of the North Sea and the wind's cool caress – it is anticipation of this that keeps me going amidst the madness of crowded cities.

The memory of my final visit to Shetland, all those years ago, has never left me. I had just turned eight, or maybe nine – my exact age is unimportant for it is the wildness of that summer that I remember with a trembling heart. The thrilling, calming sense of freedom that I had never imagined a child could feel, so distant from the confines of my stuffy upbringing and the boredom of the regimented, respectable household in which I had my place. Over time I have come to equate that sense of wildness in my soul with the earthy lure of the islands; long have I imagined myself working wool beside the fire with Auntie Jeanie, drawn by the kindness of her heart away from a life that was never mine. My own heart swells with joy at the thought that soon I will see her again. She will fold me in her homely arms and I will be safe.

He will never find us there.

But I must try to push the thought of him from my mind. The marks left by the blows that he dealt me have now mostly faded. If only the memory of him would vanish, too.

I see Neil and the stranger sitting side by side on the bank, beside the mooring rope. They are not speaking together as I approach, stepping lightly off the boat with Boo in my arms and enjoying the feel of the cold, wet grass under my bare feet, but there is no tension within their silence. The stranger is barefoot also, and despite the cool rain he has taken off his jumper and turned the sleeves of his shirt up to his elbows. My eyes are drawn to the patterns of black lines and dots that adorn his forearms, etched into the brown canvas of his skin. I pull my eyes away – I must not be caught staring.

Neil pulls a face at Boo and is rewarded with her steady, curious gaze.

'We could do with getting going, Neil,' I say. My voice sounds small, self-consciously shrill.

'Dennis up, is he?' Neil grins; his long legs begin to make the series of exaggerated movements that will get him to his feet. 'I'll round up our things.'

Malik follows Neil's example, though markedly more slowly. There is a weariness to his movements as he rises.

'Can we. . . ?' I begin to say, before he has even made it to his feet. '. . . Can we give you a lift anywhere? We have a van.' I gesture with one hand in the vague direction of our unseen vehicle.

He hesitates as he looks at me. I feel my cheeks flush, yet note that he, too, appears uncomfortable. He glances from me to Neil, to the ground, shifts his feet, swallows. When eventually he speaks, his voice is low and quiet and his accent strange.

'Can you take me north?'

'North?' Neil echoes.

'As far north as you can.'

For a moment no one says anything, then Neil claps his hands sharply together. 'You're in luck, Malik: north is just the direction in which we are headed.'

2

Rasmus

1949

He ran his hands again and again over the contours of Ketty's swollen belly, felt the life that stirred within, and buried his face in the curtains of hair that poured over her breasts. He ran his hands lower, felt her body shudder at his touch – heard her sigh.

The journey across the ice cap had been a failure, a waste of time, this much he understood now. Nothing had gone wrong, but... that was just it: they had faced no hurdles, come across no challenges over which they would have had to use their audacity and skill just to survive. There could be no need for heroism when all ran smoothly. And if they had faced any difficulties – he thought with a coldness through his veins – how would he have got through it anyway? How could he have broken through the numbness of his soul to become the epitome of a Great Explorer?

He pushed these thoughts away. Felt the texture of the skin blankets on his own bare skin. The warmth of Ketty's skin against his. The rawness of their encounters and the soon-to-be life that they had created, that had formed and grown in the cave of its mother's body while he had journeyed over the endless space of the ice cap. Perhaps this had been the real purpose of his journey.

And then the baby – a boy, was born just as the first rays of spring sun were beginning to infuse those long winter days with light. A soft, plump little thing, he was; dark-haired and caramel-skinned, like his mother. Perfect. Perfect... that is, if it weren't for the strangeness of the child's eyes. One dark like those of all of his mother's people; and the other colourless, in the way that a pool of shallow water has no colour – the pupil nothing more than a tiny black dot.

Rasmus was surprised, intrigued – he had heard of such afflictions – yet he could see the unease which the infant's unfocussed, mismatched stare provoked within the community. Even Qallu would not hold the baby, his sister's child. There was something apologetic in the way he kept his distance, something cautious and fearful.

'They are saying the child is cursed,' he muttered once to Rasmus, but would say no more.

During the lengthy darkness of the nights he remembered the stories that Qallu had told out on the ice cap; they came to him now, compulsively, like moving pictures accompanied by a wash of uncontrollable, unidentifiable emotions. At these times it seemed to him that the child was indeed born of this world of spirits and shape-changers, unstoppable forces intertwined with the wilderness and the ancient ice.

He might have feared for the child's life had it not been for Ketty's seemingly unwavering love for her son. She smothered him with kisses, fed him tenderly at her breast, kept him always close to her skin and said nothing of the strangeness that others feared. Avaaraq, too, though she made no comment about her husband's ambivalence towards his new nephew, welcomed the baby into her home as she would have a child of her own. Qallu remained quiet, kept out of the way, intervening only to snatch his own young son away as he crawled towards the sleeping baby. The child screeched, angry that his path had been thwarted. Avaaraq fetched him from Qallu's arms, chastised her husband in harsh, hushed tones. And Qallu, meek – with anxious glances at the tiny, sleeping creature – slunk away into the falling darkness. Rasmus heard him return later that night, reeling drunk, and his heart weighed like lead in his chest: he had inflicted this curse on the child. He, a White Man trespassing in a world that was not his own.

3

Martha

Away from the tranquil water, and we are back to the busy roads. The cool water that falls from the sky is smeared into nothingness across the van's windscreen, blurring our view of the world beyond. Malik looks pale where he sits in the backseat; I steal curious glances at him in the rear view mirror, as he in turn watches the rain-soaked towns slide past through the window. Neil, in the driver's seat, turns on the radio, but I soon grow tired of the incessant chatter and, catching sight of the pained look on our passenger's face I turn it off again. We return to the monotone noise of the engine and the rain.

Boo grows restless in my lap, begins to cry for freedom. We have been cooped up in the van for long enough. The road we are on is fairly quiet – Neil will always favour a quieter route over a direct one when he is behind the wheel. I see sheep in the field beside the layby in which we decide to stop: scraggly balls of cotton wool in the rain. Neil turns the key, bringing the engine to a stop, and immediately Malik wrenches open the side door, stumbles out into the undergrowth and throws up in the bushes.

'I thought he was looking a bit pale.' Neil's forehead creases in empathy.

I take Boo out into the fresh air, swathed in a woollen hat and blanket. She points delightedly over the fence at the grazing animals in the field beyond, similarly clad and oblivious to the wet weather. Their peaceful slowness is highlighted by the rush of the cars as they rattle past on the road.

When we return to the van, Neil has opened up the back door and hooked the gas cylinder to the cooker to heat a kettle full of water. Malik is sitting on the back of the van, legs crossed, woollen jumper pulled on. The pattern around the shoulders is colourful, intricate; it could perhaps be Scandinavian, I think as I toy with the idea of knitting one like that for Boo – she will be needing it where we are going, after all.

Malik offers me a wan smile, ever polite as I approach.

'Feeling any better?' I ask meekly.

He nods his head, black hair damp with shining rain. 'Sorry,' he mutters. 'Not used to cars.'

He watches Boo as she potters around in the back of the van, crawling on worn corduroy knees and pulling herself up onto her feet, her stubby fingers grasping onto the edge of the bed. I had sewn her dungarees from remnants of the rust-coloured corduroy that I had used for my own pinafore dress – the one that I am wearing now; the one that I worked on during long, lonely days at home while *he* was at work, trepidation building within me with every kick inside my swelling belly. My stomach twists as I realise that Boo and I are dressed alike. I remember how cruelly he laughed the first time we both wore my creations – put on with so much pride – and said we both looked a sight. He refused to be seen with me until I had changed into something else.

I had worn the dress now as an act of defiance, an

acknowledgement of freedom... but my legs still tremble with fear and uncertainty. Perhaps it is too soon to be making such gestures? I will not be free from him until I have placed the wild Atlantic between us.

'What is her name?' Malik asks, disturbing my anxious reverie.

'Boo.' Her name is soft on my tongue, and the sound of it lifts my spirits from the mire of those recent memories into which I too often sink. She turns her head at the familiar sound of her name, smiles a mischievous smile. She bounces on her knees.

Malik smiles back at her.

'Boo. I like that.'

We do not stop for long. Neil is eager to get the day's driving over and done with. I can see by the way he keeps pushing the arch of his glasses with one finger, even when they have not slipped down the bridge of his nose, that he is growing tired and exasperated. Once we are refreshed, he leaps back into the driver's seat and soon we are underway again. Boo protests loudly at being enclosed once more, but it is not long before she stops kicking and lays her head against my chest, lulled to sleep by the monotonous rattle and hum of the vehicle. The tension in my body evaporates immediately. I glance in the rear view mirror and see that our passenger, too, has laid his head to one side and is fast asleep.

The day wears on. At long last we stop for the night in a layby beside a quiet road. The winter darkness quickly descends. It is cramped inside the van with the four of us, and yet – dare I say it – the atmosphere is almost homely, a world lit by meagre candlelight and enclosed by the steady rhythm of the rain against the sides of the van. Other than offering his help with the cooking, our guest remains silent and still where he sits in the worn upholstery of the back seats. But his eyes flicker – one dark, one illuminated in the light – and I can see that his thoughts are busy.

Neil, too, is lost in his thoughts. He empties a tin of baked beans into a pan and places it on the portable stove – the clang of metal against metal. He coaxes a spoon round and round the pan, his eyes obscured by the rising steam that fogs his glasses. Only Boo chatters, periodically feeding at my breast until finally she gives in and closes her eyes for the night.

Neil, Boo and I share the bed as usual; Malik insists he will be fine sleeping across the seats.

I lie awake while Boo feeds quietly once more beside me, between me and Neil. A half-hearted smile creeps over my lips in the darkness as I think of what my mother would say if she knew I was sharing a bed with a man to whom I am not married, though of course – I glance down affectionately at my daughter – it is not the first time I have done so.

We have thought about getting married, Neil and I, to help ourselves and to help each other. I am a single, unmarried mother with nowhere to go and Neil could more likely find a job if he were a married man, as well as enjoy the safety of a reputable guise. Only we would know that our marriage was a sham, and no one would need find out that Neil is not Boo's father. It was something he suggested himself after the last act of aggression against him as he tried in vain – tears of anger, shame and sadness spilling from beneath his glasses – to scrub the word off the side of the van. *Homo*, scrawled in red paint, in ugly capital letters. We ended up covering it with a new coat of paint, brushing over the admittance of his sexuality as he had done so many times before.

Before we left I did not even say goodbye to *him*. I had nothing to say to him, nothing that would not earn me another bruise that I would have to keep hidden in shame.

As every other night for as long as I can now remember, he is there in my thoughts as I finally drift off to sleep. And in my slumber he continues to pursue me, an endless chase through the wilderness of my dreams. The great, white bear is there again, too, bounding on huge paws over the rocks with such speed and agility that I cannot tell which of my hunters will reach me first. But the earth shakes under the bear's advance, and *he* almost has his hands on my – on our – crying daughter as I grasp her to my chest, and I am shouting for help, and the bear's claws look as sharp as knives, and its eyes are black. . .

With a gasp I am awake, sitting upright in shock. I see that it is only Malik who is before me now, sitting on the edge of the narrow bed. Although I cannot see his eyes clearly in the near-darkness, I feel his hand gently on my shoulder; his head turns towards Neil, who is still sleeping soundly next to Boo, and I know what he is thinking.

'No,' I stutter, realising I must have been calling out loud in my sleep, 'There was a bear – a huge, white bear. Chasing me. It was so close.' I falter to a stop at the strangeness of my words. I am thankful for the darkness which hides the colour that must be flushing my cheeks and spares me the embarrassment of meeting Malik's eyes. I sense that they are fixed on me. His breath is light; he does not move. I am comforted by the warmth of him as his grip on my shoulder tightens.

'Do not be afraid,' he says quietly. 'He will not hurt you.'

Then he is gone and the cold bite of the night air surrounds me. I snuggle down into the blankets and sink swiftly into sleep. My dreams are filled with the swelling sea and a gentle north wind.

———

Rolling waves, a biting chill, I hear the laughter of the wheeling seagulls off the Aberdeenshire coast. The boat pitches and rocks, and my stomach is tossed from side to side. It is too cold for Boo out on the deck where there is no shelter from the wind that drives across the open ocean. Inside, the heat of her little body against mine is unbearable. Nausea broiling, I forcefully entrust her to Neil – who protests but soon gives in at the sight of my pale face – and make my way slowly out on to the deck at the rear of the ship.

We have left Aberdeen behind, smudged into the horizon. We are headed north, tracing the east coast of Scotland: I can just make out its undulating shape in the failing light. I pull my coat more tightly around my body, my loose hair streams in ribbons across my eyes, which sting with the black smoke that belches from the chimney of the boat and merges with the wild wind. My knees seem to creak as I seek out a more sheltered spot and rest my aching bones on one of the skeletal metal chairs that line the outside wall. There is a strange feeling of calm away from the howl of the wind, though I can still feel the vibration of the boat's engine shuddering up through the chair, up the length of my spine. I cross my arms tightly over my chest, watch as the sky grows darker.

I am roused by the movement of someone sliding into the chair beside mine. It is Malik, his eyes dulled by a look of discomfort.

'Seasick too?' I ask, finding the uncomfortable need to raise my voice over the relentless chug of the engine below us. Malik nods, drawing into himself as the wind tears across us. For some time neither of us says a word, until I can summon the courage to speak. I ask what is always foremost on my mind: 'Is Neil all right?' My voice is hesitant. 'With the baby?'

He smiles unexpectedly as I say this, and his cheeks are beginning to flush with colour from the weather's bite.

'Don't worry, they are both happy.'

My body aches with relief, comforted by the words of a stranger.

'I worry so much,' I find myself admitting, 'when I can't look after her.'

'She will be happy with her father for a while.'

'Oh, Neil's not –.' The words are out of my mouth before I have a chance to think them through. 'I mean, her father is. . . somewhere else. A long way from here, from. . . this.' I hear a tremor in my voice as I nod in the direction of the swirling, wild waters around the boat and the grey plane of the sea that

202

stretches all the way to the horizon.

'I suppose Neil's the closest she has to a father now,' I add, striving to sound light-hearted in the hope that it might hide the emotion that is threatening to surface. But I can see by the way Malik's gaze lingers on me – from the corner of my eye – that he is not fooled. He says nothing, and I pretend not to notice his looking at me as I feel my cheeks flush with colour: red, the colour of shame, the shame of being a single mother and having to admit that I have failed my daughter. My stomach churns. Perhaps I have made a terrible mistake.

I close my eyes tightly against the wind until this new wave of nausea dissipates.

'When I feel seasick,' Malik's voice is close to my ear, soft, mingling with the noise of the boat. I open my eyes. 'I imagine all the creatures below us in the water, the fish, the seals, the. . . the really big ones?' He slides his hands through the air to either side of him, above his knees and mine, in illustration.

I can't help but giggle. 'You mean whales?'

He grins. His eyes crease at the corners. 'Whales. I think of them all swimming, deeper and deeper to the sea bed where they will find the Mother of the Sea.'

'The Mother of the Sea?'

'She was a woman once, a long time ago. . . '

His eyes shine as he tells the story, his English broken but his words strong. A young woman, tricked into marriage with a seagull, cast by one she loved into the depths of the ocean. . .

It has begun to rain lightly. The skin of my face tingles with its cool caress as Malik's story comes to a close. All at once we are returned to the world of the present. I steal a sideways glance at Malik: the faraway look has crept back into his eyes, which had burned with an inner fire as he relayed this strange story from a strange land. I fight the urge to lay my hand on his shoulder, to connect us, to acknowledge that we are alone and adrift in a sea that we do not know – both of us together.

Yet with every passing second I feel myself drifting further and further away from this fleeting moment of connection, until I realise that we are each adrift in our own ocean and the two do not share their waters.

Nonetheless the subject of Malik's story stays with me. I see her – the Mother of the Sea – when I close my eyes later on, to the electric lighting of the ferry's interior. Her bed is the rocks that line the bottom of the sea, her hair – black, like Malik's – snakes out from her head in curling tendrils, suspended in the gentle swell of the current; her eyes are dark and deep, her face almost white with the death that has only half claimed her. Beautiful, but so, so sad.

Boo has, at long last, drifted off to sleep beside me, worn out by Neil's excitement as he showed her around the ship. I have chosen a corner for us to lie in, as out-of-the-way as possible, hidden from the brightest lights and the lingering glances of the other passengers as I try to breastfeed her discreetly. I have made a makeshift bed with my coat. It is not very comfortable but I am so drained by nausea I barely notice. Neil's heavy breathing is just audible from where he reclines curled up in a chair, his coat pulled over his head. The rocking of the ship is soothing now, up and down, to the engine's rhythmical chug-chugging and the gentle lullaby of the murmur of the few passengers who are still awake. I pull my blanket around me.

There is a soft noise nearby, and opening my eyes I see Malik laying his own makeshift bed beside me and my daughter.

'Malik?' I whisper, my voice blurred by near-slumber, 'What happened to the seagull from the story? After he tricked the girl, the Mother of the Sea, into marrying him – did somebody catch him? Did he do it again?'

He lies down on his back. I can see his one dark eye turned towards the ceiling, yet dream-like as though he sees something else entirely.

'He tricked many people.'

'Did he trick you?'

Malik closes his eyes. 'He tricked many people.'

Boo tosses and turns throughout the night, disturbed by the glare of the electric lights. Only half-awake I manoeuvre her onto my breast every time, trying to black out the lights with the blanket until she settles down once more, only to wake again what seems like moments later. But she must sleep soundly at some point, for when I drift into the waking world towards morning I am groggy from deep sleep. Immediately my heart leaps into my throat – where is Boo? I sit up, blinking the relentless light from my eyes.

But she is there: with Malik. She appears to have draped herself across his chest, her puckered, pink lips moving silently with the flow of her dreams. He, too, is sleeping soundly. The sight is so unexpected, so strange, that all I can do is stare for a few moments as my mind takes it in. *I must not disturb them*, is my only thought.

My muscles creak with the strain of a night spent on the hard floor as I rise to my feet. I smooth down my crumpled clothes with my hands, then tease out the ruffled plaits in my hair and run my fingers through the loose knots and mousey waves.

Neil is looking in my direction with blurred eyes: a look of drowsy confusion as though he is trying to recall where he is.

'Is that you, Martha?' He squints as me. 'Where did I put my glasses?'

They are on the floor underneath his chair. I deliver them into his hands as I sit down beside him. Spectacles in place, he catches sight of Boo and Malik in their shared comfort of slumber.

'She's really taken a shine to him, eh?'

I hear an edge to his voice.

'You're not jealous, Neil?' I nudge his elbow with mine. He scowls, removes his glasses again and rubs at the lenses with the sleeve of his jumper.

Outside it is still dark, but I gather from the stirrings of the other passengers, waking groggily from snatched sleep, that the morning proper must be in its beginnings. The ferry rocks gently on an apparently calm sea.

Neil sighs heavily.

'Well, Martha, we've done it. We've escaped. If we try to put any more distance between ourselves and the people who have hurt us, then we'll be needing passports. And fuller wallets. But he won't find you here, that's for sure.' His tone is too light-hearted to offer any reassurance. I perceive also, yet choose to ignore, the tones of apprehension that bubble through his words, betraying his fear that I have brought him to the ends of the Earth.

He continues, 'Unless we find him stowed away under the wheel arches.'

'Neil, don't *joke* about that!' I snap, more sharply than I had intended, before the last of his words has even left his lips. *Pursuing us across the cold sea, and one by one he will chop off my fingers until I can hold on no longer...* All at once, vividly, I see the image of the great, white bear. The one who, I recall, weaved in and out of my broken dreams throughout the night – light footfall across the garish patterned carpet of the ship's interior – casting an unnatural shadow in the electric light. Moved silently into the snatched darkness of sleep and the wild landscape of my dreams.

'Sorry, Martha,' Neil mutters. He sighs again. 'I'm just a bit... on edge. I mean, what am I going to *do*? Who on earth will give me a job? How will we live?'

I lay my hand on his arm, try to keep my voice steady. 'Auntie Jeanie will help. She'll know someone.'

Neil looks at me, clearly now through the window of his spectacles, his eyes creased at the corners. He reaches out to take both my hands in his.

'Martha, will you marry me?'

'It won't come to that.' I pull my hands away, shake my head to show that this joke-in-all-seriousness is unnecessary

206

– unhelpful. 'We'll find a way.'

He slumps back in his chair, blows air out from between pursed lips. Boo is stirring; Malik, too. He runs his hand over her downy head as she raises it groggily from his chest, as though it is the most natural thing in the world to wake beneath the weight of somebody else's child. She looks at him, then sits back on her haunches and runs her gaze – eyes swollen from sleep – around the room. Her legs whir into motion the second she catches sight of me, and I catch her as she reaches me, lift her up onto my lap and kiss the top of her head, enjoying its familiar smell. Out of the corner of my eye I see Malik folding away his coat-bed, and something jolts within me, for I know I should not be looking.

Neil bids him a cheery *Good Morning*, demonstrating how effectively he has learned to mask his feelings. Or perhaps he is simply trying to make the best of the situation in a way I can never seem to manage.

Malik nods in response. All at once I am conscious of my hair falling into my eyes, unwashed, and yesterday's crumpled clothes, dusty from a night spent sleeping on the floor. And my daughter pulling at my blouse, demanding another feed – what if everyone sees? My body aches with weariness.

It is not long before a voice over the loudspeaker informs us that we must return to our vehicle. Back into the bowels of the boat, the sickening smell of petrol fumes, the noise of engine after engine igniting, spluttering, rumbling. When we drive out of the ferry's yawning mouth into the perpetual night and the harbour's lights, I am gripped by the uncomfortable feeling that we have travelled no distance at all.

We drive in silence, each sunk in our own thoughts. Boo, bored of this tin can environment, writhes restlessly in my lap, hangs off my shoulders, pulls at my blouse. My body is tense, a coiled spring. If only she would climb onto Malik again, let me breathe. But I am her mother, her only parent: I must give her everything I have within me, not hand her over to be entertained by a stranger. However kind he may seem. Each time she throws her strong little body around, shrieking with frustration as I try to confine her to my lap, I see him glancing over. And I am careful not to catch his eye in the mirror, in case he offers to take her from me for a moment's help – in case I blush with shame.

Rays of sunlight begin to spill into the valleys with the late-morning sunrise, shadows and light in ethereal play. Hills morph into mountains, the road dips tunnel-like down to wide bays and distant ocean horizons. I long to stop, to climb out of the van and breathe it all in. But I am anxious for our journey's end.

As we draw nearer to our destination, my memory is ignited. I recognise the small stone houses that make up the village through which we are passing; the tiny church whose doors open out onto a view of the bay; the curved, protective wall of the harbour and, finally, the cottage itself. It only comes into view as we follow the track that snakes up out of the village – nestled into the contours of the hills, the sky above and the sea below. And my father's sister is waiting for us outside the house, unchanged for all these years that have passed, as the van rolls noisily to a stop. And in a moment I am in her arms, sobbing like the child I once was.

4

'You should write to your mother, Martha.' Auntie Jeanie lays her wrinkled hand on mine as she sits down beside me at the kitchen table. 'Let her know you're here.'

I shake my head, hold my gaze away from hers.

'She wouldn't be happy to know I'm here.' I cannot calm the tremor in my voice. Jeanie takes her hand away again to pour from the teapot that has been brewing on the table. The steam curls visibly towards the low ceiling, mingles with the long, grey locks of her hair.

'She never liked you, did she, Jeanie? She always resented coming up here, and all you did was argue. Then after Dad died we stopped coming.' I bite my tongue, unsure whether I am in fact making an accusation.

Jeanie sighs, runs a hand across her forehead, creased with her remembering. 'There were many things we disagreed on, your mother and I. And after Charlie died... You know, he wanted to be cremated – he said as much when he knew just how ill he was. Said he wanted to have his ashes scattered back here in Shetland. But your mother wouldn't hear of it. She insisted on a formal burial down south.'

'Is that why you didn't come to the funeral?'

She takes my hand in hers once more, her eyes shining.

'I'm sorry, love.'

She is so much older than my mother – my mother who married a man twenty years her senior – and so much more grounded, I think to myself. All her married life she has lived in this old house, safe and secure as the seasons change around her, year after year.

I smile to myself as I hear a burst of infant giggles through the open door to the living room. Neil knows just how to make Boo laugh. The sound awakens the ghosts of memories that are not mine: a happy house full of Jeanie's children – long since grown – the childhood that I wish I could have had.

'But please write to her,' my aunt presses. 'She cares about you.'

'I wonder sometimes,' I say sharply. 'You know, she wanted me to marry *him*. She was the one who pushed me, said I owe it to my daughter to provide her with a stable family, save her from the shame of having an unmarried mother. But I couldn't go through with it. . . for Boo's sake: I couldn't bear the thought of her growing up with a father like that. Better no father at all.'

Jeanie is silent for a moment. When she speaks I hear the hint of a smile in her voice.

'You always knew your own mind, Martha.'

Obstinately I wipe the unbidden tears from my cheeks, determined to be strong, to show everyone that I have made the right decision. I had thought that here, so far from the life I had longed to escape from, I would find freedom from its haunting memories. Yet I am bruised and fearful. Perhaps we have not travelled far enough.

'What if she tells him where I am? What if he comes looking for Boo?' I say with difficulty, my chest tight. I recall Neil's inappropriate joke on the ferry, born from his own nervousness: . . . *find him stowed away under the wheel arches*. . .

A shadow falls across Jeanie's face. I shiver with the sudden sensation of cold; I know she cannot protect me. But firmly she says, 'you are not alone anymore, Martha.'

And I believe her.

There is another bout of giggles from the living room. The sound seems to lighten the atmosphere that has descended with the talk of painful things. My blood runs warm once more.

'But this new lad of yours seems nice,' Jeanie says.

'Neil's gay, Jeanie.' I don't have the strength to dance tactfully around the truth.

She falters. 'Oh.' Then hastily changes the subject. 'Your other friend who you've brought with you – what's his name again?'

I tell her, and she repeats it.

'Unusual, aren't they, his eyes?' she adds.

I nod. I want to tell her that unusual as they may be, there is a look in his eyes that speaks of kindness and. . . something else I cannot put into words.

'Where is he from?'

'I don't know,' I say, realising with surprise that I haven't even asked him this simplest of questions. 'I think he is running away from something.' I smile weakly. 'But then, so are we.'

Jeanie smiles too. 'You can all stay as long as you need to.'

'Jeanie –,' My eyes begin to refill with tears: relief at finally reaching a safe place; fear of being a burden to her.

She shakes her head, smiling still.

'We could do with some life in this old place again.'

Malik is visibly embarrassed at being invited to stay in the house. He pulls at the hem of his sleeve, stammers out a few syllables but seems unable to find the right words.

'Don't be so coy, Malik,' Neil says between mouthfuls of homemade bread, having already made himself quite at home. 'You may as well stay until you've figured out where it is that you're going to.'

No more is said on the subject. Malik, apparently eager to earn his keep, throws himself into any set of tasks that comes his way. He soon has the fire roaring in the open grate, the small sitting room infused with the comforting smell of peat smoke. He is careful not to let Boo too close. I watch, content in this new warmth, as he puts on a playful theatrical performance for her, blowing on his fingers – wriggling them in the air like flickering flames – to show her that the fire is hot and must not be touched. Giggling, she reaches for his hands and blows raspberries on his fingertips, and he collapses with laughter. It is not long before she begins to grow sleepy. Malik disappears into the kitchen and I nurse Boo, sinking in the heat of the fire, my eyelids drooping to the soothing sounds of clanging pots and boiling water. Neil is asleep in an armchair, exhausted from the long drive here.

Then the evening meal is ready; Boo sleeps and Neil wakes. Jeanie's husband has returned again from the field, peeling off his wet overalls before he joins us at the table. It is our first proper meal in days. Outside, darkness has fallen, too soon. I am too tired to think. I sit beside Malik, and his presence is comforting.

5

Rasmus

May. The ice that covered the fjord had started to break into untidy fragments, as though the ground itself had fallen away. Rasmus watched from the harbour as the year's first supply ship approached, long-anticipated, ploughing the new inky waters. The sound of cracking ice echoed like gun shots through the village. The children, assembled at the quay side in shirt sleeves despite the cold, cheered the ship's arrival. Rasmus's heart, however, was heavy.

Both Snorri and Birdie had begun to make preparations to leave. Equipment had been assembled, checked, repaired, discarded; personal possessions had been retrieved from the corners of the hut in which the three men had passed a civil yet cool winter of few words. Neither of his companions gave any acknowledgment that Rasmus might not do the same – he might choose to stay. Yet... could he stay? It seemed as though the decision were not his to make.

He would return to England, to Manchester's dreary walls. Here he could draw up as much publicity as possible surrounding the expedition – a pointless endeavour, he felt, given that they had achieved nothing. *Nothing*. The word tasted bitterly satisfying in his mouth. But with a proper written report (perhaps even a book – he could make it sound romantic, adventurous), a collection of well-arranged photographs and various articles in the right publications, he might at least receive funding for a second trip. Without Snorri this time; and certainly without Birdie. In the meantime, perhaps the dust would settle in Angmagssalik and his child's "curse" would be forgotten. Then he might return as a friend once more.

But there was also Judith. His wife. His young, innocent wife, who had trusted him to return to her from the north. Unknowingly, she would welcome back an adulterer. He dug his hand into his pocket for his cigarette case, his beating heart calmed a little with the comforting smell of tobacco as he retrieved the wedding ring from inside, fingered it tentatively – a sacred, terrifying object. He slipped it onto his ring finger, and laughed bitterly at the sudden recollection of his fantasy, while crossing the ice cap, that he would lose the finger to frostbite and the ring be made redundant.

He would wear it nevertheless, as a reminder that some things are best kept secret. At once his heart hardened with the thought: Birdie would tell Judith, if he were not there to prevent it. He must return. He would not let Birdie win.

Another baby, a girl this time; she had a different mother, yet he was a father again. Judith fed the baby powdered milk from a bottle – the doctor had told her it was more hygienic, she said. Rasmus did not mind; he enjoyed feeding the baby himself as she stared up at him with wide, blue eyes. Both of them, blue.

Then, not three years later – gone in the blink of an eye – he became father to another child. A boy. Rasmus pushed the pram along paved, narrow streets; fed the baby artificial milk in the stillness of the nights, and all the while thought about his other son – his first son – the son his wife knew nothing about. What did he look like now? Still just like his mother, probably – and she, as beautiful as ever in the timeless clarity of his memory. Perhaps he had already learned to hunt, to kayak, to fish. Or perhaps he was an outcast, cursed by his mixed heritage – by that one colourless eye.

There was something comfortable and reassuring in the familiarity of this day-to-day family life, and yet it oppressed him. He wrote articles for the National Geographic; co-authored research papers on Peary, Franklin and others, those heroes of his childhood; made a name for himself in this Western world of Polar exploration.

And year after year he felt himself suffocate, slowly, under the weight of it all.

It kept him going, his secret; the life that one day he would return to. *One day*, when the time was right.

6

Martha

Here, the days are unpredictable. The weather is wild, an unstoppable force of nature. The wind whips around the house like a prowling animal, slamming doors and whistling through cracks in the stone walls. We draw heavy-woven curtains around the window frames, try to keep the fire lit. Jeanie sings sweetly over the howling.

But there is always work to be done. Jeanie and Alastair are often out in the storms and the gales, tending to the animals or the garden, or repairing damage to the buildings. There is an old croft house across the sheep fields, which Alastair has been renovating. Jeanie mentions one evening that when it is finished it might make a good home for me, Neil and Boo. I know she means well, yet my heart sinks at the thought. I am beginning to doubt that Neil will stay in Shetland for much longer, for he does not seem at home here. Most days, waif-like and intimidated by the wildness of our current home – our new home – he cowers into a comfortable chair by the fire, buried in a book, and will not venture outside.

Malik, however, needs no encouragement to join in with Alastair and Jeanie's efforts with the house and the animals. His energy seems limitless; he is growing less pale by the hour. I help in the house where I can – cook and clean, with the baby in tow, for I feel I must earn my keep if I do not wish to live alone in the old croft house. On drier days I walk with Boo wrapped snuggly against my chest in the sling, down to the post office or the harbour, and watch seagulls wheel, as the winter cold gnaws at my bones, and I think about what it would be like if Malik were to stay, then the croft house would not seem so empty.

The daylight hours are so few that each day soon passes. As dusk begins to fall I look out over the wild waters and rain-drenched rocks and my heart grows warm with the anticipation of welcoming back those who have been out in the weather's wrath. Malik peels off his sodden overalls and kicks off his muddy boots before shuffling as close to the fire place as he can. His eyes are animated, his skin browned. He holds his arms out to Boo, squeezes giggles from her, and the geometric patterns on his forearms snake and intertwine in the dancing light of the fire.

While Boo sleeps Jeanie teaches me to spin the sheep's fleece into yarn. The wool is soft and greasy between my fingers; I create lumpy string that twists and snaps on the wheel, but I am proud of it. Laughing, I tell Jeanie that I will knit my daughter a hat that will be too itchy for her to wear.

I count the minutes until Boo wakes again, inevitably. Sometimes she is content to sit on Jeanie's lap – sometimes Malik's – rest her head back and watch me at my work. With the rhythmic spin of the wheel and the gentle heat of the fire her eyelids soon begin to droop.

Sleep does not visit me as easily, however. When the fire has been raked over and the lights all extinguished I lie awake in the bed beside my daughter and my head reels. It was agreed that Malik and Neil would share the twin bedroom, to give me and the baby some space. But I do not want space;

I am scared in the dark on my own. I find myself listening out for the creak of the front door opening, heavy footsteps tripping up the stairs, slurred swearing as *he* invariably trips over one of our daughter's play things left on the floor: the sounds that I came to dread the most.

Instead I hear the muffled footsteps and click of the door that indicate Jeanie's husband, Alastair, getting up to use the bathroom. Sometimes I hear Neil's laughter from the bedroom, over the wind's howl, and I wonder what he and Malik could be talking about. I swallow down the lump of jealousy that rises in my throat, remind myself that we are safe at least, my daughter and I – for now.

She wakes early each morning – too early. She chatters away, bounces on the bed, pulls at my hair and squeals, and I carry her swiftly downstairs so she doesn't wake those who are still rightly asleep. I wish they would wake up. I wrap myself and Boo in jumpers, turn on electric lights in the winter darkness, but my body aches with cold and tiredness.

Sometimes, Boo slides ahead of me, backwards down the stairs, smiling and eager as she crawls on the cold stone floor around the doorway and into the kitchen. One morning, after we have been staying in the house for nearly three weeks, I hear her break into a surprised squeal as I am still halfway down the staircase. My imagination reels with absurd ideas, strange surprises that this old house could have thrown up on a still February morning before the dawn. But I see that it is only Malik, though he himself appears as a spectre in the unexpected lamplight.

He slips his paintbrush into a glass of murky water on the kitchen table and picks an approaching Boo up into his lap, chides her gently in his strange, guttural language as her fingers reach out for the painting he has been working on. I can't help but look: he has painted the view from outside the house, just as I remember it in the daylight. A swirl of winter

219

colours above a stormy slate sea, the indistinct shapes of birds wheeling over dark cliffs. It is as I remember it, and yet there is something more in the strokes of his paintbrush, an otherworldly beauty that I had not noticed in this place, that I had not looked attentively enough to find. I turn my gaze curiously to the artist and those mismatched eyes that capture the beauty that I cannot even see.

'Alastair found me some paints,' he says awkwardly as I catch his eye, as though he is apologising.

'I. . . I didn't know you could paint,' I say feebly. Something sinks within my stomach with the thought that perhaps I should have been the one to ask him what I could do to make him feel more at home. Would he like some paints, knitting needles – a book to read? I do not know him at all.

I lose myself once more in the sweeping curves and contours of his painting.

'It's beautiful, Malik.' My voice is quiet. From the corner of my eye I see him look at me and I sense, with a feeling of comfort, that he has taken my praise in earnest.

'I'll make some tea, shall I?' Without waiting for an answer, nor meeting his eyes, I turn away and begin to heat up the stove. I collect the cups, prepare the teapot, anything to keep busy. My hands tremble as I try to hold the kettle steady under the stream of water from the tap. It must be the cold, I tell myself.

Malik slides a piece of clean paper in front of Boo, where she sits on his lap, and lets her make watery scribbles with the paintbrush. He runs the tip of another brush around the shapes and lines that she makes, adds to them, colours blending on the white paper. I cannot help but watch them, absorbed in their private dance. My heart rises with elation, yet is heavy with the memory of things that never were: her father could never relate to her in this way. Perhaps I am to blame: I was the one who fell pregnant; he did not want a child, not yet.

Boo grows tired of painting just as the kettle comes to the boil. I place the teapot on the table (Malik helpfully moves the paintings out of harm's way) and, giving Boo a piece of bread and butter to suck on, hoist her up onto my lap as I sit down. Malik says something unintelligible as I slide a cup of tea over to him. I must inadvertently have looked bewildered, for he smiles and repeats the word. 'It means *thank you*,' he adds.

'Tell me again.'

He speaks more clearly this time, pronouncing each syllable. *'Qujanaq.'*

I try to move my lips around the guttural sounds, but give up almost immediately, laughing in embarrassment and inwardly chastising myself for making such an exhibition of self-consciousness.

Malik, however, looks positively thrilled. 'Try again,' he encourages, his eyes bright and attentive. *'Qujanaq.'*

I copy the sounds he makes as he repeats the word after each of my attempts, until eventually his round face breaks into a wide smile.

'There! Now you can speak my language.'

My lips tingle.

I hear the creak of floorboards above us – the sound of Jeanie or Alastair moving about in the bedroom. Startled, I jump up to my feet, almost knocking over my cup of tea. I reposition Boo on my left hip, dizzy with the heat that is rising into my cheeks. With my free hand I move a spoon from the table to the sink – keeping busy, preoccupied.

'I can help you,' Malik says from behind me as I begin to retrieve pots and pans with which to prepare the breakfast.

Shamefully, I imagine he is perplexed by my sudden flustered display. As am I, in fact.

'No, no.' I strive to sound natural. 'You just, err, enjoy your tea.'

But I feel his hands around Boo, taking the weight of her from my hip. A pan handle slips from my grasp, clatters carelessly against the stove.

'Then I can hold the baby,' he says. Quite without meaning to I meet his eyes as he takes hold of my gurgling daughter. He smiles.

'You don't need to do everything, Martha.'

Footsteps on the stairs.

I relinquish my grasp, turn away before, I hope, he notices the awkward colour that I know has flushed even more deeply across my cheeks. Jeanie bids us both a good morning as she enters the kitchen. She coos over the baby in Malik's arms.

At long last the sun rises in a clouded sky. Once breakfast is finished and the animals fed, we all walk together down the lane to the church. Neil trails behind, reluctant to join, yet persuaded by Alastair's no-nonsense approach to chide him out of the house. The fresh air, at least, appears to blow some of the lines of anxiety from his face. Jeanie pushes Boo in the pram – a great, clunking thing that Alastair unearthed from the depths of one of the outbuildings. It looks to be older than me. I had helped Jeanie to clean it up, enjoying the look of joyous recollection on her face as she scrubbed at the enormous metal wheels and blew the dust off the canvas rain hood, telling me stories of when her own children were babies. I see the same look on her face now as she pushes along her great-niece. The chubby, pink-cheeked face of my daughter peers out from under her knitted bonnet, and she periodically rubs a fist into her tired eyes. I lay my hand on the sleeve of Jeanie's coat, wordlessly asking her to walk a little slower in the hope that Boo might fall asleep before we reach the church. She slows her steps, winks at me discreetly, and my heart glows with the notion that she has understood without words having to pass between us.

She looks beautiful, I think to myself. Fresh-faced and bright-eyed, her grey hair wrapped into an elegant bun sitting at the nape of her neck. Loose strands of hair flutter freely about her forehead, streaming in the wind – wild and free, I imagine, the reflection of her soul. She does not obscure her face with make-up, dye her hair unnatural colours or wear fake nails like my mother. She is the most beautiful woman I have ever seen. My heart swells with anticipation as I recall her promise, that morning, to take me into Lerwick one day to buy some cloth so that I can sew a plaid dress for myself like hers, or a woollen pinafore, and maybe even a checked coat. My spinning, too, is already beginning to improve. Jeanie says I can earn some money from selling the yarn that I spin from the Shetland fleeces, once my work is good enough.

We park the pram just inside the church doors. Malik lingers behind to help me tuck the blankets around Boo's peaceful, sleeping body. My bare hands are stiff from the cold; they brush against his as we both strive to make my sleeping daughter comfortable. The warmth of his fingers against mine causes me to shiver inside my coat. He catches my eye, he smiles.

The sound of the organ has already begun to ring out from inside the hall. It plays louder as Malik pushes on the door, holds it open for me. Thankfully, Boo does not wake. I slip through the doorway and into a pew at the back of the small church, watch Malik as he closes the door quietly, and I glow with warmth as he offers me another wordless smile before sitting down beside me. I slide the coat from my shoulders, brush the windswept hair from my eyes.

Most of the pews are filled with people, old and young; I can see the back of Neil's head, beside Alastair's, a few rows in front. Only Malik and I have taken a seat on the bench at the back. Alone together, so it seems. I revel in the heat of him beside me, so welcome after the wind's cold breath. He has pulled off his jumper, rolled up his shirt sleeves. He slides his hands inquisitively over the leather cover of the hymnbook that he has picked up from the pew, and I imagine tracing my fingers along the black lines inked into his forearms, following their pattern over his dark skin. The heat of the full room rushes to my head.

Inappropriate thoughts, and in a church of all places; inappropriate thoughts in which I long to lose myself, in these glorious moments while my daughter sleeps and I remember that I am so much more than just a mother. My own mother would talk of sin if she were here now, placed between me and this man whom I hardly know.

Try as I might to alter the course of my thoughts, I am acutely aware of his still, calm presence throughout the service. After the final hymn and prayer – during which Malik remains silent and I, consumed by sinful thoughts, only mouth the words with little thought – a tea trolley is wheeled up the aisle. Feet move, clothes rustle, and conversations begin. I look up as Neil appears beside the pew. He blows out an exaggerated sigh from between his lips, slumping his shoulders forwards, though I can tell from the glint behind his glasses that this is largely for show.

'Might as well stay for a cuppa,' he says, 'since we're here.'

Alastair strolls up behind him, and with a slight incline of his grey-bearded head, motions for Malik to accompany him. I rise to my feet along with Malik, and watch them slip away into the gathering. Both few of words, I think – they seem to get along so well.

Boo is still sleeping soundly in the pram: I inch open the door, as quietly as I can, to check. The coldness of maternal guilt spreads through my warmed body as I realise that I had not given one thought to my daughter during the service, as I sat beside Malik. The pram could have blown away and I would not have known. I *cannot* be anything more than a mother – just a mother. My heart sinks with the knowledge that Malik, too, must see me in this way. He is fond of Boo – that I can see – and I am simply the one who loves and cares for her.

My feet drag a little as I walk back inside the church hall. Neil pours us both some tea as I return, snatches a handful of chocolate biscuits.

'So I'll tell people she's my daughter, shall I?' he says casually, his mouth full of crumbs. 'And you're my fiancée, only we can't afford to get married just yet. And we're going to have two children – a boy next, of course. And we attend church every single Sunday without fail, always have done. Perhaps if we tell them that, they'll overlook the sex-outside-of-marriage thing.'

I try not to smile. 'I think we'll tie ourselves in knots with all that pretence.'

Neil shrugs. 'Or perhaps you could say that your "fiancé" is in the army, currently deployed somewhere in Russia. Missing in action, even. Or a prisoner of war.'

I accept as he offers me another biscuit.

'And you?'

He thinks for a moment, rubbing the bridge of his nose.

'I could be your half-brother, a worn-down banker from the city looking for a more fulfilling way of life up in the Wild North.'

'You'll be needing a haircut for that to stand,' I say, brushing a lock of hair from his shoulder.

He grins. 'But what about Malik?' he furrows his brows, as though this story of pretence is a particularly difficult one to conjure.

I run my eyes over the room's occupants. It is not difficult to spot Malik: black hair quite unlike anyone else's, skin so many shades darker. He appears to be in conversation with a middle-aged, smartly dressed man, oblivious to the many curious glances that are thrown in his direction. Alastair stands by, nursing a cup of tea, following the discussion with his kind, dark eyes. Occasionally he exchanges a few words with the man, nodding his head, looking to Malik. I get the impression that the other man is acting as an interpreter.

'We could say Malik is a foreign dignitary on a cultural exchange visit to Shetland?' I suggest.

Neil snorts. 'Dressed like that?' He watches the animated conversation for a moment longer. 'What do you think they could be talking about?'

My curiosity is awakened, but I do not get the chance to voice my wandering thoughts for Jeanie appears by my side, takes my arm, and leads me to awkward greetings with friendly-looking neighbours.

Malik says nothing about his conversation with the man in the church. Yet I can see that he is not deliberately secretive, only quiet as usual; hesitant, perhaps, with his use of English.

We sit around the fire as the sky drips with darkness, stomachs full from Sunday dinner; on this a day of rest. Coffee brews in the pot. Alastair disappears from the room and returns with a bottle of Scottish whisky and a jumble of crystal glasses. He pours a measure for himself and one for Neil, then holds up the bottle, offering it around the room. Jeanie and I decline – I have never liked whisky; besides, Boo is feeding intently at my breast.

'Whisky, Malik?' Alistair asks in his broad Shetland lilt. Malik shakes his head. 'Just a wee dram?'

Malik shifts his knees in apparent discomfort at Alastair's questioning, averts his eyes towards the fire beside which he is sitting, cross-legged on the rug before the hearth.

'My mother drank, a lot,' he says apologetically. 'It killed her. Her brother, too.'

For a moment, no one speaks. Alastair nods in understanding, a gesture which Malik, returning him a meek smile, seems to appreciate.

Neil raises his glass, his cheeks pink and his eyes shining from below his mop of hair.

'This is good stuff, Malik – medicinal. It will cure you rather than kill you.'

I glance over at Malik, fearing Neil may have caused offence. Untactful jokes are his speciality, after all. But Malik only smiles again, his shoulders relaxed once more and the warmth of the glowing fire illuminated in his eyes.

'And it will help the baby sleep,' Neil adds, sending a wink in my direction. I look down at Boo. Her eyelids are beginning to flutter with slumber.

I carry her carefully up to the bedroom and lay beside her on the bed. A quiet place: I hope that she will fall asleep for the night and I might return to the warmth of the fireside and the nervous comfort that I feel in Malik's presence. Boo has just closed her eyes and slipped off the breast when I hear the click of the bathroom door, and moments later Neil's head peers into the bedroom.

'She asleep?' he whispers. The dim light of the lamp reflects in his glasses, obscuring his eyes and making the sight of his disembodied head all the stranger.

I nod. I shift away from Boo, slide my feet off the bed and onto the floor, and begin to button up my blouse.

'Something on your mind?' He would have returned downstairs otherwise, waited for me there.

He slips into the room, twisting his fingers together in thought.

'I want to help him, Martha,' he says, his voice hushed as though he does not want those downstairs to hear what he has to say. 'You know, I've been thinking about why I'm here, what my purpose is here. And I think that's it: I am meant to help him, then everything else will become clear.'

I do not want to question his reasoning, bizarre as it seems to be; there is only one thing that is foremost in my mind.

'What do you mean, *help him*?' My heart begins to sink heavily as it occurs to me that I already know the answer to this question.

'Help him to get to where he needs to go. You know –,' He points a finger towards the ceiling. '– North. Like he said. I'm sure that's what he must have been talking to that man about, in the church.'

My stomach twists with sudden nausea.

'You want him to leave?'

Neil moves closer to me around the foot of the bed. 'I don't want to get rid of him, Martha, it's just –.'

'Then why do you have to interfere, Neil?' I interject.

227

Neil stops in his tracks, looks at me through the interplay of light on the lenses of his spectacles.

'You know he can't stay here, Martha.'

'Jeanie says he can stay as long as he wants,' I contend. There is a shrillness to my half-whispered words that I do not like.

Neil shakes his head.

'He has his own life. You know that. Maybe even his own family, I don't know. But he is looking for something – *somewhere*. And we should help him.'

I do not know what to say. My throat appears to be closing up, choking me. I do not want him to leave. My feelings must be obvious, for Neil sighs, drops his shoulders.

'Oh, Martha, you didn't really think he would stay, did you – for you? *The tall, dark stranger.* Well, not tall, but. . . '

'Don't patronise me, Neil.' I keep my voice steady this time, study the floorboards. Neil chews at his lower lip and for a moment or two neither of us speaks. Then he sighs again, heavily, pushing at the bridge of his glasses with one finger.

'We should do what we can.'

I nod silently. I know that he is right.

7

The man from the church greets us warmly as he ushers us into his home, out of the wildness of the weather. He shakes Neil's hand, then mine.

'Jasper,' he says. He ruffles Boo's fine hair affectionately as she pulls off her damp woollen hat and throws it onto the floor. He welcomes Malik as he would an old friend, and at once they are talking together unintelligibly before Alastair is even through the door. Their conversation sounds different to Malik's distinctive native tongue which I have heard him speak to Boo. Jasper notices me and Neil watching awkwardly, listening without understanding, unsure what to do or where to go in the narrowness of the hallway.

'Your friend speaks very good Danish,' he beams, his accent thick and slurred. 'Come in, Alastair, my friend!'

We hop out of wet shoes, shuffle along the wall; through a doorway into the kitchen. Jasper's wife receives me with a kiss on the cheek, makes a fuss over Boo, delivers something sweet into her little, fat hands and puts the kettle on the stove. We sit together, alone, at the kitchen table. She plies me with homemade scones and we talk together about our children – what else when we do not know each other?

It is warm and comfortable in her company and beside the heat of the stove, yet my body aches with an irritable restlessness. The others have vanished into Jasper's study: the men discussing important worldly matters while the women make their tea, bounce the babies on their knees and keep their noses out of everything. That is the way I was brought up, after all, I think resentfully. I try my best to swallow my negative thoughts; try not to think about the inevitable fact that soon he will leave... Malik. The cake sticks in my throat.

I have just finished my tea when Neil pokes his head around the kitchen door. 'Come and see, Martha.'

I leave Boo with Jasper's wife, my daughter contentedly sucking on buttery scones, and follow Neil. The walls of Jasper's study are lined with bookcases, each one packed with books; from battered leather-bound volumes to small, crisp paperbacks. There are maps tacked up onto the single bare wall, some annotated, some evidently mediaeval, showing a strange, illustrated view of the world and its continents. A historian, Jasper's wife had told me of her husband. Semi-retired now.

The historian himself is intently scanning one of the bookcases as I enter, and does not look around. Neil ushers me over to an old wooden desk. I nearly trip over the typewriter and pile of books that have presumably been temporarily moved onto the carpet to make room for the large map that is spread across the surface and spills over the edges of the desk. Its two top corners are anchored to the desk by glass paperweights. Malik pours over it, moving his hands over the oceans and islands: Great Britain, Shetland, Iceland... He places his finger down, looks at me with bright eyes.

'This is where I come from.'

I lean across the desk on my elbows, to see where his finger lies.

'Who'd have thought it, eh?' Neil pipes up from the other

side of the desk: 'Greenland! Didn't think anyone lived there. I thought it was just ice.'

I glance up at him through the locks of my hair that have fallen out of place, sweeping the North Sea, but as usual it is difficult to discern whether he is being facetious.

'North,' I say quietly, turning my head to Malik. He is level with me, fingers still resting on the crass representation of his homeland. His eyes meet mine, so close that it feels as though we are sharing something secretive, and my stomach lurches. He is from a different world, a different time: there are so many questions that I long to ask him and yet I cannot find my tongue.

I am torn back to the here and now by Jasper's sudden exclamation of triumph. Malik and I straighten up as he deposits an open book onto the desk and taps his finger against a printed monochrome photograph.

'There he is.'

He draws back to allow Malik to see. I notice that there are creases at the corners of Malik's eyes, the brightness vanished, a heavy thoughtfulness as he views the picture: three men standing side by side on an apparent sea of ice, dressed in bulky fur parkas, their feet and shins tied into large skin boots.

'There *who* is?' asks Neil, moving around the desk and craning his neck to see the point of interest, evidently not noticing Malik's sudden detachment.

'My father,' Malik says flatly, his voice only just audible. He does not look up from the photograph.

Neil leans in closer and pushes his spectacles up the bridge of his nose so that he can better read the text that is written beneath: "*Polar explorer, Charles Rasmus Stewart and companions Snorri Eggertsson and Robert 'Birdie' Smith, 1948.*"

He snorts, mutters, 'I see why they called him *Birdie*, that one. Well, well,' he adds, straightening his back, 'Our mysterious stranger has an origin.'

Malik does not smile, nor respond in any way – has eyes only for the photograph; I wonder if he has heard Neil's meaningless remarks. I dare not ask if I can take a closer look, not just now.

'Is that who you're looking for, Malik?' Neil continues: 'Your father?'

Malik shakes his head.

'He's dead.'

'Oh.' Neil's cheeks colour slightly in embarrassment. 'Sorry, man. Sorry to hear that.'

'I read it in the paper,' Jasper offers by way of condolence. 'A heart attack, was it? – very sudden, they said.'

'He killed himself.' Malik says it matter-of-factly, without looking up. An awkward silence descends in the room and reigns for some moments.

'Who is this, Jasper?' Malik points to one of the other monochrome men, further ignoring the topic that has just been uncomfortably broached.

Jasper moves in to take Neil's place.

'Snorri something. Let's see, what was he called... yes, Snorri Eggertsson. An Icelander.' He straightens up, rubs the backs of his hands, one after the other. 'I think I might be able to get hold of his address, if that would help you? I have contacts at the Polar Research Institute in Cambridge.'

Malik looks up at him with an intensity that unsettles me. There is a singlemindedness to his gaze, an indication that he has already forgotten everything around him. He answers Jasper in Danish.

I do not feel right being in this room; it is not my place. My throat is tight, the bookcases are imposing, closing over my head. I am dizzy from an unexplained heat. I slip out into the hallway, through the front door and gently close it behind me. I stand on the doorstep, spattered by drizzle, rushed at by the wind. Gradually, the heaviness lifts from my chest.

The bay is spread out below me under low cloud, drenched in water – the sea smudged by the wind into indistinct, murky colours. It could be one of Malik's watercolours, I think to myself.

My chest hurts.

I start as I hear the sound of footsteps at my back. Malik slips through the half-open door, apparently not wanting to let rain into the house, and gently pulls it to behind him.

'Are you all right, Martha?'

I nod wordlessly. The loose hair around my face blows across my eyes in damp streams. I tuck the flyaway locks behind my ear. I will not, *cannot* bring my eyes to meet his: I fear I may say something, do something that might give away my feelings.

'I'd better go see to the baby,' I mutter, and step towards the door, my movements awkward and self-conscious. My arm brushes against Malik's as I pass, and he lays his hand against the sleeve of my jumper – the wool decorated with droplets of rain – as if to stop me. My gaze slides up to his, momentarily.

'She's all right, Martha.'

But I cannot stay out here, with him. I wrench open the door with shaking hands, swallowing unshed tears, and return to my daughter.

———

I hear Neil's words on repeat inside my head, a looped tape that I cannot switch off: *we should do what we can to help him.*

One morning, the following week, I bundle Boo into the over-large pram, swathed in all her blankets and woollen layers – as is now customary for her mid-morning nap – and set off with a pounding heart down the lane. I catch sight of the distant figures of Alastair and Malik in one of the sheep fields, and involuntarily I glance down at the basket beneath the pram to make sure that the envelope containing Malik's paintings is still there. My breath catches in my throat. I will make sure to replace them before he returns from the fields, before he notices that they are missing.

The curator handles the paintings with near-reverence as he slides each one from the envelope and onto his desk. He peers at the rolling watercolour hills and tempestuous sea through spectacles perched on the end of his nose. I am light-headed; my heart hammers still. Boo sleeps soundly outside, wrapped up against the wind.

'These are really something,' he says at length, glancing up at me over the rim of his glasses. 'You say your friend painted them?'

I nod, encouraged by his praise.

'Yes. Malik. You might have seen him around the village. Black hair. Um. Eyes are different colours.' I twist my fingers together awkwardly.

The curator pushes his glasses back into place and smiles at me warmly.

'Well, Martha, you can tell Malik that I would very much like to exhibit his work here – it's all for the community, after all. I dare say we'll manage to sell a few.'

I leave the pram outside the front door as I arrive home, Boo still sleeping soundly. It is later than I thought, and Jeanie is preparing lunch. Alastair and Malik sit together at the kitchen table before a selection of pieces of leather, needles, thread and leather thongs. Alastair's brows are drawn together in concentration as he inspects what appears to be a boot, sewn from some sort of skin or hide and decorated with strips of coloured leather; he runs his fingers over the sole where, at the ball of the foot, the hide has been worn through entirely, leaving a smooth-edged hole. Neil lounges on a chair at the end of the table, his nose in a book, though he peers over the top of his spectacles at the array of tools and materials on the table.

Malik looks up as I linger in the doorway. He smiles warmly; his eyes are bright. I can only give a brief, awkward smile in return, conscious of the paintings that I clutch under my arm, hidden inside their brown paper envelope. My throat is tight. Immediately I jog upstairs and into the bedroom that Neil and Malik share; slide the paintings back into their rightful place in the drawer in the desk where Malik sometimes works; stumble into my own bedroom and sit heavily on the end of the bed, trying to regulate my ragged breathing.

Later in the evening I sit beside the fire, watching Malik from the corner of my eye as he works: he runs the thick needle deftly through the hide of his boot, entwining the cord around the curves of the heel and toe. It is not long before he has finished: the sole is replaced, the boot mended; joy brims from his eyes as he inspects his work.

'Look, Martha.' The weight of his body sinks into the sofa beside me. The furniture is old and worn; I am almost pushed on top of him as the cushions shift. I tense, hold my own body in its place, though I do not want to.

Without speaking he proudly shows me the new stitching on the sole, and the pieces of dyed sealskin that decorate the top of the boot. I watch the way in which his hands move over the softened leather, cradling its weight, smoothing supple creases. I nod my head in appreciation of his work, unsure of what to say. Then the words rise, almost unbidden: a confession.

'Malik, I, err... your paintings...'

He looks at me expectantly, waiting for the remainder of the sentence to struggle out past my lips.

'The curator at the community gallery – the one in the village – he, err, wants to exhibit them. He really likes them. Thinks you might be able to sell some.' I look away, conscious of the awkwardness in my voice. 'I just thought as well, you know... it might help you. If you're needing money to get back home, I mean.'

I attempt a smile, to show that I mean well. And as I meet his eyes I find that they are looking so directly into mine that all further words of explanation escape me. I cannot look away.

'Thank you,' he says quietly.

The sound of Boo's waking cries reaches my ears. I jump to my feet, tear myself away from the heat of the fire, the heat of him.

I take the stairs two at a time, shivering in the dark and the cold. February is almost at an end. Then, spring will come. And I know that now he will not, cannot stay.

———————

Malik's paintings look wonderful, mounted on the walls of the gallery. Some of the views are ones that I recognise: snapshots taken from the door of the cottage during a storm, or from the path along the cliff where we sometimes walked together, in comfortable silence on a still day. In more than one of his paintings I can see a watercolour figure in a sheep-filled field in the distance – it must be Alastair going about the day's work. In the bottom corner of one of the sweeping landscapes I see Neil's campervan: an orange smudge blotted onto the winding road. On another I can just make out the figure of a woman standing on the hillside and looking out to the wide sea, her long skirt billowing in the wind and her hair blowing about her face. *It could be me*, I think, and my stomach lurches.

But I dare not ask Malik about the painting. I look over again to where he stands at the other side of the busy room, in conversation with yet another of the exhibition's guests. He drums the fingers of his right hand against the top of his thigh – the only sign as to his nervousness – and I smile to myself each time I see him gesture with his hands as he speaks, knowing – although I cannot hear over the general chatter in the room – that he is trying to find the right words in English.

Unintentionally, I catch his eye as he looks across the room. He smiles, and I see him apparently excuse himself from his conversation with a woman who I recognise as a friend of Jeanie's. He walks over to me, his footfall soft, clad now in his sealskin boots, pulled up over the hem of his jeans as usual. When he had finished mending his strange boots – *kamiks*, he called them – he gave his other boots to Neil, joking that he never wanted to see them again. I had wondered what it could mean, the relief that I had seen in his eyes as Neil took the boots from his hands.

He stands next to me, but we do not speak. I am conscious of my hands, my arms dangling with nothing to do or to hold, for Jeanie has taken Boo from me and is carrying her around the room, bouncing her on her hip. I can sense Malik's eyes on me, but I cannot look at him. My heart is hammering. It seems to stop altogether as I feel his hand on my arm.

'Come with me, Martha,' he says, close to my ear so that I can hear him. I allow him to lead me through the gathering of people and through the door to the curator's office. It is quieter in here, and empty save for the two of us – alone together. I stand awkwardly as he reaches for his backpack and lifts it up onto the desk in the middle of the room. He rifles through it and pulls out a paper folder. As his eyes meet mine I see within them a glimmer of nervousness.

'I made some other paintings,' he says quietly, as though he is admitting a secret to me alone.

He passes a small wad of papers into my hands. I take them carefully, hardly daring to breathe, for I can sense his eyes on me as I run my gaze over the uppermost picture. My self-consciousness, however, is quickly forgotten. The style of his painting is unmistakable, yet these watercolours depict somewhere different to the bleak hills and stormy waters of Shetland. A place where the hills have morphed into distant mountains, and the world is infused with the blended colours of sunlight upon ice and snow. Similar to his paintings in the gallery, some are simple, sweeping watercolours of light, colour and landscape; others also depict the people within these places, single moments captured in time. In one scene I see a black-haired woman breastfeeding an infant; in another a man is sprawled on his belly near the bottom of the frame –

wearing kamiks, similar to Malik's. He has raised his rifle up to his shoulder, ready to shoot a seal that lies some distance away on the ice, apparently oblivious to the hunter. I see colourful wooden houses pitched upon the black-white of rock and ice, sleds pulled by dogs that look like wolves, and I think how strange and how magical this world is, from which he has come. I can picture him within this landscape – his real home – and my heart swells with joy and aches with sadness, both at the same time.

'Malik,' I say in awe. But I get no further, for as I reach the last painting my heart skips a beat once more. The landscape is nothing but ice – skilfully and simply painted – and in the distance stalks the single, solitary form of a great, white bear. I can sense the power of the creature from the watercolour brushstrokes.

I shake my head in disbelief.

'I. . . I keep dreaming about a bear, just like this one.' I stammer out an explanation to Malik, laughing a little to show that I am aware of how ridiculous this sounds. 'I've never even seen a bear.'

I look at him, and he smiles warmly but does not laugh.

'You don't know the strength you have inside you, Martha.'

I keep looking at him, wordlessly, wondering what he could mean. Then there is the sound of footsteps. I glance over to the door, and there is Neil, leaning the top half of his body around the doorframe and into the small office.

'Ah. There you are.' He grins at Malik, throws him a wink.

'Baby wants you, Martha,' he adds.

I suppress the urge to stride over to the door and knock the glasses from his face. *Could I not just have this one moment?* I sigh inwardly. Of course not. *The baby needs me*; Malik is leaving, he has to return to his home that he clearly pines for – I feel the longing for this place seeping from the paintings that I still hold in my hand, angled away from Neil's gaze as though to protect Malik's secret. I am certain that he would not stay with me, even if he knew how my body aches in his presence. *The baby needs me* – yes, it's probably for the best.

I slide the paintings back into his hands and smile apologetically. I can feel his eyes on me as I leave the room, reluctant to return to the busy gallery. My body is here, but my mind is somewhere else.

———

Neil and I stand together in the busy harbour. My eyes sting from the smoke that billows out of the waiting ferry as it swallows up one queuing car at a time, and I cannot stop the tears that spill onto my cheeks. I am losing another friend. First Malik, now Neil.

'I don't want you to leave,' I sob as I grasp Neil's hand in mine. 'But I want you to be happy.' Neil embraces me again and I bury my head in his chest, thinking that I would have said the same words to Malik when he left the previous week, had I had the courage to do so. I had suspected then that Neil would be leaving soon, too, though he had not yet said as much. I try to apologise for bringing him to this place, but he only shakes his head.

'Don't be silly, Martha. We escaped – together – remember?'

When he releases me from our embrace, I see that his eyes are clouded behind his glasses.

'You'll come and visit, though, won't you? A city break.'

I smile, nod my head. 'Yeah, of course.'

I feel a rush of warmth through my body, for I know that there will be much more for him down in London. He can be free in the city; live the way he wants to.

'Write to me when you get there,' I add. 'Don't make me worry about you.'

'Love you, Martha.' He plants a soggy kiss on my forehead. Then he hops back into the campervan, slams the door shut and blows me another kiss through the open window.

I wave tearfully as the van rumbles away into the vehicle deck of the ferry. I walk back into the ferry terminal, where

Jeanie is waiting with Boo in the pram – having already given Neil a fond farewell before allowing the two of us a proper goodbye. She slides her arm around my shoulder as I wipe away my tears with the end of my coat sleeve.

'All right, hen?'

'Maybe I should be going with him,' I choke. 'We've always been in this together, me and Neil.'

Neil and Malik – my two friends – both of them gone.

'He's not leaving you forever,' Jeanie says comfortingly.

I know that she is talking about Neil, still my heart skips a beat as I think that she could mean Malik. Neil had told me more than once that I must move on from my thoughts of Malik, accept that he had travelled back home, yet I cannot shake off the feeling that he might come back. He *could* come back. 'It's not like he's from outer space,' I had said to Neil, half-jokingly. But he had only raised his eyebrows, and my insides had twisted with anger towards him for failing to give wings to my hopeless dreams and forced optimism.

And now, it is only me and my daughter.

'Oh, Jeanie,' I sob in a sudden tide of sadness and self-pity. 'I don't want to get in your way.'

'Martha!' Jeanie chides gently, rubbing her hand against my arm. 'Leave the baby with us, then – she's a joy.'

I catch her eye and smile back at her through my tears.

8

Rasmus

May 1973

He could tell by the succinct knock at the door that it was
Birdie. The man did not come often, yet always uninvited;
Rasmus felt the weight of his presence on his soul before he
even arrived. He imagined that Birdie alighted on his front
doorstep from nowhere, folding away his great, white wings
and turning his beak towards the ground – to all appearances
a friendly visitor.

Rasmus hesitated in the hallway. It occurred to him that he
could pretend he was not at home. He imagined his unwanted
visitor stalking around the outside of the house, sticking his
beak through the cracks where the windows had been left
slightly ajar, searching – and the thought made him shiver.
No, he would answer the door and calmly tell the man that
now was not a good time. And he need not feel guilty, for
this was the truth, though he would certainly not mention
the reason. His family life was no business of Birdie's. He
wished sometimes that it were no business of his, either.

Truth be told, he did not miss his daughter, though she had not been gone long, and his veins still bubbled with anger and guilt. Had he driven her away? He was not sure. They had argued. But then, they had always argued. She was a defiant, headstrong girl, Marianne; they had always struggled to see eye to eye. And the boy... he was the complete opposite: such an apathetic adolescent, it made Rasmus despair. Drank too much, smoked too much, played his records too loudly, refused to get a decent haircut.

'I'm sorry, but now is not a good time,' Rasmus began to say as he opened the door. But he got no further than the first word before Birdie strode in, hunched his shoulders to shuffle off his coat and proceeded to peer with beady eyes into the hallway.

'She's not here,' Rasmus said sharply, irritated with himself for failing to be more assertive, as always.

'Oh, shame,' shrugged Birdie.

Rasmus pursed his lips. He did not like the way that Birdie looked at Judith. He knew what that look meant, even if Judith insisted she did not see it herself.

Birdie showed no signs of leaving, despite Judith's absence – an obvious disappointment to him. Rasmus found himself making a pot of tea in the kitchen while his visitor took a seat at the table, apparently making himself quite at home. For a while neither of them spoke. Rasmus could think of nothing to say; his body felt drained and his heart felt heavy, as it had now for longer than he cared to remember. He could not shake off the numbness that gripped his soul. There was an atmosphere of inevitability to Birdie's visit, he thought: a strange sense of finality that accompanied his presence. Rasmus imagined that he were entertaining a visit from the Grim Reaper himself.

'There's plans for an ethnographic research expedition to Angmagssalik,' said Birdie, as Rasmus took a seat at the kitchen table, placing the teapot between them. 'There's talk of having you on the board of trustees.'

242

'An expedition?' said Rasmus weakly, knowing already that he was too old for such things now.

Birdie looked up as he poured his tea, his sharp, watery eyes seemingly reading deep into Rasmus's thoughts.

'It's too late now, Rasmus,' he said darkly. He set the teapot back down on the table with a low thud and gurgle of water, then looked up, raised his eyebrows sardonically. 'All these years, yet you've never been back.'

Rasmus faltered, unsure whether this was a question, a statement, or perhaps an accusation. Then all at once he understood the glint in Birdie's eyes.

'But you've been back, haven't you?' he said, striving to make the question sound natural, to keep his voice from shaking with an emotion that he could not understand. 'To Angmagssalik.'

Birdie took a sip of tea, leaned back in his chair.

'I work in shipping, Rasmus, of course I've been back.'

Rasmus swallowed. 'You haven't mentioned it before.'

'Didn't think it was important.' Birdie shrugged his shoulders in apparent dismissal, yet Rasmus could see that it was a performance: the man was enjoying this, putting on a show. He had the feeling that this was to be the final act.

His hands shook as he poured himself a cup of tea.

'There's nothing for you to go back for now, Rasmus.' Birdie spoke again as the silence endured for longer than Rasmus had intended. 'It's changed: that way of life you were so obsessed with – that's gone now. No one lives like that anymore; people don't need to hunt or keep dogs. They need money instead, now – they need jobs, only there aren't any. They drink. Everyone drinks.'

Rasmus felt dizzy with nausea; he did not want Birdie to continue. But he needed to hear what the man had to say, he needed to know...

'And... and Ketty?' Rasmus's voice was hesitant. He knew now that he feared the answer.

'Ketty's dead, Rasmus,' Birdie replied. 'Too much of the old drink. Her brother, too. And his boy: he put a rope around his neck. Couldn't see what his future could possibly bring. And who can blame him?'

Birdie had turned his eyes away, his former arrogance replaced with a sadness that could not be disguised.

Rasmus watched him. He felt only a sense of emptiness that grew steadily by the second as though it had always been there, as though he had never before felt anything in his soul, and never would. His whole life – an empty shell.

His voice spoke as if from a great distance.

'And the boy? Ketty's boy?'

Birdie looked at him again, and steely-eyed, set his cup down on the table.

'You thought you were special, did you? The only bedfellow? I kept her bed warm as much as you did.' He paused. 'I'm ashamed to admit it now. But we're all human, and all men get lonely sometimes.'

Rasmus shivered. *I kept her bed warm...* He had said it so casually. As though it meant nothing, changed nothing. His throat was dry.

'And the boy...?' he said again.

Birdie shrugged his shoulders once more.

'Could be mine, could be yours. I don't think Ketty even knew herself. But he won't remember either of us, he's no longer a child. He's no one's.'

Silence once more. Rasmus stared at the table.

'Still,' Birdie added quietly, 'Your wife deserves to know. You've kept quiet about it for long enough.'

Rasmus rose slowly to his feet. 'I think you should leave now, Robert.' He spoke calmly, could not bring himself to make eye contact.

We are all human, Birdie had said. And all these years Rasmus had felt as though he were trapped under the wing of the monstrous white gull, waiting until he had gathered enough strength to fight his way to freedom. He saw now,

244

with a lurch of his heavy heart, that this creature he had feared was nothing more than a man. It was the depths of his own imagination against which he had been fighting this lifelong battle.

Birdie appeared to hesitate.

His gaze fixed on the table top, Rasmus inwardly braced himself for one final fight, for unkind words and raised voices. Instead he heard only the muted scrape of the chair on the linoleum floor, footsteps that passed him swiftly by, the soft click of the front door. And then Birdie was gone.

PART THREE

Malik

'There's something I think you should know, Malik.' Snorri turned away from the window, breaking the reverie that had kept him silent for some time. I did not move from my chair, fearing the sudden look of vulnerability that crossed his face as he spoke to me.

'Since you've come this far, I think it is best that you know.'

He clasped his hands behind his back, appeared to grow smaller under the weight of what he was about to say.

'Of course, everyone knew about Rasmus' relationship with your mother, it was no secret. But,' he stopped, sighed heavily.

My breath caught in my throat – in that moment I knew what Snorri was about to say.

'Robert – *Birdie* – was also... *involved* with your mother.'

I dragged the air painfully back into my lungs. *'Involved?'* I shuddered at the sound of this word, heavy with emphasis.

'I can't tell you much more: I tried to stay out of it as best I could,' Snorri continued. He began to pace before the window, shaking his head. 'He was perhaps just trying to get at Rasmus. I don't know. I never understood the feud that those two had between them.' He stopped, looked over at me. 'But you understand what I'm saying... don't you?'

I understood. And I wished that I did not. *Involved.* Involuntarily my hand crept up to touch my right eye – the cursed one. Aqueous blue, full of water, the shallow eye of the gull. Just the same as *his* eyes, hideous and cold, above his beaked nose.

'Of course, no one can know for certain.' Notes of an apology hung in Snorri's voice. 'And I don't know what difference it would make anyway. What's done is done, and I'm sorry you became involved with all this.'

'Did. . . ' I struggled to find my voice. 'Did Rasmus know?'

Snorri shook his head, shrugged his shoulders, both at once.

'Not at first, no. I have reason to believe that Robert told him the truth many years later. Perhaps that's the reason he. . . The icing on top of the cake, as they say. The thing that tipped him over the edge.'

'The reason he killed himself?'

Snorri looked at me, evidently uncomfortable to hear such things said so plainly.

'There was a darkness within him,' he said firmly, in explanation. 'Depression. He said so himself. I believe he hoped that it would not follow him to the north. . . but one cannot escape such things.'

I nodded. I would have risen to my feet, to take my leave of the weight of the conversation, but my body had become numb. I feared my legs would not carry me. It did not matter to me, who my father was. Not anymore.

My stomach completed another sickening twist with the realisation that the man known as Birdie had not come to me as a complete stranger on that day in Angmagssalik, when I had sat mending my kamiks on my front doorstep. I had seen him before; he was a phantom presence in the hazy memories of my early childhood. An occasional visitor – an unpleasant guest – a "friend" of my mother's. It was no wonder the sight of his eyes on that day had filled me with such dread – a nameless dread that only now did I understand.

I glanced at Snorri. He had been watching me as I sank into the timelessness of memory.

'Thank you,' I said. 'For your time. And your honesty.' With both my hands on the desk I pulled myself to my feet; I could not stay in this room any longer.

'You can stay here tonight,' Snorri said, with no hint of a question. 'It is the least I can do.'

I shook my head. 'No. Thank you. I should go. I have to go.'

He walked over to the desk, looseness in his movements, seeming to sense defeat. He picked up a book from the table, began to flick through the pages.

'I'll make a call to the embassy – we can get you on the next plane home from Reykjavík.'

The chairs were horribly uncomfortable, a crippling place to spend the night. I tugged my mended kamiks off my feet and attempted to create a bed across the chairs with my anorak, but still I did not sleep. Every few minutes I would glance over to the door, expecting to see Eqingaleq strolling into the quiet, deserted airport. But there was no sign of him, and I knew in my heart that I would not find him here.

Soon I would see the fjords of Greenland. The pack ice would just be beginning to break up at this time of year, leaving open water for miles and miles, to the east and to the south. . . What kind of a welcome could I expect? There were few who would have missed me. I had sold my dogs. I still wore the curse with which I had been born, for all to see in the unevenness of my eyes. I missed Qallu and his kind-heartedness, but with him now gone from this world forever, I did not feel as though I were returning home. I was more an outsider now than I had ever been.

I knew that my daughter would not remember me, or at least would not understand the nearness of my life and hers, the way in which we were connected. I had been gone for over a year. She might remember me as the strange man with frightening eyes; she might remember the suffocating, hostile

251

atmosphere that descended in her family home whenever I was present. I'd had to beg to be allowed to see her. And I doubted, since I had been gone for so long, that her mother would accept me back into my daughter's life, even if I were to beg as before. She had a new father now, I recalled – a real father. This was much better for her; I did not want my innocent daughter to have to shoulder the burden of a broken family, a half-absent father with a curse, a father who was an outcast.

I closed my eyes and tried to picture her, imagine what she would be like now, as a toddler. But I could remember only baby-plumpness, and at once I saw the image of Boo, laughing as she sucked on the paintbrushes that I had left lying around. And Martha prising them from her little hands and apologising to me breathlessly, as though anxious that I might be angry with her, or the baby. Neil had told me about Boo's father, about how he used to hurt Martha – it had brought tears to my eyes – when Neil was not looking. I had not mentioned my own daughter's existence – to Neil, or to anyone in the house – for fear of what they might think of me. Perhaps they might think that my daughter was kept away from me for the same reason that Boo was taken away from her father, to a place of safety. I feared that they would have stopped me, too, from being with Boo.

And yet, in the end I was the one who had left Boo behind. I had held her in my arms on the quayside, before I must board the ferry which would take me over the broiling sea once more, to Iceland this time. I had not wanted to let go of the solidity of her little body – for where she was, there was Martha also.

I missed the familiar comfort of Martha's presence. I missed the freshness of the sea wind over the low Shetland hills, the way in which it blew through Martha's fine hair and stirred it up into wild streams which she would tuck away behind her ears over and over again. I missed the warmth of the fireside in the evenings, the weight of Boo's head against my chest, her eyelids fluttering as she watched the gentle

252

whir of the spinning wheel. Martha's hands teasing the wool into yarn, her laughter when she made a mistake. Boo would stir slightly at the sound of her mother's voice.

I thought about the paintings that Martha had helped me to sell. She had seemed so apologetic for taking my paintings without my knowledge. My thoughts were heavy with regret that I had not told her how grateful I was to her, how touched I was. I recalled the strange, comfortable nervousness that I had felt as we stood side by side at the opening of the exhibition – my exhibition. I could not speak; I could only watch as she chewed on her bottom lip, chapped with the cold of early spring, wishing she would look up at me.

Why would she not look at me?

I remembered how my insides had broiled just like the ocean as I had watched her look through my paintings of Greenland – the ones that I had not shown to anyone else. I could no longer avoid admitting the truth to myself, the way I felt about her. And I knew that this time it had nothing to do with drink, or the means to a desired end. Yet as I thought back to my brief encounter with the girl I had met in the bar with Michael, the fateful union with the woman who was then to carry my child, and – most painful of all – the mistaken clash between Sun and Moon... I feared that to act on my feelings might cause harm once more.

Eqingaleq would have helped me to understand my thoughts, had he been around. Without his guidance I did not have the confidence to trust myself. So I had said nothing to Martha, only suffered inwardly, paralysed, over the weeks leading up to my departure. And what could I have said to her, anyway? I knew that I had to reach Iceland, I had to find Snorri; still I wished that the remaining days I had with Martha would not pass by so quickly.

I had been waiting for the spring, when the ferry would run to Iceland once more. But I left in winter-cold rain. At the quayside I shook Neil's hand, and Alastair's. Neil bid me good riddance – one of his awkward jokes, I presumed, given the tightness of his grip on my hand and the look in his eyes that I could only interpret as sadness. Alastair grasped my hand in both of his as he assured me with all sincerity that I was welcome in his home anytime. A lump began to rise in my throat, and stuck there as Jeanie embraced me in a way that my own mother had never done. I could not speak, not even to Martha as I embraced her last of all: Martha and Boo together. I wished that someone could have taken Boo from her at this moment, for I longed to hold Martha tightly. But perhaps this would have been more painful. I wrapped my arms somewhat awkwardly around mother and daughter, my cheek to Boo's head. She turned her face to mine and I kissed her on the forehead. Then, before I could think about what I was doing, I kissed Martha on the cheek, too. I turned away quickly, so that I would not have to see her reaction, but I felt her pain nonetheless, aching in my own heart.

Afterwards, I watched as Lerwick disappeared into the smudge of mist and rain. My heart was heavy, but warm after the send-off I had received. I had left Greenland as an outcast, missed by nobody; later I had fled the grey city under a cloud of shame. I had stayed in Shetland for only a few months, yet I felt as though I were leaving home –

– I swung my legs off the edge of the plastic airport chair so quickly that I almost fell onto the floor, hit by the sudden realisation that it was not the beak-nosed man who was now foremost in my thoughts. He had been there for so long, a constant predator, that I had taken his presence for granted.

My thoughts had been clouded by the shame of my past misdeeds, mistakes committed in darkness and drunkenness, overshadowed at all times by the seagull's great, white wings. He had taunted me and I had believed that I was worthless. But he did not haunt my thoughts any longer.

I paced up and down the row of empty chairs. The coolness of the floor against my bare feet brought some calm to the heat of my thoughts. I thought of Martha: reminiscences that flowed in like the tide, pushing aside the agony and self-doubt that had pursued me until now on webbed seagull-feet and the dogged chase of wolves' paws. I thought of Judith, too, and the kindness that she had shown me when the beak-nosed man had brought only pain. One day I would show her my thanks, for the warmth that she had brought into the darkness of my soul.

But for now, I thought, I would tell Martha what I had done, and the wrongs that I had committed. I would explain to her, at last, who I really was and where I had come from. And perhaps she would forgive me, where Judith surely could not.

I knew that I had followed the path that was laid out for me: *fate*, as Eqingaleq had said. But I understood now that in following it I had, in the end, travelled too far to the north. Thankfully, I had some money left, saved up from the paintings that Martha had helped me to sell. If I were to hitchhike back to Iceland's east coast – to the ferry terminal – I could be in Lerwick within the week. With this thought, I pulled on my kamiks with shaking hands, hoisted my bag onto my back and half-ran out of the airport building and into the breaking dawn.

Lerwick was beginning to stir in the morning light as the ferry docked after the few days' journey I had endured on the North Atlantic. The crossing had been calm, the ferry cradled in the gentle arms of the Mother of the Sea. I watched gangs of belligerent gulls, swooping and shrieking over the stone harbour, and smiled: the sight and sound of them no longer instilled fear in my heart. Making my way down the gangway, relieved as always to place my feet back upon solid earth, the blood rushed to my head as I caught sight of a familiar figure.

And where the hell have you been?

The words rushed out indignantly, though I noticed even as I spoke them that I was not at all surprised to see him in this place.

Eqingaleq grinned with his ever-present, mischievous humour. He was leaning against the harbour wall, evidently quite at ease, for his smooth face did not show a single crease of worry on its canvas skin. He spat out a piece of seaweed on which he had been sucking and tossed the remainder of it over his shoulder, into the water.

I've not been anywhere. He grinned again. The fur of his bearskin trousers rippled like grass in the wind.

I wrenched my backpack off and threw it onto the wet stone ground.

You know I've been looking for you. For quite some time, in fact.

Then you can't have been looking very hard.

With a sigh I rested my back against the wall, stood beside him, looking upon the stone houses of the town and the undulating island hills beyond.

Come back for her, have you? He spoke casually. *If she'll have you after all that you've been up to.*

I could hear the mischief bubbling in his voice; he may even have thrown me a wink. But I did not look at him, would not give him that satisfaction. I pursed my lips together to quell the unbidden smile at the corners of my mouth.

So you were here, were you? All this time?

We looked at each other, his black eyes boring deep into my being.

I was with you, he said, *only you chose not to see me.*

I closed my eyes for a moment, savouring the peace brought by his words. When I opened them again I saw him wink, and this time I smiled from ear to ear.

It's good to see you again, my old friend, I said. And picking up my backpack, I started to walk.

My feet carried me along the road that led up and out of the town. I could see the rise of the hills beyond the houses, grey in the morning light, and I pictured the cottage beyond them, on the island's opposite coast. It was likely that I would see Alastair first, feeding the sheep out in the fields. Perhaps

Martha would be there with him, for she had said that she felt quite at home amongst the sheep. She had laughed when she said this, and her eyes had lit up, and her cheeks were coloured from the cold, wild air, and I was sure she must have noticed me looking at her.

I was so caught up within my thoughts that at first I did not notice that Eqingaleq was no longer at my side. I spun around in a panic, fearful that he had left me again. But he was sitting only a short way behind me, on a low wall by the side of the road, one leg crossed casually over the other. He looked at me, and I raised my arms questioningly.

You're going to wear another hole in your kamiks, he said.

He was right. It was a long way to walk.

You're not thinking straight, he chastised. *It's no wonder you ended up out your way, in Iceland.*

I walked slowly back to where he was sitting, digging my hands into my jeans pockets as if trying to hide this small part of myself away from the anxiety that began to slip back into my mind. We had not yet talked about my meeting with Snorri.

Who do you *think my father is?* I asked him hesitantly.

The wind seemed to drop as I waited for his answer. My heart stumbled irregularly, yet around me the world was peaceful. The road was empty – of both people and cars – and I could see fields now, beyond the houses. We had almost reached the boundary of the town. Back towards the harbour, the ferry continued to belch black smoke into the clear air, the rumbling roar of its engine carried away inaudibly by the wind.

I looked back at Eqingaleq, sensing that his gaze had not left me. He shrugged as I caught his eye.

The only thing that matters is what you do now, he said.

I nodded. My heart stilled. Then through the gentle rush of the wind I heard the sound of a car approaching. I held my arm out, my thumb stuck up in the air. The car indicated, and trundled noisily to a stop beside me. As the driver leaned toward the opened passenger window I found that I recognised her: a neighbour from the village to which I was headed.

'Are you going to Jeanie's, hen?' she asked.

I nodded, and with a smile she bid me take a seat in the front of the car.

We passed most of the journey in an amicable silence, accompanied by the sound of acoustic guitars and voices singing in harmony on the crackling car radio. My driver made some attempt at instigating a conversation over the music and the chug of the car engine, but I could give only one-word answers. She did not ask me where I had been, or give any indication that she had noticed my absence in the village. I realised that I had been gone for little more than a fortnight, though to me it felt like an age had passed since I had bid Martha goodbye. Perhaps I would find her in the little cottage in the fields, the one that Alastair, Neil and I had been fixing up. Perhaps Neil would be curled up there in his chair, hiding from the weather as usual. I had missed his company and his sense of humour, and how much he cared for Martha and her daughter. Though I knew that he loved her in the way that one loves a friend. He had told me all about that – about his interest in other men – and I had hoped he would not notice my blushing cheeks, for such things were not discussed where I came from. I wondered what Eqingaleq might have to say on this topic. I glanced at his reflection in the rear view mirror – to where he was sitting in the back seat – but saw from his pained expression that his attention was fixed on the swerve of the car along the winding road and the nausea that it conjured.

My stomach turned somersaults as the village came into view at last, and with it the grey, stormy plane of the North Atlantic – which stretched all the way to my own country, unseen over the horizon. I knew I would never set eyes on the frozen fjords of Greenland again, and although I ached with sadness at the thought, I could accept, now, that I was in the right place.

As my sweeping gaze took in the landscape, I caught sight of a figure up on the hillside – the figure of a woman – and my heartbeat leapt up into my throat. It must be Martha – just as I had painted her – windswept, in the wildness of this place that seemed to suit her so well.

'Could you drop me off at the post office?' I asked my acquaintance. The best place from which to follow the path up the hill. We were there in a matter of seconds, and saying a rushed *thank you* and *goodbye* and *see you again soon* to my driver, I set off up the hill as fast as I was able.

I heard the noise of the car engine rumble away into the distance – the only car for miles, it would seem. Martha must have heard it, too, for as I glanced up the hill I saw that she had stopped in her tracks. Although I could not make out her expression, I could sense her surprise and uncertainty as she watched me approach.

Have you even thought about what you're going to say to her? Eqingaleq wheezed from where he followed a short distance behind me, panting as he tried to keep up. But I did not turn to answer him; my feet continued on the mossy path.

I dared not look ahead, for I feared seeing her expression. What if she were not happy to see me? I felt the beat of wings over my head, and I knew that it was Eqingaleq, flying past me in his raven form. I followed the swoop of his black wings from the corner of my eye and saw him alight a little way up the hill, behind Martha, and I realised with a rush of warmth and relief that she had walked down the hill to meet me. Within a few more steps we were standing face to face.

My breath came quickly; my heart beat like a shaman's drum.

She brushed the flyaway locks of hair from her eyes and twisted them behind her ear. Looked at the ground, looked up at me.

'Did you forget something?' she asked. Her smile wavered nervously and her gaze flickered here and there, but I saw that

259

her eyes shone unmistakably. And my heart gave a sudden elated leap within my chest for I knew then that I had followed the right path.

Well? I heard Eqingaleq say. My eyes shot to where he was standing, just behind Martha's shoulder and in his human form once more. He raised his eyebrows.

Go away, I hissed under my breath. It was still a little ragged from the climb up the hill.

But he did not move, only lifted the corners of his mouth in a mischievous smile. *I'll tell you what you forgot,* he said, and he puckered up his lips and to my alarm made a lunge towards Martha.

I moved quickly, pushing him away with one hand and placing the other on Martha's shoulder – for I was not about to let him get away with such a stunt. He cursed as he stumbled on the mossy ground and immediately he had righted himself he gave me a shove back, towards Martha. I felt the warmth of her nearness, the tingling in my fingertips where they touched her shoulder, and before I knew it my lips were on hers. I forgot about Eqingaleq; I forgot about everything else except for Martha.

As our lips parted, quite naturally, I caught sight of Eqingaleq's on-looking figure from the corner of my eye, and Martha's gaze fixed on me in a look of surprise. Disbelief, perhaps. I feared I had overstepped the mark.

I swallowed. 'Sorry,' I said. I let my arms fall back to my sides. My breath had slowed, but still did not come easily.

Sorry? Eqingaleq shrieked. He jumped up and down on the spot. *Don't apologise to her! Why are you apologising?*

I did not know what else to say to her. Martha, too, appeared to be speechless. But she had not moved away from me, and we were still standing close enough together that the wind did not blow between us, and I felt giddy from the warmth of her.

You should have had a drink before you got off the ferry. I heard Eqingaleq's voice intrude upon the stillness of the moment. *It would have steadied your nerves – it always worked before, remember?*

I tried not to listen to him. I noticed instead the gentle rise and fall of Martha's chest with her breath, and the stray hairs that fell across her forehead and brushed against her lips.

'Did you not find whatever you were looking for?' she said hesitantly. 'Up north?'

I shook my head and looked to the ground. 'Well, yes,' I corrected myself, and my blood ran cold momentarily as I recalled my uncomfortable meeting with Snorri. 'But I wish that I hadn't.'

As I spoke I heard the swooping cries of gulls far above us, echoing across the emptiness of the landscape. And below, the barely audible crash of the rolling tide.

I felt the touch of Martha's hand on mine, where I had let it hang hopelessly at my side, and the warmth spread wonderfully through my body once more.

'Will you stay this time?' she asked.

I looked at her. Her eyes were shining. I nodded and took hold of her hand, pressed it tightly in my own.

All at once I felt a rush of air as Eqingaleq – a raven again – swept his wings up into the air. I watched as he shot upwards with an elated cry – so loud that Martha must have heard him too, for I saw that she followed my gaze. The seagulls above us scattered, shrieking in alarm as the raven rocketed into their midst. And with its black wings outstretched it swooped and somersaulted in the slate sky.

Acknowledgements

I would like to thank my dad, Nigel Bidgood, for telling me so many stories about Greenland throughout my childhood. Your enthusiasm for the Arctic and the beautiful photographic slideshows of your expeditions, set to all your favourite music, are the reason this book has come about. Twenty years later I still think of Greenland whenever I listen to *King Crimson* or *Jan Gabarek*.   And thank you for accompanying me to East Greenland for the first time, where all the stories became real.

I would like to thank all the kind people who helped make my summer stay in South Greenland possible and so memorable.   Notably, *Narsaq Museum* curator Karina Frederiksen and your lovely family, and my friend Karta Kristoffersen, who looked after me so well and gave me my first taste of whale meat!   I would also like to thank my friends in Shetland – Francis and Outi, Raddi, Mary, and Chris the crofter. My heart is still in Shetland, and I hope I can make it back again one day soon.

Many thanks go to Phil and Tracey at Wildpressed Books for believing in me and my writing. This book would never have been finished without your continued support!

About the Author

Holly grew up in Derbyshire but has always been drawn to the sea. She has written from a young age. Her love affair with island landscapes was kick-started on a brief visit to the Faroe Islands at the age of eighteen, en route to Iceland. She was immediately captivated by the landscape, weather, and way of life and it was here that she conceived the idea for her first novel, The Eagle and The Oystercatcher. Holly studied Icelandic, Norwegian and Old Norse at University College London. She also studied as an exchange student at The University of Iceland (Háskóli Íslands) and spent a memorable summer working in a museum in South Greenland.

She decided to start a family young, and now has three small children. Holly helps run *Life & Loom*, a social and therapeutic weaving studio in Hull. She likes to escape from the busyness of her life by working on her novels and knitting Icelandic wool jumpers.